Praise for IDEA33- A Revolution

"Humanity's ever-present sliver of hope fights for a finger-hold against the machine."

"The world that the three heros and their companions inhabit is frightening, vivid, and yet a potential reality. A Revolution makes me want to throw away all electrical devices and go for a 2-week rainforest hike."

"Prepare for the adventure of 'not so distant' future. The IDEA33 series offers new hope to the next generation of gamechangers on this planet."

"In today's reality we see the precursors of the world we witness in A Revolution. The hero's struggle for a better future lights the reader's way toward hope in a wickedly controlled world."

"Never predictable, always interesting, the IDEA33 trio of Dous, Terra, and Heli are back for more adventures. Poignant and funny with lots of surprising twists; *A Revolution* is impossible to put down."

"With poise and promise Henke delivers another stunning installment to the IDEA33 series with a powerful message for a Greener world."

IDEA 33
A REVOLUTION

IDEA 33

A
REVOLUTION

Sheala Dawn Henke

Printed in the United States of America
First Printing, 2015
SDH Publishing
ISBN: 978-0-9912363-2-9

http://sdhenke.com/

Dedication

To our beloved Mother Earth

Acknowledgements

A dear friend and Art teacher, Molly Babcock painted the image of a spark for me during the early publication stages of Book 1 in the IDEA series. Since then this image has surfaced as a true calling and obligation for me to work harder to ignite the minds of young readers. Education is not only the foundation of everything I've accomplished over the last couple of decades, but my heart's home. I am forever grateful to my students who light the way for me each and every day. I can only hope that I am lucky enough that they may serve as the beneficiaries to every story I write for years to come.

I also wish to thank the original group of the Muses, a group of young writers who not only have played a critical role in the evolution of this series, but who have grown to understand the great power of their own words and the mark they can make on an untold future. It has been an honor to watch them evolve into the next generation of messengers to provoke a lasting impact on the world.

To my friends and colleagues at Bennett Elementary who have supported me along the way. Cyd Johnson, kindred friend and teaching partner who understands this 'other' aspect of my life and encourages me to apply focus on my passion for writing.

To my editors Kerrie Flanagan and Jennifer Top who suffered tirelessly through each and every passive verb, wordy passage, and flip flop of who's whose. Also, to others in the professional sphere who so graciously volunteered their time and energy to this project. Dr. Bob Seney and Kelly Larson who each made their own dent in the reader's and writer's market by supporting debut authors like me. And to the remaining long list of Beta Readers including James Sack, Maria Lobeski and my own mother Dianna Butler whose eagle eyes homed in on every last detail in the book's earliest edition. These unsung heroes each offered invaluable critique which spoke to the heart of my learning process and articulated priceless opportunities for growth and improvement for future endeavors. You all give new meaning to grass roots publishing!

To my family who bless me in and around all of the corners of my life. You meet me with support, love and teach me to find grace in gratitude. You all serve as anchors in my life and who not only hold me accountable but nudge me on.

Ever-present in my heart are my husband Jay and two boys Canyon and Cache who provide nearly every ounce of joy in my life and give me more strength and love than I can possibly contain. Your love spills out on every page!

Ultimately, the blessings that have unfolded through this experience are a true testament to what I believe deserves the most credit. Call it what you will, God, Allah, Brahman, Gaia or more simply the essence of Light, it was with the fortitude and grace and something outside of myself that these words ever met the page.

Foreword

Sheala Henke has done it again with this next installment in the Idea 33 series. In this book, IDEA33 A Revolution, Heli, Terra and Dous continue on their predestined quest to save our planet from destruction. As with the first book, Sheala weaves together a fascinating story filled with intriguing characters.

I have known Sheala for a couple of years and it has been a joy watching her grow as a writer. I met her when I worked part time at an elementary school in Fort Collins where Sheala was (and still is) a teacher. When I found out she was a writer, I connected with her to let her know about Northern Colorado Writers, the organization I founded in 2007. I wanted her to know that if she needed help or support with her writing, she might want to consider looking into joining the group. It took a few months, but she eventually did.

She soon made the decision to self-publish her book series and hired me to help her with the process. Her successful Kickstarter campaign funded her venture. I quickly learned that when Sheala makes up her mind to do something, she wastes no time. She jumped right in, spent many late nights and weekends working on the book. Over the course of five months, she would send me a couple of chapters to read through and critique while she worked on the next section. She then went back through the whole book again to make final changes. We took a couple of months to format the book and got it ready for the book launch.

The first book was a success and I know Sheala learned a lot about writing and publishing. When time came for her to write this second book, she was more prepared with an outline, a more flexible time table and stronger writing skills. The process went more smoothly, and the result was another amazing book.

What I love about working with Sheala is her enthusiasm for her writing and her willingness to do whatever it takes to make it happen. Her energy is contagious, and I am always recharged after meeting with her. She is passionate about her stories and it shows in the final books. I also appreciate how my vocabulary has improved thanks to her. Because of her own love of reading, she has a stockpile of unique words at her disposal that frequently send me to the dictionary.

Sheala's passion for our world and the concern she has for what is destined to happen if we don't start taking better care of it, is an underlying theme in all the books in the series. She weaves it so well into the storyline that you never feel like you are being preached at; instead she gets you thinking about important issues and problems. IDEA 33; A Revolution is the perfect read for those looking to expand their world views with a quality work.

I feel grateful to have worked with such a talented writer and I look forward to helping Sheala with future projects.

Kerrie Flanagan
Kerrie Flanagan is the Director and founder of Northern Colorado Writers, an accomplished freelance writer, writing consultant, publisher, writing instructor and author. Her recent articles can be found in The Writer, Writer's Digest, and in the past four Writer's Markets. She is the author of *Planes, Trains and Chuck & Eddie*;

Write Away: A Year of Musings and Motivations for Writers; and *Claire's Christmas Catastrophe.* In addition to her own work, she has helped nearly a dozen writers self-publish their work and guides writers to reach their full potential. She teaches writing classes throughout the year in Colorado and Wyoming.

http://www.KerrieFlanagan.com

Preface

On the value of Origins: "The most powerful words in [any language] are 'Tell me a story,' words that are intimately related to the complexity of history, the origins of language, the continuity of the species, the taproot of our humanity, our singularity, and art itself."

Pat Conroy

For me, the Muse arrived long before any words ever rested on the page. Expression took its time, settling into my bones and today I've come to recognize the familiar voices that continue to echo through my writing. They are the voices of my students after more than fifteen years of teaching and each imprint has had a resounding effect on my achievements.

In the beginning, my intentions with writing the first installment of the IDEA33 series were simple. I wanted to explore the process of writing a story in a simulated 'walk through' with my students and I wanted it to be about them. In my mind, at the time it seemed so elementary of a task that I never assumed it would take on a life of its own outside of the walls of my classroom. Despite my obliviousness to where this would lead me one day, the idea had all of the ingredients for success. The combination of my passion for writing and the fact that I had a story to share with young all too willing eyes and ears set the ball in motion. But the real adventure began when one of my former students asked, "Are we going to publish this someday?" In that moment little did I know what power the Muse would have over me. What started out as a grassroots effort to bring the story to publication, has evolved into a fellowship of young readers and writers sharing their love of the craft while the story continues with the completion of the second installment of the trilogy.

Personified, my Muses come to life as a group of young teens and secondary level students who have opted to join me on this journey. They each have dedicated personal time to the project and continue to pursue their own goals as developing writers as well. With monthly meetings during the school year and weekly meetings over the summer the group has grown from an intimate assembly of 8 originals to over thirty members ranging in ages of 9 to 15 years old. We gather, we share, and we support one another as the foundation grows, plotting the points toward our goals and offering a safe and supportive platform for feedback. In this rendition of 'Pay it Forward' I can only hope that one or more of these individuals might take this experience into their lives to evaluate their own successes in a broader changing world.

Jon Bard with Write 4 Kids speaks of the 'Tribe' authors actively cultivate as artists and writers. He states that the relationships authors build with their readership can evolve into a connection that becomes less about the books they write and more about the kinships they share. In this case our 'Tribe' was initiated with a common passion and I see my role as their teacher to foster the building blocks for success and feed them well. What I have learned from each of them is a priceless lesson in sharing, but it resonates most in the wellspring of support and a communal environment where we all flourish.

Inheritance

"Tracy didn't have time to tell you everything," Mr. Cruise said. His eyes jumped over to Justin.

"Jacque will make his way back. It's not a matter of if, but when," Justin confirmed.

"Should we even be having this conversation?" Heli nodded toward the marble glow of a lens perched in the corner eaves. It peered down at them. IDEA's eyes were always watching.

"We've taken care of the details...for now. This conversation stays off the record," Mr. Cruise said. Justin nodded, providing Heli with some assurance.

"What exactly is it that we're keeping off the record?" Heli asked.

"It's no longer safe for the three of you here." Justin's eyes jumped between them.

"What are you saying?" Heli felt the stone seat harden beneath him before he stood up. Terra sat nearby. She reached up. Her hand tenderly grazed his hip before it slipped into his hand——enough to ground him.

Mr. Cruise let out a somber sigh. "None of you really understand the magnitude of what you've done do you?"

"What happened to us in the Strata shouldn't require an audit." Heli paused and looked to his friends.

"It certainly left its impression," Terra whispered.

Cruise looked at them. "You haven't spoken a word of what happened since that day with either one of us. You all walk around here like ghosts. And other than your reliance on one another, you keep to yourselves. We wanted to give you time to work it out on your own terms, but we also want you to know that we're here to serve you now. I believe it's time we speak of the incident."

Heli muttered softly under his breath. "The incident? So, IDEA's watch dogs suddenly grow a heart after all this time? Decided you finally give a damn now the Alpha has abandoned you?" His voice rose. "I'd say if anyone walks around here like ghosts it's you two. And honestly, we really don't know who it is you serve."

Dous fidgeted uncomfortably in his seat. "Something you care to add?" Heli asked looking over at his friend.

"It's their job Heli."

"And whose bankroll do you think they depend on?" Heli looked back at Justin and Mr. Cruise. "I've been trying to figure you two out since this all started, and I doubt we'll ever really know the truth. But what I'm certain of is that you never worked for us." He sat back and stared at them. "Besides, what's the point in dredging it all up again? We did everything you wanted and like you said before Tracy was an unfortunate casualty. We all have to live with that."

"She would have wanted to know," Cruise said.

"As we confirmed before, we are the only ones privy to this conversation. We need to understand more of what happened in there. It's been the focus of a lifetime of work," Justin added.

"Well sounds like you're due for vacation then." Heli smiled.

"So much anger...still locked up in there." Mr. Cruise took a step back.

Here we go again. Heli projected.

"What is it you want from us?" Terra asked. "I mean, if you're asking us to tell you how we feel and explain what it was like in there, that doesn't just happen between strangers."

"I sincerely apologize if that's the way you see it. Our roles have always been to relieve the three of you of some of the burden," Cruise said.

Dous let out a deep sigh, "You want to know what it was like? Okay…swimming." He looked at Justin. "It made me think about the water at first. Like, the moment you dive in and it wraps itself around you…you're a part of it and it's a part of you. Except all of that was gone after that thing spit me out…as if it knew my imperfections and was laughing in my face." His hands rested on his immobile legs. "I used every ounce of will to stay and those same barbed hooks that pulled me out couldn't hold on to Tracy. It was my job to get you all out. What use am I who can supposedly manifest what I want from the universe, but I couldn't do a damn thing to save her. What a crock."

"The entry," Heli exhaled. "It was palpable. Like having all five of your senses come alive at once but imagine you suddenly and exponentially develop billions more. The extremities of pleasure and pain in there…" Heli paused, "should've been impossible. We were all holding on for dear life…"

Terra nudged in with her thoughts as she squeezed his hand and added, "Plain and simple, it was absolutely terrifying, but the crazy part is that I think any one of us would've stayed for the eternity it promised," she paused. "None of us have ever seen a real thunderstorm. My grandmother had memories of the electrical dry storms before they developed the Synthasphere. She would tell me how you could almost anticipate the next stroke of light that would lace the sky in raged streaks. Her eyes would move up searching when she described it. I could always see a mixture of fear and pleasure flash its way across her face. Then, she'd cushion the story to tell me how the sinking feeling of any unknown only makes you want to dive deeper." Her voice trailed on in a whisper, "You really want to know what it's like to be pried apart by the fingers of angels? She shook her head and closed her eyes as tears streamed down her face.

Mr. Cruise swallowed hard before he spoke, "You all went in acknowledging centuries of the damage done. To affect the release, you had to become the pathway itself. Beyond that, it would have been involuntary, like the muscle movement of your heartbeat. Palpitations of the heart require no thinking," Mr. Cruise explained.

"So, is that why it felt like we entered a black hole?" Heli muttered.

"Quite the opposite," Cruise argued. "A black hole would denote the absence of something, energy and light for example. The Strata sent you into something more along the lines of an implosion of all that is, and together you were the sum of it all. It was no simple task for any of you to have gone in, but an even greater surprise that you made it out."

"Well I wouldn't go as far as to qualify this as a miracle. Just the dumb luck of a maiden voyage. It certainly didn't get on without its sacrifice," Heli said.

"Dumb luck, eh? I'd like to hear you say that to the first known voyagers of flight into what at one time was the uncharted territory of air and sky? Like them we know little of the dynamics of this environment, but now we know that there are ways to access it."

Justin lifted an eyebrow. "Tracy may be gone, but she was correct in her assessment of the three of you. We've analyzed the results. The Regeneration is conclusive. Not only have each of you successfully entered and emerged from the Strata unscathed, but evidence of the shift is appearing all around the globe. The atmosphere is healing."

Heli pulled his fingers through the matted strands of his hair. "I could've told you that the moment we came out of that thing, but I guess IDEA always needs its confirmation. Get to the point."

Cruise looked up, "Do you know what happens when dying stars collide?"

"A boiling tragedy," Heli joked.

"A new star is born," Dous answered.

"Exactly. She didn't die in vain. She died to see that you moved on. In the short time you've been here you've accomplished what we weren't sure was even possible. Unfortunately, there was not enough time to prepare you for the aftermath."

Mr. Cruise's eyes bounced between them, "Your attachment to one another took less than thirty-three days as you reached time line targets. This was all in preparation to enter the Strata successfully."

"You're talking about the prophecy. We know...our relationship, our connections, the Cor and all that. Tracy explained everything." Heli nodded. "How it was necessary."

Terra looked at him, a sharp gaze in her eyes.

"Tracy was our only source of information. We weren't given clearance to anything more beyond where we are today. And the three of you have spent the last three months adapting to what happened as if it were over, but this is only the beginning, from our estimations. Entering the Strata wasn't just some rite of passage for you all. Your entry and the regeneration were only a preliminary measure of what the prophecy may be referencing with the inscription," Mr. Cruise said.

"Figures there would be more to all this. It doesn't end here, does it?" Dous asked.

Cruise made a little coughing noise. "We've studied each curve in every character transcribed in that document. Like Justin said, a lifetime of work."

"The Zenith Creation," Terra interrupted. "The moment of new beginnings. Something like that."

"Something like that." Justin stared back at her.

"You're right, this doesn't end here," Mr. Cruise went on.

"Is this your polite way of getting around to tell us 'There's the door?'" Heli fumed.

"You said it yourself. We got the job done, we turned things around." Dous fumbled with the knobs on his wheelie, taking it out of lock mode. He rolled forward to the edge of the table. "Wasn't that the point of the entire mission?"

"We don't even know the extent of the entire mission. The problem is that Jacque is one of the few who does. As cozied up with the Regulation as he is we have to take the threat of his return seriously. There are people in his corner who would make it their business to take full advantage of that fact," Justin explained.

"If we can't stay here then where do you suggest we go?" Terra said, squeezing Heli's hand harder before releasing him.

Heli edged his way closer to the table, "So this is our reward? We risk the impossible, come within an inch of our lives to alter the prophetic end of all times and this is how IDEA repays us?" Heli stopped. Mr. Cruise moved around the barrier of the table separating them to approach Heli.

Justin began, "We won't be able to…"

Cruise held up a firm hand to stop him. He looked up at Heli. "Jacque has plans for the three of you. We are certain of that. With what little we know of the details, we can assure you that his intentions go far beyond what you or I could ever imagine. I believe you, above anyone else, would understand this." The familiar squinting twitch returned as he stared back at Heli.

Justin leaned in. "We can no longer protect you here. We don't have a choice in the matter. Your only safe option is to leave."

A pause hung in the air like a burr set against Heli's skin before Mr. Cruise finally added, "There is another place."

***

Spattered shards of tan and grey went flying past, offering the only distinct measure of the hovercrafts's velocity as it went careening along the empty byway. The thought of leaving IDEA and being relocated and tossed into the vat of another unknown only added to Heli's unease.

He peered out the tinted window of the vehicle, scanning the shroud of dead arid space as his thoughts spilled, making no attempt to censor them, *When do we get to live our lives out from under this rock?*

We're here...under that rock with you, remember? Dous pressed in. Heli kept his gaze out the window.

As always, Heli sent, his thoughts weary.

Still here, Dous projected.

Heli rolled his eyes, lolling his head back around toward his friend.

He watched Dous yank at the front of his Hodgesuit. Its form to fit design must have been clinging a little too tightly. "Is it warm in here? It just feels so…" The hovercraft suddenly met an air pocket and the compartment jumped as he spoke, cutting him off.

Crowded. Heli tapped at his head, finishing the thought for him.

If I have to sit here and listen to you two bicker for another second, I'm going to lose it. It's been nearly six months. We should've gotten used to this by now, Terra shared.

"Can we just agree to speak real audible words while we're stuck in here? The close quarters make it hard to filter." Heli rested his head back against the seat.

"Somebody woke up on the wrong side of the bed this morning," Dous said.

One thing they all could agree on was that it wasn't always optimal having others carve into your thoughts at any time, even with those whom you've shared a primordial bond.

Heli lifted his head, "I just think it's important that we stick to some of our original agreements."

"Oh yes...how could I forget?" Dous sat up straighter and spoke counting on his fingers, "Derived from Ruiz's ancient Toltec wisdom and the four agreements." He cleared his throat. "Number one, be impeccable with your thoughts. Two, don't take anything personally. Three, don't make assumptions. Then, of course the fourth, and my all-time favorite, amended with precautionary measure by yours truly," Dous bowed chivalrously, "always place the greater good in the highest priority."

"I think it might be time for a fifth amendment," Heli said. "Not getting up into other people's business."

"Fine, but don't come pining around when I opt to shut you out."

Heli slapped his hand against his chest, "That hurts."

"I'm starting to wonder if a mindful shunning might be just what the doctor ordered," Dous joked.

A quiet laugh escaped Terra's lips. Heli turned to look at her, realizing that the joke was on him, and if Dous could opt to shut him out, so could she.

Heli could feel his shoulders ache as he rolled them back and twisted his neck in the cramped space. As difficult as it had been to enter the Strata, a portal through which they had successfully regenerated their dying planet, learning how to manage their expanding gifts as a result, might prove to be even more difficult.

"If we can survive going into that thing, then we can certainly figure out how to manage this. Personally, I'm more worried about Jacque," Dous said.

Heli squeezed his eyes shut. Terra's hand stiffened in his. The mere mention of the man's name sent a flare of anger through him. Lighting the fuse and building up steam. His friend's words sank in, tainting the safety in this space.

"It's happening again." Terra slowly edged her hand out from his.

"Can you even feel it coming on?" She asked.

Heli began rubbing both of his hands on the pant legs of his Hodgesuit. The heat was there before he had even produced enough friction to cause it.

"Agh-Yes! Can we change the subject please?" All it took was hearing that name to propel Heli into the throes of a murderous fantasy. Gripping his thighs, he envisioned the heat wrapping itself around his enemy's brittle neck to end it once and for all. He slid down and put his head between his hands. The shame slipped from his voice uncensored, "All he has to do is creep into my head and then this 'thing' happens." Heli held up his hands in front of him, expecting them to somehow spontaneously combust.

"Just breathe. Think of something else, something that might help you relax." Terra took in a silent gulp of air.

Dous added, "There has to be a way to get control of it."

"Control it? I don't even know what it is. I'm afraid to even be this close to either of you right now." Heli closed his eyes.

"There has to be a way," she offered. Heli slowly reopened his eyes.

"I'm sure there is, but I'll be dammed if I know how to get around it." He drew in a sharp breath and brought his hands down again, this time tucking them into the side slings of his Hodgesuit.

Terra slid closer to him and slipped a hand under the crux of his arm. "We're not worried that you'll hurt us, if that's what you're concerned about. We just want to help."

Clenching his teeth Heli projected the thought, breaking his own rules, *A little late for the intervention. I almost killed Justin and what I nearly did to you...*

A vision flashed through his thoughts, the violent recall of Terra's shrieking screams just as she had reached out to touch him as he fell unconscious to the Chronovirus.

Terra leaned into him. "You were sick. You can't blame yourself for that. That virus was encrypted to kill you."

"They were still my actions and I take full responsibility for them no matter what state I was in." He looked at her and his mind reeled at the recollection of Justin's whitened scars, wrapping around like icy tendrils over the tops of his fingers and the back of his hand. Justin was the only one to wear the mark of Heli's fury, but it could have just as easily been Terra to suffer by his hands.

"Maybe this place...wherever we're headed, will help us find some answers," Terra offered.

"I appreciate the optimism, but where ever it is they're sending us, it isn't likely going to provide us with the answers I need." Heli turned away from them to stare out the window again.

There was another long pause before Dous spoke, "Why couldn't they at least tell us where they're sending us?"

Terra squeezed Heli's hand—urging him back before she answered Dous, "I know it feels like we're hiding out like thieves, but it's the only way to be sure Jacque won't find us. And Tracy…" She stopped, "This is it. It's all we have now. At least we're together," she said. Heli felt the pinch in his throat as he swallowed the memories of the home they had made at IDEA back down and rallying he said, "Their instructions were clear…" he paused, swallowing hard, "maybe it is for the best. No one else knows about this place. Not even…Jacque."

Dous argued, "How do you know? I mean supposedly we were only safe at IDEA, right?"

Terra's eyes fell on Dous, "Justin said he'd place his life on it; that if Jacque even knew about this place, it wouldn't exist." She offered some relief by adding, "Tracy would have wanted for us to be safe, not under the guise of that man. He's not operating on a full set of scruples. He'll send us back in there. You know that right?" Her eyes burned with intensity and Dous's bleaker blue eyes shifted to her.

"I know, but will you look at where we're headed?" His hand swung out batting at the window. "It's no-man's land out there. What kind of safe zone is this?"

Heli followed his friend's gaze out the window, a mystery of chromatic earth tones in a spray of green hues slowly encasing them.

Heli slid up to the curve of his seat, its upholstered edges less forgiving at the moment. "Tracy entrusted whoever these others are with our safe keeping because she knew it was the best place for us. I guess it's time we trust in that."

Dous nodded. "Keep telling yourself that, but Tracy's not here anymore. And since when did this role reversal happen?"

"It's out of our hands now." Heli felt the thin thread of truth to what he said and looked at his friend.

"I suppose that if you're willing to put up with this, then I should be able to accept it too." Heli turned and settled back into his seat. He looked back at Terra, her honeyed irises wide and trusting. He sucked in a sip of air while her stare engulfed him, and he read her reply. *Well done.*

***

Heli's attention is drawn to Terra's hand squeezing his as she shuddered, waking him from the early trials of a dozing sleep. "How much longer do you think? "

"What a surrealist nightmare." Dous aimed his gaze out the window. "I think this hov might have a glitch in its programming."

"I'm sure it's an unregulated area if it's been kept a secret this long. We should be there by nightfall," Heli answered and sat up straighter.

"High hopes. And I thought I was the optimistic one." Dous resituated himself along the curving seat, pulling up his satchel and plopping it down on his lap, digging around and peering inside. "Well, on these rations we should have been there a while ago."

Dous's ever-reliable focus on when and where their next meal would be never ceased to amaze Heli.

Letting go of Terra's hand, Heli crossed his arms in front of him and lifted an eyebrow toward Dous. "Who let you be in charge of the food? I don't know if that was such a good idea."

"What? You think I'd leave you two high and dry? I am good at sharing," Dous countered.

"Whatever's left." Heli narrowed his eyes on his friend.

Dous smiled back as he reached to pull the stash out of his pack and handed it over. "Satisfied?"

Heli shook his head approvingly, accepting the tribute, and turned to look back out the window before Dous spoke again.

"Just remember, you two have each other. I have…" Dous shuffled through the bag to pull another item out, "this sandwich." And he quickly unwrapped it from its insta-degrade coating before coming down on it with an enormous bite. He looked at Terra who sat wide eyed staring back at him. With his mouth full he managed to muffle, "Gonnuf…eat yours?"

"We're gonna need to find you something else to occupy your time, especially without that pool of yours," Heli said.

Dous grimaced, his mouth happily still chewing, and he finally swallowed. "Something'll turn up. I might just have to apply a little focus, that's all."

"Like the last time you asked for what you wanted from the universe?" Heli lifted an eyebrow feeling a little twist in his stomach still holding the uneaten sandwich in his hands.

"That wasn't my fault. I had no idea I could possibly taint the forms of manifestation. I just wanted to have a little fun with it, tweak the system a bit. I never thought it might have ethical limitations. Besides, it's not every day you find out that you have the ability to make things happen. How was I supposed to know there was some universal code I needed to follow?" Dous shrugged.

"Tracy warned you," Heli said.

Dous reached and laid a hand on his stomach, "Yea, well I think the lesson spoke for itself. Those stomach cramps lasted for two days after eating my share of those berries."

"Careful what you wish for, right?" Terra added and smiled back at him. "Just glad Heli and I only indulged in the few that we did."

"I know, I know, it's not like I haven't heard it before or that I'm a glutton for punishment." Dous rolled his eyes. "I just didn't think that my little impression stamp on their production would have such severe consequences."

"Everything we do has consequences. You haven't figured that out yet?' Heli gazed out the window onto streaking rivulets of green where immense groves of timber and overgrown vegetation flew by.

The foliage had become denser, and the vehicle began to slow its expeditious pace. They were entering an area not marked for transport, obvious by the scraping and tearing of branches from trees and shrubs gripping at the hovercraft frame.

"Why doesn't the Hov move up over the top of this stuff?" Dous asked.

"Probably programmed to stay low."

Heli could feel the pressure from the cage of plants that surrounded them, stripping at the flesh of metal encasing the vehicle and the only barrier between them and the treacherous thicket. It was getting thicker. Terra's hand met the windowpane as if she were peering out at a long-lost friend, fearless and grinning from ear to ear.

Heli was shielding his ears, as she turned to him, speaking louder than usual. "This is amazing! I thought I'd never see more green than at IDEA, but this is unbelievable!" She hopped up onto her knees, like a small child peering out the window to get a better view.

"The programming on this thing must be way off!" Dous yelled with his hands cupped over his ears as the Hovercraft careened through the brush.

Heli brought his hands down to absorb the sights and sounds that were forming, a vibration he could feel right down through the core of his body. Just as it began to take on shape, the vehicle halted, rotating in a full 180 degree turn to come to a stop. They had settled in on a small clearing. Ahead of them the crevice of a narrow path carved into the bivouac of sheltering trees. Heli and Dous both turned in their seats to join Terra and get a better look out the front visor. The space had them surrounded by high arching trees—ghosts of an ancient past hovering around the space.

"There's nothing here except…" Dous's words trailed off and they all watched a woman miraculously appear out of the bracts in the branches. Sidling into the clearing to get closer to the vehicle she peered in, curiously squinting at the passenger compartment on the side mount. Heli knew she couldn't see anything past her own reflection through the shield of tinted windows. She moved clockwise around to the front of the craft. He noticed that she was a mature woman, but in her eyes was a glimpse of a youthful past. Her long trailing silver hair moved like downy feathers over her shoulders

She can't see us, can she? Terra's thoughts rolled out.

"She knows we're here," He whispered back.

"Well that's unnerving," Dous blurted.

Who is she? Terra projected.

The woman turned, revealing a grotesque tracing of a scar like a luminous snail's trail down the side of her cheek. Terra let out a small gasp. The woman's eyes stayed pinched and her nose crinkled up as if she had gotten a whiff of something unidentifiable.

"They're here!" She called like a woodland crow out to the trees.

Appearing out of the same crook of foliage where the woman had emerged came a man. He walked slowly over toward them. He was twice the woman's size, in both height and girth, with a tinge more youth in his gaze. He answered her call, but stood at a distance, peering toward the hovercraft, his chin held high, "Aye."

They were no ghostly mirage, but real live people.

What do we do? Dous froze, while they all watched the strangers from inside the safety of the hovercraft compartment.

"Must be the greeting party." Heli shifted his weight to sit down and turn toward the door. He hesitated, indecisive on how to proceed. He looked at Terra still perched up on her knees, staring out curiously.

"You two stay here," Heli decided, sliding past her.

"Excuse me?" Terra backed away, adjusting to face him. "We came here together, remember?" Her eyes were drawn into a scowl.

In no hurry to wave the white flag and expose them all just yet, Heli said, "I want to check it out to make sure it's safe."

"Safe?" She mocked. "Okay, let's rewind, shall we? May I remind you of the last time you tried to keep us all safe?"

He hardened his stare, "This is non-negotiable." The silence between them and the short breath that escaped her while he watched her deflate back into the seat was difficult to ignore. He pressed the button on the release hatch, never looking back to see her reaction and slid out while the door slid closed behind him.

The silent strangers both shifted to look at Heli, but stood erect, splicing him with their wide-eyed stares.

"Hey," Heli offered quickly and halted, feeling the tips of his fingers prickle with a buzzing heat. He shifted awkwardly waiting for a response.

The man spoke first. His voice was a deep baritone so low Heli could hardly register the utterance. "Welcome."

His approach was assured as he took three steps forward. Nodding his head, Heli observed the sheen of his silvery grey buzz cut and how it glowed in a tiny pocket of sunlight poking through the towering trees. His overly pronounced chin jetted out below a pair of emerald green eyes locking in on Heli, a distinct regality in his gaze. Both hands remained interlocked behind him.

The woman stretched her head around to look at their vehicle. "Your friends, they're with you?"

"Uh…" The side door slid open. Heli looked back to see Terra emerge.

"Yes, we're all here," Terra shoved past Heli. He stumbled, instinctively moving a hand out to graze her side. She pulled away without looking at him, rigid to his touch. Her arm stretched out to meet the man's. This time, the stranger proffered a hand of his own out to her.

Heli hardly noticed how Dous slid only his legs out to sit in the open gap of the door frame.

Her delicate fingers folded into the stranger's. "Hello, I'm Terra n' that's Dous. I see you've already met…him." All humor empty in her voice. Her eyes flickered between them. Vying for her thoughts, and realizing she would likely shut him out, Heli angrily bit his lip to hold his tongue.

"We're glad you made it here safely. My name is Cue and this is Emeal." He reached his free hand back toward the woman who edged in closer to stand next to him.

"Pleased to finally meet you." The woman's hardened stare softened as she approached Terra. Her eyes lifted with a smile, showing where each wrinkle had originated.

"I'll be sure to notify your friends at IDEA that you have arrived." Her voice had a sinewy quality.

"Already sent a com-trip." Heli held up his CS card and the woman looked at it through squinted eyes, then shot a quick glance back at him before dismissing the comment.

"Come, we have much to show you." Cue let go of Terra's hand and both he and Emeal turned to disappear into the brush.

Heli stood back waiting for an opportunity to catch Terra's attention, but Dous spoke up, "Can somebody give me a hand here?" He was still wedged in the open slot of the door. Heli had nearly forgotten all about him.

Terra looked back at Dous, once again bypassing Heli with a curt nod. He could feel her temper flaring out in a spray of pins and needles set to penetrate as she flew past him with her chin held high.

Numbly Heli turned to help gather more of their belongings and pulled Dous' wheel chair out from the rear compartment. As he set down their bags and began fumbling with the knobs, his finger slipped and was caught in one of the handle ratchets. Wincing, he shook his injured finger and stole a glance Terra's way. She was looking at him directly now, but in no way did it comfort him.

Serves you right. Terra's thought projected over the waves of cooler air.

Hefting a load of their baggage over his shoulder, Heli watched as she turned away from him again. He edged his way in her direction, a common reflex in an attempt to make amends.

Terra stood taller as he approached and whipped around to face him when he was up close. She stared hard into his eyes and her seething anger took his breath away. Heli could already feel the electricity between them, unspoken words shredding him from the inside out, a teasing torture to his restraint. He looked down to see if she was up on her toes, her chin held high to meet him at the neckline. She had certainly changed since the first time they had met.

He realized while looking back, keeping his head down, subordinate to her gaze, how little he really understood her. Her mood swings, her reactions, but most of all her power over him.

"We do this together. Is that clear?" Her pointer finger pressed hard against his chest. He resisted the urge to pull her closer. He quickly relayed a thought, an involuntary grip hold, tethering him to her. *You're so…* His mind spiraled, staring into her bold eyes to finish the thought, *beautiful when you're angry. Oh? Is that why you do this? To get your kicks?* Her mouth curled, considering him. *Well, you ever do it again and you'll have more than a bum finger to deal with.* She was angry, but her eyes glowed like embers of a fire, and she turned away before he was through relishing in it.

On an exhale, Dous sputtered, shuffling both of his legs in front of him, "If you two are done with your little love-spat, I could use a hand here. My butt's numb."

"Sorry." Heli shook his head.

"Where'd they go? Do they expect us to just follow them in there?" Terra asked and nodded toward the small entrance in the brush where their hosts had suddenly appeared and more recently disappeared. Heli offered a hand to Dous, aiding him to move onto Zuke. He shifted and peered at the gap in the branches. He could see a cleared path beyond the first layer of the thicket and reached to grab their bags, maneuvering Dous toward the passageway through the trees.

"Come on." Terra ambled his way. Together they approached the passageway. Heli held back, and she didn't seem to think twice before crossing the threshold first.

Among the Frey

"Agh!" A loose twig spliced through the skin above Heli's left eye as it flew from its cocked station. His hand darted up to where he had received the lash, feeling the smooth trickle of blood slide along his finger tip. He stopped to look at the shiny cast of crimson, quickly reminded of his own human frailties.

"Dous snuck up behind him, Zuke's wheels nudging Heli's calves gently from the rear. He turned to look down at his friend. Dous's whole face pinched up, "Oh man, that's a bleeder. You okay?"

Heli checked himself, nodding slowly, hardly registering Dous's comment before his attention was drawn up ahead of them. Terra was quite a few paces in front, nearing Cue. Heli quickened his pace, assisting Dous up the incline to make his way toward her. Cue stopped and turned around to face them. Heli casually wrapped his arm around her waist and drew her close while she leaned into him for support. Cue's eyes darted between them.

"You all look…" He paused "tired. We don't have much further to go. We've reserved a covert for you where you'll have some time to settle in and rest." Cue led them all up the brow of the hill.

Heli's primary focus had been to get Zuke and his passenger up over the final leg of the path, so when he finally could see over Dous's head he noticed a stack of stones near the crest of the hill.

"What is that weird noise?" Heli asked. "Birds?"

"Yea, but I haven't seen any…" Dous started.

Heli looked back over his shoulder to see Terra following them close behind as he made a final push up the lip of the mound. Suddenly his attention was drowned out by Dous's exclamation, "Whoa! Toto, we are definitely not in Kansas anymore!"

"Toto? Who are you…?" And then Heli saw it too. He dropped his hands to his sides, so stunned by the sight before him that he didn't notice Dous rolling backwards until he felt a jab in his side from Zuke's handles. He quickly grabbed hold of them again.

"This is crazy." Heli hitched up Zuke's breaks with a swift kick of his foot.

Terra had caught up with them, breathing heavily as she came around from behind, "Where on earth are we?"

The sight had stopped them all in their tracks. The parcel of land revealed more than just the greenery surrounding it. As opposite as night and day, the quiet hum of the forest volume rose coming alive now with bustling people moving in a network of purveying commerce. Heli watched with interest as those around them seemed to maneuver in a collective rhythm, a colony of life bursting at the seams. People, loads of people. Of those who scuttled by, only a few exited briefly from the swarm to acknowledge them and then their business would have them rushing off again.

"No Hodgewear?" Heli asked. He noticed right away that the citizens of this enclave all wore similar style coverlets with short capped sleeves in varying lengths, covering them only down below their knees.

Cue dodged his question, "Welcome to the Frey."

Among the masses, each individual hosted a wash of neutrality, camouflaged by the natural hues of tan, green and grey causing them to blend in with their surroundings. There appeared to be only one striking exception to the rule. They each wore a unique band of brightly colored beads around their neck. This slight variation, seemingly the only feature distinguishing them from one another. Cue's was the thickest, a cache of blue, with vermilion and yellow ties trailing his neckline in wavy rivers of contrast. Heli rubbed the sleeve of the slick body armor he wore.

"Come." Cue motioned to have them enter what appeared to be the center of the main square.

Heli dropped their bags and he looked at Terra who raised an eyebrow. Dous twisted around in his seat like he was lost. "What is this place?" He asked, scanning the mirage of commerce.

From what Heli could ascertain in the distance to the north-eastern rim, was a quartered plot of land where gardens were situated on the grounds. It out-scaled any plot of managed greenery he had ever seen before, even on and around the grounds of IDEA. Along the periphery to the east were mounds of what appeared to be underground earth-ship trench dwellings. Heli scanned the view and watched how people would disappear intermittently into one of the ground suites only to reappear again a few minutes later out of another. Children ran about everywhere; the sounds of their chirping and laughter and the chiding of adults bonded to them added to the chorus. Heli had never been comfortable around small children, but he watched with mild curiosity at the way Terra eyed them smiling. Like ants in their colony, subsisting in the layers of the earth, everyone here, including the young ones at play appeared to have a purpose.

Cue spoke again, "This is our community gathering space, and each member contributes to what we have here." He raised a hand toward the gardens, "And those are our life's blood." Heli instinctually lifted his hand to touch the scratch that had recently crusted over, healing already.

"These gardens, they're legal?" Heli asked, drawing his hand back down still gazing out across the Frey.

Cue stared back at him. "Depends on how you look at it."

Terra cut in, "These are rogue greeneries alright," and she shook her head slowly up and down and darted off in the direction of the gardens, as if being pulled by some invisible string. Heli grabbed their bags and stepped up his pace to keep up with her and the others joined them.

"Hey wait for me!" Dous called to Heli.

Heli jumped back, "Sorry. She's gotta stop taking off like that." Heli grumbled, fumbling with the load and Zuke's handles to push Dous forward.

"She seems pretty comfortable here. A little more spring in her step." Dous observed.

Heli gripped the handles a bit tighter pressing on to catch up with Cue.

"So, you grow all your own food here? No regulators manage any of this?" Heli asked. Terra stood along the edge of the plot, her eyes opened wide on the expanse of bounty before them.

"We manage what we have here with a citizen survey and follow up with reasonable distribution to our citizens in equal shares." Cue answered.

"Vegetarians?" Dous asked, seemingly disappointed.

Cue nodded to the west, "Our livestock is tended to just down that hill, right below the waterway aquifer storage.

"You capture water?" Heli asked.

"We use underground basins for storage to limit evaporation rates and provide the best application of recovery. Our aqueduct lines siphon our water for irrigation and everyday use." Heli looked out toward what he had assumed were fortification walls encasing the area, realizing that they were actually man-made channels for water transport.

"Quite the set up. I've never heard of anyone managing water this way." Heli scanned the perimeter of the site.

"Likely not something you would have seen in limited historical hall cubes. The technology albeit ancient, is one of the best sustainable water transition systems to date," Cue nodded and flicked his eyes with a tempered smile and kept walking.

This is more than just a rogue greenery, Heli leaned in to transfer a private thought to Dous and Terra. *Remember what Justin said about this place, if anyone from the outside knew about it, it wouldn't exist. If they're hiding this, what else do you think they aren't telling us?*

Cue cut in, "What some see as an illicit cause, we consider revolutionary. We live here in this space by our own set of rules, communally regulated, sharing what we alone can cultivate in a collective effort to survive. We're self-sustaining, and we place no drain on the outside. We leave no trace of our footprint on their precious AG Regulatory terms. I'd say we're all better off."

"A win, win of sorts?" Heli wondered aloud.

"Well…yes, and we pride ourselves on it. Everyone here does their part to provide what they can to benefit the system." Cue nodded toward a passerby, a man who looked to be carrying some assortment of rigging. As Heli moved his eyes up from the man's tote, he noticed the way he stared back with two dark eyes, a gleaming intensity. It was only then that Heli began to observe the interested looks they had all been getting from just about everyone who walked by.

"System? Commune you mean? Sounds like something out of a Change-Maker society manual," Heli said.

Before Cue could answer, Dous interrupted, "What's that over there?" He pointed toward some kind of a watch tower. It was covered by the same foliage that surrounded them lower to the ground. The only hint that it wasn't a natural part of the grove were the small circular windows.

"Our survey station." Cue pointed out.

"How is it possible to hide something like this? Those on the outside certainly have the technology to weed you out," Heli asked.

"This is so much bigger than the small plot my mother kept but it never took long for them to come hovering around and we'd have to turn it under. How do you keep this hidden from them?" Terra eyes never left the garden.

"We're not living under some cloaking device if that's what you're suggesting." Cue quirked a slight smile and his tone shifted, "But as much as the outsiders and their regulators have faith in their controls, their superstitions remain intact."

"A bit cryptic isn't it?" Heli asked.

"Not at all, if you're familiar with this region and its history." Cue paused, looking back toward Heli as he went on, "This area has long been believed to be cursed. That's what keeps them away…a nice cozy pocket of ignorance, leaving us with the perfect opportunity to take full advantage of."

Heli noticed how Terra had moved in closer, leaning into him for support. He began to feel the same force of nature pulling on the fibers of every muscle in his body. Ragged with fatigue and still loaded down with their belongings he said, "I think we'll take you up on that rest now."

"Yes, we have some time before the evening meal at sundown. We can discuss this more later. Emeal will lead you to your covert." He stretched out a hand in the direction of the trenched mole holes Heli had observed earlier.

Emeal slid in between them as Cue moved out, relieved of his station. Without a word, she waved for them to follow her. Heli turned and saw Dous struggling against Zuke's wheels caked with clotted dirt from the terrain.

"You need a hand?" Heli asked.

"I don't know how I'm ever going to get around in this place," Dous murmured and he shrank in his seat. His voice was a shrewd version of itself.

"Here, I'll get you up the hill at least." Without waiting for permission Heli took hold of Zuke from behind and pushed Dous up the incline.

On their way up the slope, Dous lifted his head. "This place... it isn't exactly what I had in mind for a relocation destination."

Heli leaned in close placing a heavy hand on Dous' shoulder, *Well, knowing you as I do, you'll find a way around this.*

When they reached the coverts, Heli could see the terraced uneven lines of earth-ship dwellings come into view. The structures were like horizontal rivulets running across the face of the hillside. The facade gave no clue to the size of the space which extended back into the mound of earth. On each level, of which there were three, there was a ledge-like pathway cut into the dirt mound to serve as a small extension deck. They connected like the spokes of a wheel along a pathway of trellised rows. Etched into the earth around them were three lines converging into one. A single lane eventually brought them all together with a switchback path zig-zagging down from both the right and left sides of the slope.

Dous was quiet, unlike himself. Heli watched him, wondering.

He knew that if Dous was working his magic the answer to his next question might serve to smooth his friend's dour mood. "Does your aquifer have a surface spring?" Heli asked Emeal suddenly.

"Yes, right at the water table, just below the groundwater flow there's a small storage pool."

"Could you swim in it?" Dous's head popped up, a smile replacing his frown.

"Sure, but most of its storage volume is under a permeable layer of rock, and the temperature...well, it's very cold. Only about 18-20 degrees Celsius." She looked between the two boys curiously.

"But swimmable? I mean, with the proper Hodgewear; it wouldn't pollute the source?" Heli asked.

"Well, no swimming in it wouldn't likely taint the water, but it's no lake by any means. The water that seeps up into the spring basin is about forty meters long and twenty-five meters wide. What doesn't go directly from the underwater basin into our aqueducts for community consumption is stored there to irrigate crops." Emeal pointed toward the garden and looked back at them. "What remains is used to water the livestock we keep. Why do you ask?"

Dous had come alive again, sitting on Zuke. He looked at her with a lopsided smile. Heli could read his thoughts. *Abracadabra! Manifesto Presto!*

Don't know if you can rightfully claim that one. That pool has been here longer than you or I have. Heli pressed down on Dous' shoulder unnecessarily.

Hey, I'm just getting started. Now all I need is something to keep me entertained. Dous projected the thought before Emeal pinched her eyes on them both. Terra cleared her throat. Heli and Dous both jumped, realizing how their inner dialogue had initiated an uncomfortable silence that was cause for suspicion.

"It's for me. I would be the only one swimming. It helps me keep up with things." Emeal's eyes shifted over to Dous and down toward his legs. Dous projected what only Heli and Terra could comprehend, *Little things—like my sanity.*

Emeal nodded toward him. "I see." She turned away to call out to a young girl who was scrubbing some kind of fibrous material in a large cistern near one of the shelters. It steamed off as she worked. She withdrew the wet material as it clung to itself and she clipped it up along a long line of other unidentifiable parcels. Heli had seen this sort of community wash and dry in historical film cubes once. He became fascinated by the simple use of pure manpower that had been taken over by machines so long ago.

The girl who looked to be about their age approached them swiftly, wiping her hands on her tawny fitted tunic. She wore the short garb in the way most of them did: plain as day but striking somehow in its modest style. The tips of her lighter hair were a bright cobalt blue slicing out in spikes along her shoulders, an unusual accent to her features that set her apart from the others.

"Mianna, I'm wondering if you would be available to take Dous on a little tour of the Frey's spring basin before the evening meal?" Emeal nodded toward the girl.

"Of course. I was just finishing up." Her voice trilled with animation, and she caught her last word with an intake of air, holding back unbidden enthusiasm, behaving as if she were being bestowed some honor that she didn't feel she was deserving of.

Her eyes spun between them, unsure of how to proceed.

Dous sat staring with his eyes open wide on the girl and suddenly he rocketed from his position, speeding on Zuke's wheels to greet her.

"I'm him...I mean, that's me." He shook his head absently. "I'm Dous." He sort of cringed, muttering to himself softly with an exhale. She smiled down on him, her pale blue eyes inquisitive enough.

"Shall we?" He reeled his way around and past her in the direction of the waterway. She looked back at Emeal and then to Heli and Terra, shrugging once more before skip-stepping to catch up with him. They exchanged a few words out of earshot and Heli considered trying to get a read on Dous's thoughts but thought better of it. At that same moment Terra reached to take Heli's hand, eying him cautiously and smiling back at him. Reading his thoughts, she offered him the reward of a gentle squeeze.

Emeal interrupted, "Don't worry about him, he's in good hands." Heli projected a quick thought, *Yup, made to order hands I'm sure.*

"They'll meet up with us for our sundown meal." She led them both up a slight incline toward the door to one of the first level coverts. Heli stood back, waiting, staring at Terra and then casting a glance toward their guide, feeling an odd twinge of awkwardness forming.

"Excuse me?" Terra's voice softened, "Will we be sharing the same covert?"

"Yes. Will that be a problem?" Emeal looked at Terra and then to Heli, seemingly unaffected by their concern. "We have limited space here. We're working on plans for the next installation of coverts on the other side of this mound," She nodded to the side of the hill, "but at this point, we have to make due with what's available. We all share accordingly."

She set her chin up and raised an eyebrow. "There are two separate chambers in the covert. You may divide them in whatever way suits you. An indoor fire circlet may be lit in the evening and early morning hours. Timer controled rationing of the unit's bioethanol is automatic during operational hours."

"We'll be fine." Heli nudged Terra, pulling at the curve of her waistline to move them into the small alcove of the covert.

Emeal nodded and stepped back from the threshold. "Happy rest then. We will see you at sundown." Her eyes went to Terra first, then landed on Heli before she turned and disappeared into the shadows of the path leading away.

Entering the low-lit space and emptying his hands of the load they carried, Heli felt the kind of morose exhaustion that might have him losing his temper if he didn't get some time out from the busy Frey. He reached with a hand to the side mount on the wall to signal the sensors and raise the lighting as they entered. A heavy earthen odor instantly filled his lungs to match the view.

"It smells like vanilla moss and heaven in here." Terra relaxed in Heli's grip the moment they crossed the threshold into the center chamber.

Together they looked out on the expanse of space beyond the covert entrance.

"Not quite the little pocket of dirt I was expecting," Heli said. The entire room was a cast of priestly greens interspersed with the lighter fare of alabaster tones.

"This is no pocket of dirt. It's amazing!" And she let go of Heli's hand to prance forward toward where a free-standing fireplace sat centered among a sunken lounge area. "I could get lost in here."

"You're okay with this arrangement?" Heli asked.

"Yeah." She turned around to look back at him. "Are you?"

"I'm...fine with it, just not sure it's such a good idea."

"Why not? You survived having Dous as a roommate," She offered and sat, sliding her hand along the face of one of the cushions.

"Yea but having Dous as a roommate is one thing. This is altogether different." Heli wanted her to agree, or at least give him a glimmer of her thoughts at this moment, but she shielded him for some reason.

"Heli we've been together for nearly a year. This doesn't feel that unusual in the natural progression of things and we don't really have much of a choice in the matter." Terra glanced back up at him.

"So, here we are." He swallowed while his stomach did a flip.

"Here we are," Her lip twisted into a grin and she moved one of the cushions to leave an open gap next to her. "Maybe..." She paused, "we just relax and know that it's out of our hands," she patted the space next to her. "We enjoy the moment."

"Easier said than done." He stood frozen. *If I could actually stand in a room alone with you and not feel like my heart's been set on fire,* He projected.

"Speaking of fire." Her hand reached to press the sensor on the side of the center table. He watched her every move, while every ounce of him warmed with the flames. He had already imagined how easily they would both slip into a catatonic slumber among the cushions.

"I think it's safe." She looked up from the flames that were licking the edge of the glass tube and smiled. She let her hand fall down in the vacant spot again next to her.

Heli slid his hands into the pockets of his Hodgesuit and slowly made his way down the stairs toward her. The sweet smile she cast up at him gave him good cause to press on.

With some semblance of a subject change Heli sank down next to her, "I couldn't have dreamed this place up." He looked around, but his eyes were drawn hopelessly back to her. "I wasn't sure you could stand being cooped up in here for long."

Heli sucked in the peat moist air watching her.

"Oh, I can certainly stand it." She rolled her shoulders, "I'm just afraid that if I fall asleep now, I'll never wake up." Terra's airy voice was low and smooth as she slid down into the conclave of pillows surrounding them.

He bypassed the opportunity to speak again and leaned back beside her. She shifted in toward him, wrapping herself around his edges. Their bodies fit together like the grooves of a woodworking joint, intertwined into one solid dovetail fit.

He kissed the top of Terra's head as the tension withdrew, fading into a cloud of sleep he might never wish to wake from.

Another

Waking in the dark, Heli felt a still sense of reluctance to stir. He winked one eye open to peer down at Terra cradled in his arms. She was wrapped up comfortably against him like a paper doll, light and fragile, as if the slightest movement might rouse her and tear her from his reach. Perhaps it would be better to stave off consciousness and allow the shadowy contours of the room to bring him back to the timeless, effortless space he'd just left. *If she's dreaming...*

Terra's small hands pressed up against his chest and twitched as she began to stir. He watched as her eyelids fluttered slowly up and closed again.

Mmm...That helped.

It still surprised him how communicating with her this way always inspired a spellbound thrill in him, a colorful truth only they could translate. The sun was down, he knew, and he could feel it in the same way he felt the settling of his own bones in their sockets. Did they miss the evening meal? At this point he didn't much care. He could fast until the morning sated by the mere fact that he held all the sustenance he would ever need in his arms.

"Forget dinner. Let's just stay here, like this," Heli caught his next words in his throat, *forever,* and she burrowed into him deeper.

"But Dous…and we need to go out and meet these people. Besides, how are we ever going to learn anything about this place without getting out there?" She pushed up onto one arm. Heli still lay on his back staring up at the ceiling, a canvas of mudded stucco.

"I don't know. We could just live like hermits in our little hole here." He felt a smile coming on and he squeezed her tighter.

"Ha, ha," She muttered.

"But seriously what do you think about all this?" Heli asked. She pushed off him and swung her legs around to sit up. She was still within reach. He let his hand fall next to her and gently drew a line with his finger up from her wrist to her elbow. He watched the goose bumps prickle across her skin.

"I think we can't go making any assumptions yet." She stopped and looking down at Heli's hand on her arm, "And...I think you'll need to stop doing that if we're ever going to make it out the door," she continued to fumble around the cushioning making her way to the center to stand.

"Are you coming? Or shall I tell them you're being held captive by a mad mesh of pillows?" She picked one of them up and tossed it at him. He was quick and sat up in the instant it took to catch her pitch.

"I'd really rather stay here and finish this pillow fight," he said and her eyes narrowed in on him.

She continued walking away from him toward the door, "Don't even think of reading my mind right now."

He took a deep breath, jumped up and rushed to catch up with her just as she was reaching for the sensor, ignorant to his advances. She startled when he took hold of her one last time around the waist, spinning her around in a pirouette to face him, "You know, those pillows might come in handy when you have to fend me off." He let his forehead come down to meet hers. "This arrangement could become difficult."

"Don't worry, we're stronger than that." She peered into his eyes, meeting them this time without contest. But a hint of the tease rested in the shine of her gaze and she carefully removed herself from his embrace, firmly taking his hand and pulling him out the door with her.

***

They walked down the path toward the flickering incandescence that seemed to spread out to every angle of the meadow. From the center of the Frey the fire's torch emitted a glow that offered a cast of silver haze over each stranger's face. Heli held Terra's hand tighter and they merged into the assembly of tipping heads, to be engulfed by the crowd. Dous came into view about ten meters ahead of them. He was seated on Zuke, pulled up at the edge of the wall near the flames. The fire pit's cylindrical glass casing towered above them, nearly fifteen feet across in diameter and as tall as an old-time silo. As intoxicating as the warmth was, each fiery tongue licking the transparent wall of the inferno made Heli wish they weren't standing so close.

A familiar voice cut through the cast of voices surrounding them, "Hey guys!" Dous rolled forward from the burning backdrop.

Mianna stood by, withdrawn and scanning the crowd.

"You guys get some rest?" He asked, and his voice squeaked a bit.

"Yeah, sorry we're late," Terra said.

Heli looked at Dous. *Have a nice tour?*

Yea, Mianna just took me down to the water, remember? Dous answered and looked back at her waving an inviting hand. She smiled. Approaching them her gaze never left the ground.

Terra let go of Heli's hand to offer it in greeting, "Glad to see a familiar face. It's great that you could show Dous around. I'm sure he gets tired of being stuck with us all the time." She shared the rest in a thought, *I think the new social scenery did you some good.* Dous's lip curled.

Mianna nodded and looked down at the ground while her sandaled foot swirled in the dirt. "Wonderful to finally have you all here. We've heard so much about you."

"Heard about us?" Heli asked.

"Yes, my father…you met him earlier…when you first arrived," she said.

"Cue?" Heli confirmed.

"Yes, well he's kept the Frey informed of your contributions. We're all very grateful," she said.

"What contributions?" Heli turned to look out among the nameless alien faces in the crowd that seemed even more distinctly foreign at the moment.

"What you've done to provide a much-needed change. Dous told me of your time at the institute where my father grew up." She darted a glance around between them as if attempting to read the confusion in their stares.

"He didn't tell you?" She whispered this time and looked around through the endless crowd, a teaming stream of people.

"Tell us what?" Heli asked.

"We all know who you are. Where you came from," she offered.

"Who we are?" Heli arched his back to stand a little taller.

That would explain the looks. Terra angled her head toward the group of strangers surrounding them.

"What looks?" Dous spoke, looking around again, and then his thoughts came pressing through.

Guess I'm used to it...people staring.

"What exactly is it you know about us?" Heli stared hard into Mianna's bewildered eyes.

"I...I need to go find my father." Mianna turned and quickly bent down on her knee to get eye to eye with Dous. She laid a hand on his arm and he froze. Only the slight twitch in his eyes gave him away.

"It was a pleasure being your escort." She stood tall again and dusted off the sides of her coverlet. "I'll see you around." And her eyes lingered on his for a moment before she moved off in the opposite direction.

"She's an odd one," Heli said.

"What do you mean?" Dous's eyes didn't leave her as she had disappeared into the crowd.

"He means nothing" Terra interjected. "She's lovely and very polite, and it sounds like she wants to help us get acquainted with this place." Her eyes came down forcibly on Heli and her words projected, *Lay off.*

"I know she didn't exactly volunteer to help me out, but I think she's...."

Heli threw up a hand out in front of Dous to stop him. "Sorry, I was rude."

"You, apologizing. Wow! Quite the step up. I think this place might be having an effect on you too," Dous joked.

"Don't press your luck. I admit I was kind of...," Heli stuttered.

"Ungracious," Terra finished for him, and Dous lifted a pointed finger, "And...obnoxious. Sums it up nicely."

"Tch! I'm not that far off the mark. You don't really know her or any of these people. But I do think it's wise for us to find out what we can about this place and she seems all too willing to oblige. Just keep doing whatever it is you're doing. She seems to have taken to you," Heli added.

Dous looked at Heli. "Since when did I need your permission to make friends here? And I like her too, but...not like that, I just met her for Pete's sake!" *And don't you even think I'm gonna use this relationship to settle your suspicions about this place.* Dous bridled his thoughts.

"Relationship? Oh, it's a relationship now? And I have good reason to question their involvement with hiding us here. Even your girlfriend admits it. It's not like we're your everyday guests." Heli mocked him, lifting his eyebrows.

"I've only known her for like…a day," Dous said and looked down to hide the scarlet surfacing on his cheeks.

"Careful, I only knew the two of you for a split second before I was bound to you for life," Heli replied.

She might be the better alternative. Dous shared.

"Okay, you two, are we done here? I think we've all established where we each stand with all of this," Terra intervened, "and the only thing I've come to realize sitting here listening to the two of you bicker is that I'm starving." She grabbed hold of Heli's arm and reached to cup one of Dous' hands lightly under the crux of her arm. "Time to eat!"

Capacities

"At least we survived a full week here." Dous reached toward the bowl of fruit centered on the communal table. He plucked a fuzzy fleshy object from the choices that had dwindled down to a few slim pickings of fruit and half torn away bits of bread in baskets.

"What are you talking about? You've had that cozy little suite all to yourself the entire week," Heli said.

"Yeah, and you volunteered to sleep out on the couch."

"Had I known we were calling permanent bunks I would've reconsidered," Heli thought it was best to keep the fact that his evening ritual had for some time consisted of late nights spent with Terra where they could sneak off to explore the grounds long after the Synthasphere had retired.

"I guess if you're up for a switch, it's only fair," Dous offered.

"Na, wasted space." Heli flicked a glance at Terra, satisfied with the flush of pink that took over her face.

"You were home late last night," Terra commented to Dous as she continued to glaze over the assortment on the table. He looked up at her, surprised, and then glanced at Heli.

"I didn't even hear you come in," Heli added.

"Uh...yeah. You were sleeping, I didn't want to wake you. Mianna took me to the lab so I could try on the thermal Hodgesuit she's been working on," he answered and proceeded to nit-pick through the food options with a more studious approach.

"Funny, she doesn't even wear them herself. None of these people do. Why would she be dealing with specialized Hodgesuits?" Heli glared at his friend.

"I didn't get that much information. Besides, I was just grateful that she went through all the trouble to get me that one. I'm kind of losing it without my daily sprints," Dous said.

"And how was it?" Heli asked casually, picking through the tidbits, and coming up empty handed.

"How was what?"

"The suit? The water?" Heli felt Terra tug on him. He ignored her.

"The thing actually works," Dous said.

"Pretty high grade for a swim suit in a place like this." Heli scanned the crowd.

Dous paused, and Heli turned and could see all traces of humor leave his friend's face. His thoughts came searing through, *Sorry, I didn't think to dig any deeper. I'll keep that in mind the next time she does something exceptionally nice for me, just in case there's a hidden agenda behind it.*

The scowl on Dous's face disappeared and his eyes suddenly grew wider to fall on a new focal point. Mianna stood about ten meters away talking to a woman slightly set apart from the influx of people in the growing mecca. The woman wore some kind of bulging sack in front of her. Only with closer examination did Heli realize two tiny feet sticking out on either side of the sack. She was wearing the child like it was an extension of her garment.

Heli's focus returned and Dous suddenly sat a little taller. Without another word he shoved Zuke off to merge into the crowd with one final thought before he was out of reach, *Excuse me, I've got better things to do than take abuse from you.*

"You have to stop doing that to him." Terra looked at Heli.

"What's so wrong with showing a little precaution? It's not like we don't have good cause to be suspicious of these people. And besides, like she said herself, they all know about us. But we don't have a clue who they are." He nodded toward Mianna, who now had her hand on Dous's shoulder, introducing him to the woman with the baby.

Terra looked over at them. "Is that woman wearing a baby?" She quirked her head.

"I have no idea. These people have a strange sense of fashion." He pretended not to have noticed.

Actually, it kind of makes sense, Terra thought.

"Why do you always have to take his side?" Heli asked.

"Not that; how she wears the baby so they're always together. It's like she's holding it, but her hands are free to go about her business." Terra shook her head, then looked back at him, "It's really none of our business what Dous does with regards to her. We need to give him a little space."

"We don't know these people and there's no way I'll be making myself at home just yet. It puts us all at risk," Heli aimed at being more convincing.

"If you never took risks, you'd still be alone," she said and reached a hand to place it on his shoulder. It slowly traveled up to his neck and her eyes softened, "He needs room." Heli let out a puff of air, looking away from her.

"Look, I know how you are with new people. It'll take some time, but you need to trust him. He's not going to put us at risk by making friends here."

Avoiding her gaze, Heli looked up at the sky to notice a color of cerulean blue it had never adorned before.

Do you always have to…, His thoughts were cut short as she moved in up close to put her arms around him putting a dent in any discord. When he brought is head down her lips met his.

A throat clearing came from behind them. Cue stood waiting. "Sorry, I was hoping to speak with you. Mianna expressed that you wish to consult with me. I'm available now if you can tear yourself away." He seemed to be concealing a smile behind his hardened stare.

Heli turned to look at Terra; she nodded, and Cue spoke again addressing her, "Emeal is down at the quarry along the eastern rim. She's looking forward to showing you around. We've heard you may have some skills that could come in handy down there."

"With rocks?" Terra asked.

"Oh, it's much more than rocks," Cue answered.

Terra glanced at Heli and squeezed his hand. *We have to put our trust in good people.*

He nodded slowly. *I'll come find you after this.* As she moved away, Heli clenched her hand like a lifeline. She squeezed back and the tension in him faded as she gently let go and made her way down the slope beyond his reach.

"So where to? Or do we hash this out right here and now?" Heli asked, and he looked around at the circle of people swarming about.

"I assumed you wanted to have a conversation, not a confrontation? I know Mianna may have been more than forthright in sharing and I believe you feel that I owe you some explanation. So, walk with me. I want to show you something." Cue turned, leading them in the opposite direction of the center square.

"Your daughter doesn't hold back much," Heli said as he caught up. "Just how much do they all really know? I mean, they look at us like we're…" He paused trying to find the precise words.

Cue finished his sentence for him, "Icons."

"I was gonna to say Freaks, but okay." Heli exhaled.

Cue lifted a hand as they walked and rubbed his chin like he was checking to feel how clean shaven he was. "You three are very important to all of us. The Frey wouldn't exist without our belief and connection to the prophecy. And so, to call you icons or heroes, or even the Cor for that matter, it's simply in reference to the value we place upon what you represent in this world."

"Well, you seem to be pretty important around these parts," Heli said.

Cue nodded. "I serve my purpose." There was a wryness to his smile.

"Mianna said you spent some time at the institute, at IDEA?"

"She did, did she? Hmm…well yes, we spent some time there."

"We?" Heli cocked his head.

"Emeal and I and...there were others at that time," Cue confirmed.

"So...you knew Tracy?"

"I did," Cue answered abruptly, "and with what more you need to know, we should finish this conversation in my station. It's just up this way."

Cue turned and began heading up the incline toward the watch tower hidden among the thicker bushes and groves of trees. Heli skipped up to walk alongside Cue, who took one step to every two Heli could meet in stride.

They approached a narrow staircase that went up at a steep angle, a ladder to the sky. It ended on the mounted platform of the encased tower. Cue led the way while Heli followed.

"Nice treehouse," Heli joked.

"I like to think up here," Cue said, and Heli watched as Cue walked along the perimeter of the circular space.

Machinery lined every inch of wall space in the station. Wall to wall; the mother-load of motherboards. They had entered an encasement housing the largest interfacing system Heli had ever seen. His eyes began to water as he watched the busy fractals of light randomly flicker around the room on each of the lower dashboards below the dark screens. He stood still in wonder. There was nowhere to sit, and he waited for something to beep or buzz and signal them on.

Cue proceeded to squat down right in front of Heli on the solid flooring. It looked very uncomfortable, yet his legs were crossed, monk-style, as if he were settling in for his daily meditation.

"Sit," He commanded. Heli stalled for a moment before doing as he was told.

"This computer houses everything we need to know about the outside world. That's how we were kept informed of your progress."

Heli remembered the tower overlooking the Strata.

"You were in direct contact with Tracy here?" Heli asked.

"Yes. She sent us daily reports along with visuo-file attachments." He looked directly at Heli through fathomless green eyes, "I've been waiting for the confirmation of your achievements for a very long time, watching you, learning who you are," he said.

Heli wanted to move from the subject while under the pressure of such small confines. "This thing we did, I've already noticed the changes. When I look at the sky...there are colors I've never known before and I don't have to think before I breathe. The evidence is everywhere."

Cue let out a smiling sigh. "Our second chance. The Regeneration. You three made that possible."

"I know your people can see it too, but what about all the others? Those living outside the Frey? When will they begin to see?" Heli asked.

"It's already happening. I've been in contact with other stations such as this all around the globe and they're seeing the same evidence as well," Cue confirmed.

"Other stations?" Heli asked.

"Yes, there are a few other sustaining settlements much like this one, but they are too few and far between and most remain in isolated seclusion or in hiding," Cue answered.

"Well if the news is traveling, then its good news, right? It worked. Time to reap the benefits," Heli commented.

"Reap the benefits?" Cue looked him over with an evaluative eye.

"Yea, things are going to be okay. The world isn't going to come to a horrific end and people can move on." Heli already knew just how untrue his statement was and his gut twisted with the knowledge that this was far from over. He drew a hand up sliding it through his hair.

"For the change to be permanent, we all must decide." Cue squinted at Heli.

"How do you plan on making that happen?" Heli asked.

"That's the tricky part. It's something that will require an evolution of thought and teaching. We all have to want the change badly enough to be willing to make the necessary sacrifices for it."

"Sacrifices? I thought that was the whole reason we did what we did, so that others wouldn't have to make that sacrifice," Heli said.

"You don't really believe that do you?" Cue asked.

"Look, all I know is that people who don't bend easily, eventually break. And if that's your plan for a brighter future, you're no better than the Regulation."

Cue paused, one eyebrow popped up. "Decisions don't always have to be black or white, there's always room in the middle for grey."

"I'm confused, I thought that we were brought here for our own safety and now we're talking about...I don't even know what we're talking about." Heli stared at Cue, his fingers were feeling a familiar flush of heat.

Cue's left hand fell open out toward Heli, his palm faced down. "Do you recognize this?

Heli observed the mark on the loose skin between his thumb and forefinger. He knew the familiar curve of the unfinished circle. "Your people wear it."

"But you've seen it before?" Cue inclined.

"Yes. It was all over the institute."

"This mark represents you—the three of you. It's your symbol. These people all wear it because they believe in it. And they believe in you and the message you bring," Cue said.

"I don't feel like the messenger," Heli said, mollifying his tone a bit.

"In the circle, there is believed to be the essence of enlightenment. It refers to the beginning and end of all things. But within," he tapped the inner part of the imprint with his index finger, "the interconnectedness of everything."

"I don't get it. How is it supposed to represent us? Why didn't Tracy tell us about this? I just assumed it was some kind of branding."

"It has ancient ties to beliefs long abated in our world. This knowledge was sacred to her and as you know she had valid reasons for the secrets she kept," Cue said.

"I'm sure she would have told us at some point," Heli looked at the mark again.

"She ran out of time." Cue dropped his head. "And you are not only a representation of everything she held dear, but its manifestation proven by your effective entry and exit from the Strata. It's why she did what she did and risked her life to go in and assure your safe passage." Cue nodded.

"Why was it just Tracy and the others? Why not you? Why leave her to deal with this essentially alone?" Heli felt his chest constrict.

"I haven't set foot on those grounds since the day I left many years ago," Cue confessed.

"But why? She should have never been left to handle all of that alone."

"I will share my reasons with you in time, but Tracy was the only one who could stay to prepare you. Her qualifications were in her gifts and like the three of you, her mission was one of chosen obligation. She understood this; she had her choice in aids and was able to meet every challenge with an equally thorough response."

"That explains the Bobbsey twins," Heli muttered in a short breath.

"They are hardly that." A strange bewildered smile took over Cue's face. "But yes, she selected them as her aids and IDEA's representatives supported the decision."

"IDEA used her," Heli said.

"No, they needed her, and she did her job as a willing participant. As for 'Justin and Mr. Cruise', they have their own reasons for remaining loyal to the cause."

"But Jacque," Heli shook his head, "he buried her alive in there."

Cue's voice was firm. "Although we would all like to lay blame on that man for the event of her death, all my reports show that she went in voluntarily to see you all through. Her death was a valiant effort to bring about the critical change. He deserves no credit for that."

"What's the story between the two of you?" Heli asked.

Cue adjusted his position on the floor, artfully shifting their focus, "I can't get into all of that now, but as you spend more time here I will help you come to understand. You've only just arrived as our welcomed guests. Our primary objective starts and ends with keeping you safe. Please allow me to handle the details in achieving that." He leaned forward to stand. "I have a few things I must attend to now, but I would love for you and your friends to join me for the noon meal."

Heli shook off the feeling tied to the abrupt end of their conversation. "O...kay. Is there anything you would like us to be doing in the meantime? I mean, we might be your guests, but we certainly have the ability to earn our meal ticket."

"Actually, yes, you might join Emeal and Terra down by the quarry. She can show you some of the operations and you can think about ways you might wish to contribute." Cue nodded and continued, "Thank you...for offering." Seeming genuinely surprised, Cue reached out to offer Heli a hand as they both moved to stand. Staring at the mark again, Heli ignored Cue's offering.

"I've seen this all before you know," Heli said, "I went round and round with Tracy when we first arrived at IDEA."

Cue's slanted green eyes flickered. "You don't trust easily, do you?"

"My circle is small, if that's what you mean."

Cue lifted his hand again to study the mark, his shoulders dropped, "Our circle here will remain open." He looked up at Heli.

"How familiar were you…" Heli felt a crack in his senses, but he went on, "With Tracy? I mean, if she wanted us here then I'll abide by her wishes, but the only way my circle expands is if you're upfront with me."

"We were as close as two friends could be."

"Really?" Heli asked.

"Purely plutonic, I can assure you. We trusted one another with our lives. She was family to me and I would gladly have laid my life down for her if I had been given the opportunity." Inhaling he seemed to be working to expel some other thought.

"So, I have nothing to worry about and I should trust you. As long as we're here, we're safe, right?"

Cue looked at Heli again. "That is one promise I intend to keep as long as I'm standing."

Heli held his tongue to keep from saying anything more.

"Please, enjoy your stay here." A lighter breath escaped Cue's broad chest and a smile returned to his face, "We only want for you to feel at home and comfortable in your new surroundings."

"Safe and sound." Heli whispered.

"I will look for you and your friends at the noon meal." Then Cue disappeared down the pocketed hole where the steep stairs met the ground below.

Heli sat alone for a time, with the cold granite eyes glaring back from all angles of the switchboard surrounding him. Empty faces mirroring echoes of information. Untold secrets—secrets about him, about all of them. And he was familiar with this kind of negotiation. The spoon-feeding, just enough information to keep them there. He could taste it; a subtle bitterness like silken citrus on the pallet, familiar and fading into a delayed astringency until he was ready to experience its full flavor.

It was time to go, and he started down the staircase. Every step added to his predominant urge to climb back up into the hovering chamber and hunker down until he could sense the all-clear.

The Quarry

"I'm sorry about Heli. He can be a bit…" Terra paused to look at Mianna, aiming for the right words, "abrasive sometimes." She wiped her soiled hands together, *Like steel wool*, she thought. She carefully removed a tuft of a wild plant poking out of the aggregate along the rock face where they had been sent to forage.

"He doesn't like me. It's obvious." Mianna looked up.

"It's not that, he's just…" Terra shook her head unsure of what to say.

"I get it," Mianna said, "He doesn't know me, and he doesn't trust me." She continued pruning sprigs of the wild thyme that grew out of the cracks of limestone.

"It's not that he doesn't like you, he's just like that around new people," Terra tried.

Emeal had left the two girls alone to gather greens along the sloping wall of chiseled stone handholds.

Terra laid a hand along the craggy rock surface, a daunting step ladder made of stone, feeling along the tiny hairline of new sprouts. In actuality it was a goldmine of botanical arrangements. Every crack burst with emerald trails of thriving flora. Emeal had explained how old quarry sites such as this, where the land still wore scars of a savage past, could now serve as nurseries to rare and valuable plant species. Those in the Frey foraged the area to gather the ingredients for medicinal and culinary use.

"Quite a work ethic here," Terra said.

There were others working along the wall, each in their own boxy scaffolding, filling containers that hung on the rims of the handrails. Terra eyed her own collection that had not yet met capacity but was filling up nicely.

Mianna looked over Terra's shoulder. "Our community thrives on the energy of productivity. There's something to be said for having a purpose beyond yourself and working hard in spite of the challenges."

"I'm just impressed by how it all comes together so well here. Almost seamless." Terra shook her head. "I can tell you one thing, it's not like this where I come from." Terra's hand lingered on a crack in the wall.

"It isn't perfect here either. We all just really want this to work. Mostly because all of our lives depend on it." She kept picking while she spoke. Her fingers delicately pinching.

"I happen to believe wholeheartedly that perfection is a disease. I would never suggest that anything is perfect, but there's...balance here. You all hold it together so well."

"My father and others in our community have spent many years preparing an environment to sustain all of this," Mianna admitted.

"Well, I've never felt like I fit in anywhere, but this place, your people...I think it's a very noble existence."

"Noble?" Mianna shrugged.

"I think it requires some bravery to accomplish the unconventional."

"The work we do serves more than one purpose. You'll see it in the starter clutches where the children play. We emphasize early on the value of independence and freedom within limits, but there's always been a primary respect for the overall communal development."

Terra watched as those in her periphery seemed to work in a unified fluid motion.

"You see that girl over there?" Mianna nodded toward one of the boxes nearly twenty feet down the scaling wall frame holding two very jubilant youths.

"The one laughing, with the boy?" Terra noticed how the girl was giggling profusely at something the boy had just said. Their chatter bounced off of the acoustic curve of the wall, volleying between partners.

Mianna shifted, reaching across to remove a sprig from Terra's platter and toss it onto another one of the many trays within arm's reach. "They've been sent to work together for a reason." Mianna lifted her eyebrows, looking sidelong at Terra.

"What do you mean?" Terra asked, and she watched how the girl's hand kept flying out and touching the boys shoulder as she bent over giggling.

"You may have noticed. We don't get a lot of free time here to socialize. It keeps us out of trouble. The work supports our socialization and often we're paired up accordingly. When the elders sense a bond, they find ways to support it."

"Elders? Like your father and Emeal?" Terra asked.

"Yes, and many others who aid in the decision making here. Creative controls." Mianna hesitated and then blew out a labored breath as if she wasn't sure if her next words should be spoken out loud.

"I never meant to get in the way, or to get in the middle of anything you have. Dous is just really nice. He's funny, you know?" And she returned to the business of pruning, her plucking more vigorous with every reach.

"Yes, he's annoyingly charming that way."

"You guys are really close?"

"Well yeah, he was my first friend when I arrived at IDEA." Terra wondered if she may have been reading more into Mianna's comment.

"He's probably my best friend. He's been great about Heli and me." Terra stumbled over her words.

"You and Heli?" Mianna stopped what she was doing and looked at Terra with wide unblinking eyes.

"I thought you knew everything about us," Terra said.

"Just general information, like how you were brought to IDEA, and how you formed the necessary bond, and the rest is history…or I guess not, since you were the ones who had a hand in rewriting it." Terra noticed the nervous way Mianna's speech had sped up and her picking resumed with a note of renewed enthusiasm.

"How do you put up with him?" Mianna asked.

"I don't know, we just sort of…happened. I didn't even like him when we first met." She shook her head.

"But you're sure now? He's the one?" She asked.

Terra felt the warmth rushing to her cheeks and didn't quite know how to answer. "Well, we're together, if that's what you mean."

"But it's obviously more than that. I mean, there's so much more to it. At least that's what I've been lead to believe."

"What you were led to believe?" Terra asked.

"The unique bond between you. From our teachings. You're…the Cor," Mianna sputtered.

Terra pulled her hand down from the wall dropping the sprigs she had been holding and many of them toppled to the ground beneath them. "What does this have to do with what's personal between us?"

"Your relationship is everything to us. Without it, we can't move forward." Mianna stared back.

"Feels like we're under some kind of a microscope here." Terra turned to stare at the rock face. "Adds a bit more pressure to the situation," She exhaled.

"I say you're lucky. What's between you is confirmed and you don't have to worry about all the other complicated stuff," Mianna confided.

"Oh, there's where you're wrong." Terra lifted her eyes to look up at the small crags set above her head. "It's much more complicated than you can imagine, even for us. All I know is that despite everything I've done to avoid it, we ended up here together. Don't get me wrong, I have no regrets, I just have to wonder how it is for everyone else." Terra peered up to look at Mianna again.

"I wouldn't know," Mianna admitted.

"You will."

"All they teach is the honey bee and the flower." Mianna clasped her hands together in front of her.

"Bees? Oh boy, I think I know where this is going," Terra said.

"No, not that. They explained it in reference to your connection. You three have some measure of symbiosis?" She seemed unsure of herself.

"I guess that would make sense. But that would suggest that we have no choice in the matter," Terra said.

"But you love him. That is your choice," Mianna seemed to want to clarify, and Terra was suddenly feeling uncomfortable confiding with someone she would have qualified as a stranger only a week ago.

"Yes, I do." And the words found their place, solid like the rock in front of her. Terra paused thinking about how she and Heli had never really openly professed their love for one another beyond playful taunts, "What about you? Are you with someone?"

Mianna blushed a healthy pink and shuffled her feet on the makeshift platform beneath them. It swayed and creaked, loosening the gravely limestone sheath they were propped up against.

"Friends can be hard to come by here." She looked up at Terra. "It's not their fault. I think they all just see me as an extension of my father. All the boys are afraid to talk to me, and the girls…well I don't really know what their problem is."

"You're different. You don't fit into anyone's mold. It's probably why Dous likes you."

Mianna's breath caught, and her lips pressed together tight before she opened them again to speak. "I'm not used to it. He acts like he's hanging on every word I say. He actually listens to me. All my weird ideas, he's…" She stopped.

Terra finished Mianna's thought for her, "The real deal. I know. It's endearingly annoying." She nodded, and her eyes traveled to the revealing mark on Mianna's hand as she stretched toward the highline of the wall.

"Those marks you all wear, they're permanent, like a tattoo?" Terra asked.

She could see now how Mianna stroked the circlet, caressing it with the lightest touch. "We're imprinted when the Frey accepts us as one of their own. It's put there to remind us of our connection and our commitment to one another."

Terra thought about how this was quite a statement to be made in such a small emblem, "So I hear you're a bit of fashionista with Hodgewear?"

"I have access to the lab because of my father. He's always allowed me to tinker with things in there. They've been stored there since the beginning, so I experiment with them. Spice them up a bit." Mianna paused, stopping mid pinch on one of the more brittle flocks along a crack-line in the limestone.

"But, you don't wear them?"

"No. That would ensure me even more of a friendless state here." Mianna hesitated, "But I don't plan on being here forever."

"You're unhappy here?" Terra pressed.

The alarm in Mianna's eyes was distinguishable as she glanced over Terra's shoulder. "It's not that, it's just that I need my own way. They're all aware of it. Even my father. I think he understands."

Terra recognized the solemn and empty glaze in her eyes. This was something she herself could comprehend. Terra suddenly felt an overwhelming urge to take this girl's hand the way she remembered Tracy had done at one time with her. Thinking twice she simply said, "I'd love to get a look at some of your designs sometime."

Mianna squinted, hesitating, and the edge of her lip curved. "Sure."

***

Heli walked quite a distance to reach the quarry and far ahead in the distance he spotted the makeshift boxes holding people scattered along the face of the rock slope. Situated two by two in each scaffold container, he could see Terra with Mianna hitched up on one of the low-level pods. Terra picked away at something on the rock mound, chatting idly with Mianna.

He quickened his pace. As he moved in closer he opened his thoughts, *Fancy meeting the both of you here.* Terra whipped around to look at him, her eyes open wide and her mouth twisted in a smirk. *Be nice.*

Heli felt the expelling of air in his throat to coax the anxiety of seeing Terra chumming up with Cue's daughter. Terra smiled down at him warmly. He wanted to melt into the curve of those lips. He was able to force a "Hi," as he stared up at them, blocking the sunlight with a fist, "What kind of slave labor is this? Doing a little spring cleaning before they churn-em' up?"

"No, the rock stays put, right where it belongs." Terra's hand patted the wall. "We're gathering greens. They grow like weeds on these old scars." Her hand moved gently along the craggy face of the stone wall. She turned and sat down clumsily on the scaffolding to abandon her perch. She stretched a dusty hand out for him to take and jumped to the ground into his arms nearly knocking him over.

I missed you. She looked up at him.

Making new friends? I'm starting to feel a bit left out. He drew her in closer.

You put yourself out. Here's your opportunity to make amends. She smiled and stood up on her toes to plant a light kiss on his cheek.

Terra was punishing him, yet he still found himself able to acknowledge the strange girl propped up on the platform. She looked down at them with wary eyes.

He directed his next comment toward Mianna, but his eyes never left Terra, "Good pickings today?" At least he was trying.

Terra looked at him incredulously, so he gave it another shot, this time forcing himself to look up at Mianna, "How about you join us for lunch?" He could almost feel the headache coming on from the strain of the muscles in his smile.

"Okay?" But her voice was unsure.

"Great! I am starving," Terra said with an endearing little chirp. He drew her in one more time for another kiss, ignoring their gaping audience.

Heli couldn't help but feel the pressure of Mianna's stare on them and he looked up to see how she studied them.

She doesn't get out much, does she? Heli looked back down at Terra.

You thought that about me once. He grimaced in response watching as Mianna hopped down to join them and they walked up the hill together.

They arrived and Dous was already filling up a plate enough for two. Confusion set in upon his features and he set his plate down on the table before maneuvering toward them.

"Didn't get the memo," Dous said, looking at Heli a bit cockeyed.

Heli held up his hands. "Don't look at me…these two had it all worked out before I arrived on the scene."

"Dous, Mianna was telling me about your swimming spot on our way here. We should all go down and take a dip sometime," Terra said.

Heli adjusted to cast her a reprimanding look. "Let's not press our luck, I doubt that pool is for personal recreational use."

"Well, there have to be other fun things we could find to do together," Terra ignored him.

What are you doing? Heli chided in with his thoughts.

I'm working on something here, just play along. The smile that framed her face never faded.

You're on your own. I'm no match-maker. Heli excused himself leaving the three of them to move toward the table of food.

As he filled up his plate, he fumbled, reaching for one of the utensils and dropped it. He bent down to pick it up. A large hand drew in to beat him to it. Cue kneeled beside him, and their eyes locked as they rose together. He politely handed the implement to Heli, "Thank you for entertaining my daughter." Cue nodded toward Mianna. "She has few friends here and it's good for her to spend time with those her age."

"Sure." Heli decided it might be best to leave out the details of how he would have ousted her in a second if it had been up to him.

"I was thinking that tomorrow we could follow up on our discussion. There's something I would really like to speak with you about," Cue looked around, peering out as if to survey his kingdom, "regarding one of your endowments which I'm sure you've been curious to get under control." His voice deepened making it very difficult to hear him, but Heli didn't miss a syllable.

"How do you know...?" Heli paused as Cue continued, "It's my job to know, remember?"

"How could I forget."

"In line with being informed about your progress throughout your trials, I was given information about many of the particulars."

"Our trials?" Heli asked.

"We'll meet again tomorrow in the tower at daybreak. We can talk more then." The hardened look he gave Heli was one an elder might give to warn a small child tempted to get too close to the fire. He moved off swiftly, only to stop for a brief instant. He set his hands on his daughter's shoulders to whisper something in her ear. Whatever he said made her smile and crane her neck up to look at him as he retreated and casually re-entered the ebb and flow of the crowd.

Heli grabbed his plate and found his way back to the group.

Casting him a quick thought, Terra asked, *What was all that about?*

"He wants to meet with me," Heli whispered back.

Meet with you? Why? She sent.

Sounds as if he may have a few pointers to help me deal with…you know. Heli held up his free hand to emphasize.

Wow, they've really done their homework. Terra's eyes darted around and then another thought came rambling through, causing Heli to jump.

Oh! Guess what? There's more. Our Mianna's a genius.

She's 'Our' Mianna now? Heli cocked his head toward Terra again and she went on. *That water suit she gave Dous. She designed it right here in a lab. Cue gives her access to it and she enhances them.* Terra stood with her hands on her hips.

So she's got you wrapped around her little finger too? Heli pressed.

Is it a crime to be decent to these people? She reached to pick at something off the shoulder of his Hodgesuit.

They don't even wear them here. Why would she care to modify them? Heli looked at Mianna again.

Terra cuffed Heli in the arm on the same spot where she had just tenderly removed the piece of lint.

"Ow!" He said cringing and looking away from her.

Why does everyone you meet have to be on trial? She pleaded, *Remember, when you told me about your family?*

He did, and he also remembered how she made a fine distraction that night, recalling how he had kissed her until it seemed like all the memories of being so unloved could melt away.

That was a good night. Quite the unorthodox approach to healing wounds. He flared his eyes and reached to try to steal a kiss, but she pulled back. He stood, arms empty, slightly stung.

Now that I know the things I know...about how your parents treated you, I've learned to overlook a lot of your issues. Heli let loose an offended breath, but she didn't let up, *I'm serious, you were a total jerk before...* She paused in mid-thought.

"Before?" Heli coaxed.

Before you made a choice. And she brought up a hand to cup his face, *I'd like to think we've evolved.*

Heli stood, still waiting, listening intently to her thoughts. *We have an opportunity here and I can feel you with me. In this place, these surroundings. I know you feel it too. And you haven't made a run for it. Maybe there's hope for you yet.* He felt her grip his arm harder.

Heli bent his head toward her, "I'm more than just 'with' you," he whispered, brushing his lips on her cheekbone just below her earlobe.

She leaned into him, *Then, let these good people in, like you did with Dous and I. Your parents, who raised you to be what IDEA intended, did what they did because they believed in the cause. But they weren't your family. You're not a product of them; you chose us. Remember that.*

Doubt

"Back late again last night?" Terra paused. Dous hit the brakes on Zuke and parked himself in the door frame. He scratched the back of his bed head before rolling Zuke over to the edge of the sunken lounge area where Heli and Terra sat together on the circlet of couches of their covert.

"Big plans today?" She continued. Heli was surprised by Terra's sudden interrogation.

"Yeah, I've got a few things on my agenda." Dous replied.

The kind of 'things' that might include a certain someone? Terra's thoughts peaked with interest as she nestled in closer to Heli.

"Mianna's…" Dous paused, the bridge of his nose crinkling, "helping me." Terra lifted an eyebrow.

"Is she aware of your little tricks yet?" Heli asked.

Dous's eyes flew up at him, "No, I'm not ready to get into that yet. Besides, she's been working on another design. I guess I somehow inspired it.

"Not another swim suit?" Heli asked.

"No, it's something different. She hasn't really shared much about it. Just getting through a fitting is ridiculous," Dous answered.

"Must be torturous," Heli teased.

"What do you think she's got going?" Terra's eyes lit up.

"Well, first of all, you can knock off the underhanded commentary." Dous looked at Heli. "And whatever it is, I get the feeling it's pretty high tech. She's got access to some amazing raw materials for hybrid operative suits and the stuff she's already shown me has some serious potential applications."

"Like what?" Terra moved up to sit.

"She's got all kinds of ideas. With one of the suits, there's these embedded nanotech particles and she uses some type of metallic fusion process. Chemical compounds in the thread-ware actually light you up like laser beams."

"So how does she power it?" Heli tried not to seem too invested.

"That's the coolest part." Dous's eyes opened wide on Heli, "There are these thread-like batteries that absorb solar energy to power it up. She kept going on about how it works using a method of converting energy into direct current electricity——metals as semiconductors. You gotta love science."

"A regular Madame Curie," Heli said.

"Wait, who are we talking about?" Terra asked.

Dismissing Terra's question, Dous continued, "I know, it all sounds crazy, but her ideas are kind of limitless with what she has access to. And she hasn't really told me yet, but I got a sneak peak at some of her mock-ups and the one she's working on for me looks like it may work as some kind of exoskeleton."

"Nothing novel about robotic suits," Heli said.

"Yeah, but this design is sleek. It won't hold you back. It's not cumbersome like other models. It looks like every day Hodgewear," Dous's voice trilled with excitement.

"A walking Hodgesuit?" Terra spewed.

"Those are some serious hopes you're getting high on." Heli nodded. Terra looked back on him, her eyes urging him to stop.

"You actually think she's making you a specialized Hodgesuit so you'll walk?" Heli probed further.

"You're like her muse?" Terra smiled.

"I don't know, she just gets a kick out of this kind of stuff," Dous said.

"She gets a kick out of you," Heli said.

"This isn't just fun and games you know." Dous looked down at his legs. "I have to believe this is possible. I have to believe in her."

"Does she ever talk about anything outside of her interest in you and these suits?" Heli asked.

"What are you getting at?" Dous asked. Terra turned away from them.

"Nothing, I just noticed how she seems to have really taken an interest in you. She trusts you. Just thought you could pick up a little more information about this place, that's all." Heli was peddling fast.

"There it is again, the way you get when you're not being direct. You're terrible at it. Why don't you just come out with it already? You think this might buy us some information." Dous's fists clenched against Zuke's armrests.

"Okay, you want direct?" Heli stared hard at Dous. "I have a feeling that there is some part of this place, these people, which they intend to keep under wraps and I think she's a part of it. She knows something," Heli said.

Dous's eyes burned into Heli. Terra stood aside biting on her nails. Dous looked at her, "Are you okay with this? She's your friend too."

"I...I think it's worth a shot. We need to learn more." She shrugged.

Stricken, Dous looked frantically between them. He spoke quietly, "I finally have something outside of us, and you want me to ruin it."

"You wanted me to be direct," Heli whispered.

"Yea, I suppose I set myself up for that let down, didn't I?" Dous's head hung low as he shook it up and down, "I would never expect either one of you to sink to this level."

"Sometimes the difficult conversations are the most important ones to have," Heli said.

"You know, you really are a cantankerous ass sometimes," Dous let out.

"Whoa!" Terra choked on an exhale.

Dous looked at Terra again. "And I can't believe you're okay with this. You one of his disciples now?"

"Dous. I...," she started.

"Forget it! Forget all of it. You can both just go on pretending to be her friend but let the record stand that I'm not okay with this." He looked back to Terra, his eyes pleading, as he turned Zuke to head toward the exit.

In Confidence

"I still can't believe what you can do with these." Dous sat up at the edge of the water storage basin. He slid his hands down the front of the Hodgesuit he wore, feeling the colder water seep its way in along his neckline where the suit clung to him like a second skin in the chilly water.

"It's good to be of some use." Mianna looked up at him shyly. She sat next to him with her knees folded in on her side like a mermaid.

"Looks like this thing hasn't been worn in ages." Dous paused, sliding his hand down the arm of the Hodgesuit he wore. "I mean, I know things have turned around, but aren't you worried about the exposure?"

She smiled and tilted her head to look at him, "Can't a girl just appreciate the notion of vintage quality things?"

"Nice try, but you have a pretty stable sense of style from what I can see. And no offense, but my dad has a few like this one," He yanked at the collar, "put away for special occasions."

Mianna traced the line of the circular mark on her left hand with her other thumb. She cupped her hands together and dropped them on her lap.

"I'm sure you noticed by now that we don't exactly live by standard regulation." She peeked up at him.

"Yea, but how can you ignore rules that are meant to protect you?" He pressed.

She stared at him directly. "You sure are full of questions today."

"Blame your father. He's the one who made you babysit me. Good thing though. I'd be totally marooned in this place otherwise," Dous said and looked around.

"Actually, I volunteered." She looked away from him again.

"Oh." He cleared his throat.

Her eyes met his again. "In fact, he really didn't want me involved at all. When we heard you were all coming…here," she nodded, "I offered to help. He got all worked up, saying I'd only get in the way, but I don't think he briefed Emeal on any of his 'plans'." A little smile parted her lips. "And then when she called me over that first day to meet you and asked if I could take you on a tour, well...I knew it would be exactly the opposite of what he would have wanted." She smirked. "Except now that I'm finally making friends, I think he's reconsidering."

"So, I'm your little social experiment?" Dous lifted an eyebrow.

"I'd rather not talk about my relationship with my father. What about you? I heard you had to leave family behind."

Dous looked out at the water and drew a swirling line in the dirt with his finger. "My fake parents you mean?"

"Well, yeah. Do you still keep in contact with them after everything that's happened?" She asked.

"Beyond the standard, 'Hi, how are you? I'm still alive and breathing' No. My mom and dad...uh, my parental units, they're good people and they raised me with as much love as they were prescribed to give, likely more, but I'll never really know if it was real," he said.

"Why do you call them that?"

"What? Units?" Dous realized how the term he had used to describe them was likely as foreign to her as it was to him when he first learned of his origins.

She went on, "You're for real. I can't imagine that doesn't come without some impression made by the people who raised you,"

"Yeah, that's just it. They were always bound to one thing and one thing only, raising me according to plan. I can't explain it. It just changed things between us when I learned the truth. You couldn't understand," he confided.

"You're right, I don't."

Her words raked up against him and he wriggled in his position on the ground next to her to put more space between them.

"It's like having the rug pulled out from under you. I came down a lot harder than I thought I would. I guess the reality of it is, is that I'm still not over it."

Dous took a moment to focus on the dark shadowy hues of the water in front of them, before raising his head. "But I can't say it's completely hopeless. It's been a heck of a journey so far."

"Fair." She nodded.

"I had a sister you know? For some reason I've never had a doubt about what was between us."

"What's her name?" Mianna asked.

"Maisy." Dous felt his heart constrict.

"Did she know about all this? About you?" Mianna asked.

"I highly doubt it. She'd never be able to keep this from me. She was the most important person in my life before I met Terra and Heli. I haven't seen her or spoken to her directly since our last visitation. That was a while ago while we were still living at IDEA."

"You miss her." Her voice carried out into the distance as a whisper. "I never had a sibling. Always wanted one. I had the romanticized notion that it might be the closest window into knowing myself." She scooted her legs around in front of her, leaning in to wrap her arms around her knees.

Dous watched her in silence and when she peeked up to look back at him he swallowed back the sadness he saw in her face, "Is that why you chose blue?" He reached up and touched the blue tips of her hair, "I don't see any fancy salons around this place." He let his hand linger longer than necessary in the slick streaks of blue.

"Another hobby of mine—mixing it up." Her eyebrows lifted. "Keeps them all on their toes."

"Them?" He asked.

"Everyone. My father, Emeal, even the kids my age. They all lack…luster." She frowned.

"Why blue?" Dous asked.

"My mother's eyes were blue." She shrugged.

"Yours too." He watched her more intently this time without feeling the urge to look away and noticed how her cyan irises twitched with his comment.

"Your mother's gone?" he asked.

"She's dead." Her face went flat. Her long legs stretched out in front of her and she looked down spreading her hands out along the lap of her skirt. She adjusted and leaned over to stand. "We should be getting on. Come on." She reached a hand down to aid in him getting up onto Zuke.

As she lifted him up Dous asked, "So it's just you and your dad then—no other extended family here?" He angled his body so she could support him up onto Zuke.

"No, just the two of us and Emeal, among the nearly eight hundred other members of the Frey. Maybe it's closer to a thousand by now. I don't know, I stopped counting." She sighed.

"What happened to her?" he asked, pretending to be preoccupied with the knobs on Zuke.

When he looked back up she was staring straight at him. It wasn't a challenging stare, but it was as if she was trying to unravel some code embedded in his question. She caught her breath before speaking. "Being a part of something important can make a person vulnerable. It opens them up to risks they might otherwise never have taken," she said.

"What do mean?" Dous asked.

"She was a lot like me. Out of sync with the world around her. Her father, my grandfather, was the leader of one of the original bands of Change Maker Societies. He head-started the first of many new settlements during the years of unrest," Mianna explained.

"Unrest?" Dous asked.

"Regulators did their job of keeping that out of the historical film cubes too. You wouldn't have known about it since you were on the outside, but before the Blend; before there was any confirmation that the Cor even existed…that the three of you existed, people were bound to one of two things, the new Regulation or the prophecy. Many of the independent Change Makers were secretly in line with this opposing view. The precious few who were aware of the details of IDEA's mission were all living in the shadows, knowing that their time was limited." She paused for a breath. "Other groups were forming, adjusting to living off the grid. But even more than that, people were just simply hoping to escape from the controls of the AG Regulators."

"But all that's changed now." He nodded to assure her. "We have a fresh start."

"You mean what you brought back?" She looked at him with a glint of expectation in her eyes.

"What we brought back?" he asked.

"Hope. Finally, real hope." Her face went long again, "But very few understand what this means. So, we face a new challenge," she said.

"What sort of challenge?"

"Spreading the word and then surviving the fallout." She pressed her lips together tightly. "Every soul who lives among these trees will be considered a traitor and will never be accepted back into society. That includes me."

"But that's crazy. You were born here. I wouldn't think there'd be anything more challenging than facing the apocalyptic end to everything. Now that the pressure's off and there's time…" Mianna cut him off shaking her head.

"We're a stain to Regulation progress. They don't want anyone to know, and when they get wind of all this and decide to weed us all out…I don't even want to imagine." She dropped her chin and shook her head.

Dous kept prying, "What does your father say about it? It doesn't make sense. Why would he invite us here under his protection if he knows they might come after us and risk everyone in the Frey?"

"My father is an eternal optimist. He knows things, things he's never spoken to anyone, not even me. Things that I'm sure propel him to do what he does. He sees a transformation from a past based on control and fear to what he believes will bring about 'a higher vibration of harmony.' It's probably how he's made it this far." She shifted her weight and looked down at the ground again, shuffling her sandaled foot in the loose dirt.

"So what do 'we' have to do with it? Dous asked.

"He views your arrival as a signal." Her eyes shot up.

Dous blurted, "A signal?"

"A sign to loosen restrictions on access to renewed resources. Those who agree with him firmly believe that the only path beyond the resistance is to give more control back to the people." She turned to look up the path with a longing he wished he could understand.

"And your mother?" Dous asked.

"It never should have been for them the way it was. When my father was stationed at IDEA my mother arrived as one of their volunteers. That's how they met." She let her hand run through her hair, the blue tips poking out between her fingers.

"My father knew exactly what kind of danger she was walking into, but by the time he realized what was between them, it was too late. Things got complicated. They learned she was pregnant…with me. Worried that I'd become another variable to experiment with, they decided it would be better to leave."

"And you blame him?" Dous offered.

"I guess I do at some level. At least he had the decency to bring her back to her people before she died. Others joined them who needed refuge along the way. That's how the numbers here grew. My mother died shortly after my third birthday. "Her name was Arah."

"I'm so sorry," Dous said.

"I was young. I don't really remember much about her. From what I do remember she died quickly after the pain from the radiation sickness set in." Mianna's eyes remained distant.

"Your father must have been devastated." Dous looked down at his feet and asked, "How did she…" He shook his head in shock, closing his mouth when he realized it was hanging wide open.

"I'm going to tell you something…that I probably shouldn't talk about, but these marks," and she pulled her hand out to show him, "well in the lab, where I make the adjustments to the suits, we've developed other things," she confided.

"What kind of things?" Dous asked.

"It's an enhanced resin."

"What?" He scowled. "Is it permanent? Like a tattoo?"

"No, it's not done with ink, and we don't apply it with needles. It's brushed on." She shook her head. "It's interactive. Once it's applied to the skin, it enhances particular chemical impressions that occur naturally in the body. And it's the reason why we don't have to wear the suits. We don't need them." She pointed again to the circular marking.

"How in the world?" Dous asked.

"With the application of these marks we've built up an immunity along with what was already present in the skin to protect us from the assaults of the external environment." She shrugged and stood before him. "And like the shield of a Hodgesuit, we can withstand the elements."

"Like being inoculated or something?" He knew his shock was showing. "That's pretty remarkable."

"Remarkable...I suppose." She shook her head. "It's been my father's life's focus outside of keeping track of the three of you. It's how he met my mother and why the lab exists. Fortunately, he was able to transfer most of his research here when they left IDEA. It was my mother's sister who played a hand in making that possible. She was the only one who stayed behind at the institute. I never met her, but he's always spoken highly of her." Mianna's words brought flashbacks of Maisy, Dous's own sister. Suddenly the pieces all fit together.

"Tracy?" Dous's realization surprised even himself.

"Yes. She was the only other family we had. I never knew her."

"She was a good person. A lot like you actually." Dous suddenly realized how matched their sincerity was.

"There were other reasons they left, weren't there?" For a moment he wished he could read her mind, just this once, as he could with the others.

"My mother was invited soon after Tracy arrived at IDEA. It was all contingent on the agreement that she would be willing to help with the cause. She was assigned to my father's control group for early application of the mark," she said.

"Wait a minute, your mother was a volunteer test subject?" Dous rolled closer. She had somehow put more distance between them than he felt was necessary.

"Tracy was selected to take part in the mission but they had to take her from her family and her progress was somewhat marred by the fact that she arrived alone and was isolated. My mother, her sister, was willing to make the sacrifice if it meant that they could stay together," Mianna said.

"But she risked her life." Dous couldn't believe the windfall of information Mianna was all too willing to provide.

"My father didn't develop the effective formula until I was nearly a year old," she said.

"That's where all the suits came from!" Dous was so caught up in the moment that he'd forgotten that they were still on the subject of her mother's death.

Mianna peered at him strangely while he settled back down after nearly falling off of Zuke.

She continued, "People still had to wear them when we arrived." Her eyes took on a hazy distant glare. "And by then, we'd settled into a new life here in the Frey. I don't remember much about the settlement from the start, or the few others who were here before us. My grandfather died soon after I was born. Emeal came with my father and mother and she's been ever-present in my life since." She paused, "I've never been anywhere outside of this place."

Dous returned to humor. "Well I can attest to the fact that the Frey far outweighs anything the Regulators could ever provide. You're not missing much. I bet you've never even heard of Syntha-nutrients."

"Syntha-nutrients?" She smiled a little, and seeing her smile gave him new hope.

"Food crammed into a little pill that essentially gives you what you need by way of nutrition, but they're bland as hell." She stifled a little laugh and covered her mouth.

"I'm not kidding—I'd rather eat dirt after tasting real food," Dous went on.

"Sounds terrible out there." Her eyes narrowed in on him. "I guess I don't have it so bad here. Maybe I'll stick around." He felt his face warm to her smile and it revealed two prominent dimples on either cheek. She stood taller suddenly, carrying herself differently.

"But it's not like you don't have any access to the world outside. I mean, there are certainly things available here that couldn't have come from earth or sky," Dous said.

"My father has connections," she absently shook her head, "and we make due with what surrounds us to fill in the gaps between the quarry, the gardens and sheer manpower."

"But you're not happy here?" Dous asked, trying to refrain from any judgment.

"I just want to know what else there is. I didn't get to choose. This is all I've ever known. And it's not like I assume the grass is greener out there. I just need to see it for myself," she answered.

"Well, I'd hate to lose my chaperone." Dous looked up at her.

She quickly turned, the awkwardness abated, and moved behind him. He let his eyes follow her until she was out of site. He could feel the wheels jostling underneath him as she pushed him forward on Zuke. She stopped briefly. Her breath came close to his right ear and he felt his stomach swirl as her soft voice whispered, "Don't worry, I won't abandon you just yet."

In Sync

Dous stared back at Terra and Heli, his eyes drawn into a scowl to mind speak. *Why is this so hard?*

You're getting too attached, Heli tossed out the thought and stood scanning the the watery edge of the pool he had just recently helped Dous out of. Dimples of discoloration blotted the waters surface in the afternoon light.

Terra pumped Heli in the arm. *You encouraged this, remember?* Aiming her thoughts at him.

Heli directed his attention back, *We need some information and this is the best way I know to get it. If you have any other bright ideas, let me know.*

Dous's mouth twisted, letting out a tight exhale before speaking, "I can tell you two are shielding me from whatever it is your thinking. You don't need to protect me like this. I can stand on my own two feet."

Dous's bravado all but faded when Heli looked down at his legs.

"Okay, bad example. But I feel bad, she kind of unloaded on me." Dous shook one hand through his wet hair and began flicking it around in a feeble attempt to loosen some of the water still dripping from the tips of his black curls.

"So, what gives?" Heli said. This time Terra poked him in the ribs.

"Come on, I'm not a pin cushion!" He growled.

"Filter! For God's sake!" She shook her hands up near her ears for effect.

"Look, I never agreed to spy on her." Dous stopped to stare at Heli.

"It's just that I feel like I can talk to her, you know?"

His eyes quickly shifted to Terra. "She came out with a lot more than I was prepared for."

"Good! Let's hear it." Heli stopped, sidling away from Terra, pretending to cower from another blow. "Look, I know this wasn't easy for you."

"Well, although I never like to admit it, you were right. I just wasn't prepared for all of it. I felt like a priest at a confession. And Cue, he's got quite the history," Dous said.

Heli nodded, feeling exonerated, "See, I'm not just paranoid." He flipped up a hand and looked at Terra. She rolled her eyes.

"Don't get too excited. It isn't exactly a clean-cut story and it may open up an entirely new can of worms. She told me all about how her father and mother came here. They basically put themselves into exile. Mianna was born here." Dous took a deep breath and swallowed.

He looked up at Heli, "Those marks; they're more than what they seem to be too." Dous's eyes shot up.

"Why am I not surprised?" Heli shook his head.

"They have some kind of chemical property, a permanent stamp on the skin. Developed right here in the lab where Mianna works on the suits," Dous finished.

"Wait. Cue told me they were just symbols." Heli felt the heat swelling up in small bursts causing his fingertips to tingle.

"What are they for?" Terra asked.

"Well, they don't wear the suits for a good reason," he paused, "When Cue said they didn't have a cloaking device to hide them, that wasn't exactly true. This stuff gives them some sort of advantage, like some kind of chemically enhanced shield."

"Whoa. Now that's something." Heli looked at Terra again.

"Why would he hide something like that?" she asked.

Heli turned away from them for a moment so he could think, "That's what they do. All of them, Tracy, Emeal, Cue. I am so tired of us being the only ones left in the dark. Cue offered to 'spend' some time with me. I guess it's my turn to do some digging."

"Um, there's one more thing," Dous paused until he had both their attention. "Tracy had another good reason for helping them. She was family."

"What?" Heli asked, not even trying to hide his shock.

Dous propped himself up on Zuke, "Tracy is Mianna's aunt."

"Oh wow," Terra exhaled. "She actually does remind me a bit of Tracy now that you mention it."

"Mianna's mother's name was Arah. They were sisters," Dous confirmed.

Heli clicked his tongue. "She did unload. Nice work!" He pumped Dous in the arm.

Dous looked back up, "Promise me you won't breathe a word of the fact that I told you any of this to Mianna," Dous pleaded.

Terra shot Dous an empathetic glance.

"Like, ever," Dous reiterated.

"I don't know." Heli shook his head. "I don't think this grants her immunity yet. I've said it before and I'll say it again—we don't know these people and so far, no one here has been totally transparent about anything." Heli watched as Dous's face changed.

"You're a piece of work you know that? You're right! You don't know these people. You haven't even tried to get to know them!"

"Stop it! Both of you!" Terra interrupted. "Dous, I know this is the last thing you need right now. None of this is ideal by any means, but Heli's right. There's just too much we don't understand about these people and we have to push them all a little bit further to find out everything we can before we make ourselves too comfortable here."

"I've done enough damage as it is. If you need any more information you're gonna have to come by it on your own. She's a decent and lonely girl. I'm lucky she even calls me a friend. I certainly don't deserve it!" Dous flared.

"You're willing to drop it all over some puppy love crush?" Heli said.

Terra looked to Heli with alarm and Dous sat speechless, disgust written all over his face, "Call it whatever you want, but you can count me out of your conspiracy theories. I won't use her that way!" Dous turned Zuke around and rolled himself in the opposite direction.

Terra stood with her eyes closed and drew in a deep breath. "That didn't go very well." She reopened them to look at Heli. "What are we going to do now?"

"We're going to hunker down for this storm." He pointed a finger out toward Dous, "And I don't know what that might mean for him, but after it all blows over, I'll be dammed if I'll allow him to just drop everything for some girl he hardly knows." Heli's fists were pumping with heat.

"Some girl he hardly knows? How about some girl who takes an interest in him, who laughs at his stupid jokes. Some girl who might just turn out to be more than 'Just' some girl."

Heli felt his anger sifting. "You have a thick imagination." He felt the familiar stare on him, then the touch. She gently slipped her hand into his.

"Might I remind you that you yourself were quite a project at one time. In fact, I found you immeasurably flawed at first, and yet you still managed to whittle your way into my heart. Is it so hard to believe that he might have found someone outside of...*Us?*"

"You never cease to fascinate me." Heli shook his head slowly. He drew her nearer, "And did you really just use the word 'whittled?'" He placed his forehead on hers, shutting his eyes.

I rest my case. Her thoughts spilled out and he could feel her smiling on him even with his eyes shut.

Prana

Entering the unlit space, Heli gripped his tin whistle a little tighter in a balled-up fist. There was nothing like the smooth cold comfort of the metal instrument in his hand. He brought it to his mouth, ready to puff out a few notes while he waited, when the deck was suddenly flooded with light. His attention shifted as a shadow headed up the incline of the narrow stairway entering the tower.

Cue's distinguishable form slid up through the small entryway. He startled a bit when he saw Heli as he entered. "You nearly gave me a heart attack, but at least you're punctual."

"Sorry," Heli said.

"I was thinking we could start outdoors today. Get a bit of fresh air." And his arm drew out in an arc toward the stairwell he had just emerged from to lead them on.

Heli shifted from his position propped up against the solid wall and made his way over to follow Cue down and out into the open glade where the path led up to the center square.

"What do have there in your hand?" Cue asked. He kept his eyes forward as they traveled up the path.

"Oh, it's my penny whistle." Heli flicked the tube in his hand.

"Music?" Cue looked at the object and smiled.

"It's kinda right up there with air, water and shelter." He held it up for Cue to inspect.

"Good to know. I'll ask that you bring it to all of our future meetings."

Heli paused mid-stride, thinking how this might be the opportunity he'd been waiting for.

"I take it you understand a few things about my little problem?" Heli raised his empty hand and waved it in the air. "Does the offer still stand? Can you help me learn how to control it?"

"I do know a few things about what you are experiencing. It is a form of Pranic Transmission and it is manageable, but that all depends on how willing you are to take control of it."

"That's the problem, I have no control over it. It comes and goes. All I know is that it's dangerous and I've already hurt someone. I don't want to take the chance of hurting anyone else I care about," Heli confessed.

"Once you understand the nature of it and its origins, you'll have control. Any idea what fuels it?" Cue asked.

What fuels it? Heli wasn't sure.

"The operating variable that gives it power. You're already aware of your embodiment. There's quite the force burning inside of you." Cue looked at him more intently, seemingly analyzing his responses.

"Yes, I get it, but why the charge? I mean, don't get me wrong, it hasn't been all bad," he thought about the first time he kissed Terra, "but I'd like to have some gauge on it so I can get in sync with it."

"You're here for damage control?" Cue asked.

"Sure. I want to figure this thing out so I don't end up maiming some innocent person. Or worse," Heli said.

Cue let out a contemplative grunt, "Not everyone you come into contact with is all that innocent,"

"Come again?" Heli asked.

"Don't tell me you haven't wondered how you could use it against your enemies?" A taunting pair of green eyes stared back at Heli.

"Who says I have enemies?"

"With one in particular to whom I share your vile imaginings." Cue bit his lower lip hard enough that Heli half expected to see blood.

"Okay, if you're talking about who I think you are, then yea, I'd love to see him suffer by my hands, but it certainly isn't the first reason I want to learn how to control this. I need to keep the others safe. Tell me if I'm wasting my time? I'd like to just get on with this."

"Get on with it?" Cue shook his head lightly, "You're good at pushing people around, aren't you?" He slowly walked in a circle around Heli. "How does that go over with your friends? Do they like being your doormat?" The confrontation felt all too familiar.

"My friends understand me and they respect me," Heli replied.

"Or could it be...that they're afraid of you!" Cue barked as he came back around to face Heli. Standing nose to nose with an electric current alive and vibrating between them, Heli took a step back.

"They have nothing to fear from me!" Heli spoke, his anger festering.

"But they are bound to you. You do realize that, and you try, but there's always that nagging little part of you that knows they don't have a choice," Cue continued.

"What is this? You're…you're trying to upset me!" Heli spat, an abscessed wound reopening.

"And it worked. How do you feel?" Cue asked and his voice resumed its normal volume.

Heli coughed up a little air, "Are you kidding me? What if I had lost control? You did hear me when I said I don't know how to control this, right?"

"I did, and I'm fully prepared." Cue leaned in closer, causing Heli to cinch back uncomfortably. "You see, I happen to understand your little issue," he shook his hands mockingly, "because I myself know about it firsthand."

"What? How could you…?" Heli stumbled for words.

"I've been around since all of this began. I am one of the original participants to IDEA's project base. And my contribution began in very much the same way yours did." Cue's eyes dropped to the ground. "Only unfortunately one of the original three to my Cor was lost and our mission ended as abruptly as it began."

"Are you saying that you're like me? They created you? But I don't…" Heli stood silently, his mind swimming in a mash up of information.

"Who were the others?" Heli's heart flared and he could feel the stinging in his eyes coming on. He blinked hard to wash the burn out, but his thoughts kept returning to Terra and Dous.

"You've met Emeal. Thryn was our third."

"Thryn? I've never heard that name. Where is she?" Heli asked.

"She's no longer with us," Cue went on. "We went in, like you, and she never returned."

"The Strata took her?" Heli shook his head. Horrified by the thought of losing more than one precious life to that god forsaken portal.

"No, we all emerged." Cue shook his head. "But she wasn't herself after that. Something happened while we were inside. We all assumed it had been a successful mission, our bodies sound, but her mind…" He paused and a low growl escaped his throat. "It was as if something snapped and she never returned to us fully. Nearly a month later when we learned the mission failed she disappeared. Some believed that she'd gone back in on her own." He looked at Heli. "If I was certain that she were…" He stopped and rubbed his eyes as if he were waking from a nightmare.

Heli cut in, "She was lost, as in…she lost her mind? But you and Emeal came out alright?"

"Moreo or less, yes." Heli's voice became a trailing whisper.

"That scar on Emeal's face, I've seen an injury like that before." Heli thought of how he had hurt Justin.

"It was an unfortunate accident and part of the reason I wish to help you. Have you noticed a pattern connected with how it arrives?" Cue asked.

"I don't know, it seems to be emotionally triggered," Heli offered.

Cue took a step forward, looking him over. "Is it always when you're upset?"

"Well, no." Heli opted not to go into details, "but it seems to be some kind of outlier to my emotions."

"This would certainly be in line with Pranic Transmission. In your case it might be very difficult to gauge, being that it's entrained with your instinctual rhythms," Cue noted.

"Great, so it's pretty much hopeless?"

Cue's eyebrows lifted. "It will be difficult, but not impossible. You will have to learn to listen for these 'rhythms' when they're coming on."

He stopped briefly and clasped his hands in front of him. "There are certain relaxation techniques which will allow you the presence of mind to observe and accept it when it emerges that can aid in its positive acquisition. You're a musical person. You know how to orient yourself around a composition. You'll navigate this in much the same way. The skill of harnessing its power isn't completely out of your hands. It's intentional on some conscious level and I believe I can help you."

"I'll do whatever you want, if it means I can get a grip on this." Heli felt reassured by the sound of his own voice.

"You've heard of meditation I'm sure?" Cue asked.

"Sure, I know others who find it helpful." He blushed thinking of Terra in mid warrior pose.

Cue interjected, "Terra and Dous, they are a resource for calming you. Use that. You will need to learn to listen to their rhythms as well. Just the sound of their voices can sedate you when you reach this plane of energy." Cue moved in close and placed his hands on Heli's shoulders to steady him.

"Stand still." Then he began using both hands in the manner of scanning Heli from head to toe. He started at the top of his head, an air frisking of sorts, never actually touching him.

"What are you doing?" Heli asked.

"Don't move and don't speak." Cue's voice was distant and firm.

There was a flicker, a vibration, and it followed Cue's hands as they made their path up and down his body. Heli stood, unsure of how this was going to help, but afraid to move a muscle.

Then Cue stood tall again in front of him and clasped his hands together. "I was reading your energy fields. The aura seems strongest in your core. You have less than subtle energy transmitters. So strong, in fact, that you seemed to be absorbing some of mine." Cue's eyes opened wide.

"Sorry," Heli said.

"Quit apologizing. I must admit, this is something I hadn't expected. Your transmission is strongest near your heart where the magnetic field is typically more secure," he said.

"You can feel all this with your hands?" Heli asked.

"You will be able to feel it too with the proper training." Cue shot a glance down the berm of the path leading away from the tower.

"Expecting someone?" Heli asked.

"No, but I would like to run some further diagnostics and see if we can get you worked up enough to bring about the onset of an episode." Cue had moved off as he was saying this, already heading toward the tower and moving up the stairs again. Heli followed him, climbing up. As he re-entered the space he could already see Cue tapping on the screens in an orbital path around the room as they all came to life with screens lit to seize the day.

The one nearest Heli flashed in his face and he had to shield his eyes, "You want to get this going? You must be crazy."

"I need to gather some information on the level of energy you're exuding with a conduction sequence I have available in the system. It'll gather the data I need before we can proceed." He seemed immersed and was squinting in earnest at the wash of light. Tables of information drew out in long lines of code Heli couldn't comprehend.

"Wait, we're gonna do this right here, right now? I don't think that's such a good idea."

"There's nothing to be afraid of, once you know how to harness it and manage it. I'm using the Prana right now." Cue turned away from the screen to look at Heli again.

"You're kidding me, right?" Heli asked.

"What do you think powers this computer? Out here in the middle of nowhere?" Cue shot him a smile.

"That's how you stay off the grid?" Heli looked around at the screens, lit up to seize the dark, mystified.

"Mine comes on with concentrated thought and meditation. And if we ever wish to get a gauge on how to temper your condition, then we have to test it out," Cue said. Heli was starting to feel like the next in a long line of test subjects.

"This system, it can measure energy?" Heli looked down the long arc of screens and their daunting clusters of information.

"Oh, you'd be amazed by what this fellow can do." Cue gently rubbed the partition between the two screen mounts in front of him.

Standing there, it felt more like the helm of a ship from historical hall film cubes, and Heli thought the more appropriate term would be to call it a 'she'.

"What do I do?" Heli asked.

"Well, I'll need to turn on the N-sync sensors to detect and monitor your conductivity levels. They'll measure the humidity, fluid levels and acceleration shift in the air particles around you. This way I'll be able to measure the energy levels produced." Cue pressed a few more projected tiles, rearranging icons into their proper place.

"O…kay. So, all you really need me to do is get hopping mad to the point of boiling over to jump start this thing?" Heli said, half joking.

"That is exactly what we're aiming to do." Cue looked optimistic and Heli tried to fake a smile.

"So how are we supposed to prime this thing up?" Heli asked.

"We all have a soft spot. Something that might trigger a reaction like before."

"And your job is to dig around until you can get it out of me? Sounds a lot like therapy." Heli widened his eyes.

"I have a feeling it won't be that difficult," Cue admitted.

"What have you heard?" Heli joked again. "So far things are moving along without much drama."

"What about when I mention the name Jacque Punam?" Cue continued scanning the operations grid hovering out from the screens.

Heli could feel the swell almost as instantly as he heard Cue mention the name.

"There we go. See right there?" He pointed out a shift in the schematic hovering to his left, "There's a spike in your normal electron-volt patterns. You are very easily triggered by him." Cue watched the screen the way a child might watch a toy hovermobile jetting around in the air. His eyes darted from point to point.

"Is this really necessary—dredging him up again?" Heli leaned up against the only portion of the wall that wasn't covered by the face of a computer.

"Why not, he seems to be a sore subject. Or shall we discuss your parents?" Cue pressed. "They relinquished rights to you without any reservation. Agreeable people, aren't they? So how did you ever turn out to be so difficult?" His voice was a distant abrasion and Heli could feel the knots forming in his stomach.

"Okay, here we go. You want me to talk about my parents." He twisted his neck, feeling it crack. "They followed IDEA's standard orders and I made it through. No harm, no foul."

"Easy forgivings for two people who followed everything by the book, and never once broke their stamina to follow their hearts," Cue countered.

Heli could feel a flicker in his fingertips, but it dissipated quickly as they slid over the cooling metal of his whistle becoming warmer in his grip.

"You're going to need to come up with something better than that to work this out of me. I spent my entire life learning how to put up a shield to protect me from what they couldn't provide."

Cue almost looked like he might be out of material when he turned away from Heli. His back now facing him, "Then what about you and Terra?"

Hearing her name actually served as somewhat of a retardant to the ignition to his response. "What about her?"

"What if I told you that her father, Jacque, would more readily see her dead than risk losing control of his reinstatement to the project. And that because of him, the two of you will always be on the run. Have you ever considered what life will be like together under those conditions? How it might wear on what you have? Test you—pick away at every standing form you think you've created together, turning you into people you don't even recognize." Cue turned around to look at Heli directly.

His eyes bore into him and Heli sensed a burning resentment, afraid to utter one word.

"Love is fickle, it changes; it shifts. And given time…" He paused and threw his hands up shaking his head, "what kind of future would that bring? What if she doesn't…"

Heli cut him off, "Enough!" He could feel it taking over and the tube of his whistle in his hand exploded with heat, red molten metal bending easily in his hands.

Cue stopped and watched him. Heli's chest felt tight, and he struggled to take his next breath, suffocating on his own thoughts. Then, he felt them, tears, building up against his will. He reached up to wipe them away and he felt the metal cooling and the slightly warped form of the tube in his hand solidifying again.

He slid down to the floor with his back against the wall. He had his fists gripped tightly around the whistle as he held it up against his forehead. He looked up, "Who are your talking about? This has nothing to do with me or Terra. It can't. This is…about you and what you did to Mianna's mother, isn't it?"

Cue turned away swiftly and Heli watched as the man sucked in the stale air, regaining his composure. "That's enough for today, I have what I need."

Commanding an Audience

"I miss being there." Terra grabbed a pillow from the array of cushions surrounding them on the couch and pressed it firmly against her chest. She laid her chin up over the top of it and looked at Heli.

"I know, I do too," he said and he looked over at the sleeping form stretched over the cushions on the other side of the rounded sectional. "Dous seems to have adjusted."

"Tracy would've liked it here." And the sigh in her voice stopped him from acting on the impulse to change the subject. "She knew these people. I half wonder if it wasn't already part of the plan to bring us here at some point. Back to her family. It's bizarre thinking that she had such a familiar history with any of them. There's still so much I wish she were here to explain."

"She was a vault that one," Heli said, squeezing Terra's hand up to kiss her knuckles.

"What did you find out? Can Cue help you?" she asked.

"Yeah, I think so." Heli nodded. "He may be the only one who can."

"I still can't believe there were others...before us." Terra's voice and her eyes trailed off.

"So what else did he say? I mean, if he's like you, did he give you any ideas about how to manage it?" She asked.

"He thinks it's tied to more deep-seated stuff. He wants to help me learn how to become more aware of how I feel when it surfaces so I can channel it more effectively." Heli paused, "That computer they have, it's like the one at IDEA overlooking the Strata. He uses Prana to power it."

"What?" Terra looked up at him

"Seriously?" Dous suddenly chimed in as he shifted from his position to sit up.

"I thought you were asleep," Heli said and looked at Dous who was staring back bleary eyed.

"I thought I was too, until you came out with that. That's how he keeps this place under the radar." Dous's brow creased together.

"I guess so, we didn't get very far. A little time worn history got in the way," Heli said.

"I'm up for a history lesson." Dous said.

"I thought you were through with all of this." Heli quirked an eyebrow up.

"I said I wasn't willing to spy for you, but I can't see the harm in me staying up on the latest gossip."

"Well, there's definitely a lot more to the story about Mianna's mother Arah. My guess is that Mianna's been kept as much in the dark as we have. Things were definitely moving along until I mentioned his dead wife."

"Now that wasn't very nice of you," Dous said.

"Didn't she die of radiation illness?" Terra's eyes flashed back at him.

"Yea, but I think he was more worked up about what was surfacing between them before that." Heli stopped and then looked at Dous, "Mianna said that she was alive for the first few years they were here, right?"

"That's what she told me," Dous replied.

"And that coming here was some sort of homecoming for her mother? It made me wonder what would have caused the rift between them then," Heli said.

"Rift—between who?" Terra shot a quick glance his way and then looked back at Dous.

"He tried to get me all fired up by bringing you and I into the equation—like some kind of probing analysis he needed to set me off. But it wasn't about us. I could tell. And that's where the conversation ended," Heli said.

"Why in the world would he think you might get worked up about us?" Terra craned her neck to the side looking at him.

"He was trying to jump start some stress reaction and he brought up how you and I..." Heli stopped.

"How we what?" she asked.

"How things are between us," he continued careening down a word filled staircase at full throttle.

She moved out of his reach, backing away from him into the cushions.

"You can say it, you know—out loud. It shouldn't be that painful," she said.

Heli looked at Dous. "Don't look at me!" Dous said, "I'm clueless about these things."

Heli threw his head back, "You're right, I'm sorry. He brought up the fact that you and I are 'connected' and he started in on what could happen over time."

Terra took a deep breath. "Okay, and so you put him in his place, right?"

"I didn't have a chance to because I figured out that it had nothing to do with us. He was talking about the two of them. He and Mianna's mother."

"So, what about them?" Dous asked.

"Well, my best guess is that they came here, she was sick, he felt guilty, and things fell apart. Then, your precious Mianna was born and complicated things even further," Heli said.

Dous scowled at Heli. "So, she's precious now? I thought you hated her."

"I didn't say she was precious to me." Heli shook his head, flustered by the comment, "and I don't hate her."

"Let's just drop it. We need to go. Emeal wants us at the gathering at center square this afternoon." Terra scolded them both.

"That's all there is to report anyways," Heli grunted as he lifted himself off the cushions, sniffing the collar of his Hodgesuit. "I need to change. I still feel like I'm six feet under in a pile of sludge after working in those piles of compost today."

"You do that," cautioned Dous, "and while you're at it, maybe you could consider changing your attitude."

He turned, lifting one hand idly into the air to wave them both off, as he ambled up the small set of stairs and headed toward their wardrobe.

***

The crowd was growing by the minute as the masses of the Frey's citizens filled the area.

"We need to stay together." Heli clenched his jaw as a few strangers from the assemblage moved in, encroaching on their space. He could feel a constant brushing on his sides, back and shoulders as the crowd moved in solid form like a marauding mass of living tar.

"Ever been to a Trap-synth show? This is just how I always imagined it." Dous shifted on Zuke to get a look around. His field of vision must have been blocked at every angle because he finally gave up and deflated back into his seat on Zuke.

"I wouldn't know. I've never been to one either." Terra's amber eyes were bright and brilliant and although there were traces of fear written across her features, she seemed to be somehow enamored by the static volume surrounding them.

"It's a lot like this actually! Except I doubt we'll get to the part with the grunge mosh pit!" Heli yelled and he drew in a bit closer to Terra, placing his hands on her shoulders when he noticed a group of teenage boys huddled to their right looking her up and down like she was on display.

"How do you know about this stuff?" She turned and looked at him shocked.

"My cousin was in a band!" Heli spoke loudly near her ear as the thrum of the crowd was intensifying with the pitch of loud voices all bidding for the same air space.

"A band?" Dous asked.

"He's the one who gave me the whistle!" Heli yelled as they huddled together closer to hear one another.

What kind of music? Dous shifted to mind speak and Heli could hear him clearly this time.

Heli let out a breath, relieved not to have to yell, *Modern. Tech-helm drummer, laser-plucking fiddler and a lead vocalist—typical complement to the jam.*

Heli slid in to be closer to Terra. *My cousin plays the Mazari.*

"What's that?" Terra spoke again, looking at him confused.

"Digital stringed guitar—only much smaller and you wear it like an accessory in a hip holster." Heli spoke into her ear this time, up close and placed his hand on her hip.

Suddenly within the dispersement of sound came a hushed hum and Heli became aware that everyone else had stopped talking and all eyes had shifted up and out beyond them. He could see up on a podium-like mound about a hundred meters away the towering figure of Cue. Emeal was down below on the ground level, flanking him to his right. There was a severe look of concentration on her face and although Heli could see that Terra and Dous had noticed this as well, the rest of the Frey's citizens seemed to be in a trance and all eyes were positioned on Cue. There was an undeniable murmuring pressure surrounding them and Heli's instincts were on high alert to something unreadable but eminently present in Emeal's fixed stare. Not even a signal was used to quiet the crowd, but somehow together Emeal and Cue made it happen.

Dous's eyes darted to Heli. *Do you feel that?*

Yeah, what is it? Terra projected.

Heli pressed in adding, *It's like they have some kind of internalized crowd control.* Then, he muttered, this time under his breath, "Why they would need it, I have no idea."

Cue cut in almost as quickly as Heli had let out the last syllable. His voice was distant, but clear and alluring in a deep baritone, and each word seemed carefully practiced.

"The Frey has long outlived a time when all else seemed hopeless." He bowed his head with a precise pause, then lifted it again. "I ask you to come join me tonight as we move forward to mark this time, in serving a greater purpose and a higher order that we have all patiently waited for. Today we celebrate an age of rejuvenation, and the revolutionary wisdom that propels us from here into a guiding future." His eyes began to scan the crowd until they fell across Heli and the others. Heli's stomach twisted. "We mark The Cor's arrival to signal to this time!" And his hand drew out a long line leading toward them. Stunned, Heli watched as the others who surrounded them took a few steps back with whispering commentary. Heli sent his friends a quick response, *What the hell is going on?*

I think he means us, Dous pressed in.

What should we do? They're all looking at us, Terra shared.

All we can do. Heli stood still.

"The Cor stands before you—as icons we present to the world—a changing world and they will lead us to a greater day of light!" Applause rose up with Cue's voice, and like the beating of drums, Heli could feel it pounding inside of him.

"We have long prepared for a time when all people can live free from idle controls of Regulatory oppression. Even our distant ancestors understood our plight when they wrote that 'In the course of human events, it becomes necessary for one people to dissolve the political bands which have connected them with another, and to assume among the powers of the earth, the separate and equal station to which the Laws of Nature and of Nature's God entitle them. A decent respect to the opinions of mankind requires that they should declare the causes which impel them to the separation.' We preserve these precious words in this moment, and they will secure such rights as citizens of this planet and brand this time as a time for liberty and promise!" Cue finished it off by holding his marked hand over his heart, dropping his head to an overjoyed crowd cheering.

What just happened here? Heli shared.

I've heard this before. It wouldn't have been taught at Regulatory Agencies. Dous began shaking his head as if it might loosen the memory from the clutter of facts and information he carried.

Well I've certainly never heard anything like it before, Heli projected.

Those were more than just words. Oh man...now I remember where I've heard them before. Dous paused rocking gently in his seat. He kept his eyes closed against them. *I think we just witnessed the start of a revolution.*

We need to get out of here. Heli craned his head in toward his friends.

How do we just up and go? They're all looking at us. This is about us, Dous projected.

I can't believe this is happening. How did we become some sort of symbol for all of this?

Terra's question rang through Heli's head as he grabbed her hand and signaled to Dous to follow from behind. They pressed back through the crowd toward their covert. Heli ignored the stares prying in on them as they made their hasty exit.

***

"You should talk to Mianna. Find out what she says about all this." Terra looked at Dous.

Heli interrupted, "No, we don't involve her. We keep this tight, between us. She's too close to it. If we're somehow in the middle of this so-called revolution…" Heli paced the area in front of the steps leading down to where his friends sat in the circlet applying every ounce of his energy to devising some sort of plan.

"Do you think they're in danger?" Dous asked.

"These things don't come without risk, but I don't think we're gonna stick around to find out," Heli said.

"You want to just pack up and leave? We have some responsibility to these people. And where do you suggest we go?" Dous's voice squeaked on the word 'go'.

"Heli, Dous is right, we can't just abandon them. We're evidently part of the reason this is happening," Terra said.

"I know why you want to stay and help them." Heli looked at Dous, "I get it, but we may not have a choice here." He looked at Terra and she sent a thought, *What about tomorrow night? The ceremony? We're their honored guests.*

"Then we go, go through the motions and get through the night, but after that, it's time to start considering our options." Heli turned around to head to the door.

"Where are you going?" Terra asked.

"I just need a little fresh air and some time to think." The guilt settled into the pit of his stomach.

He reached for the sensor to open the door. Just as he was about to take his first step out beyond the threshold, he heard Terra behind him. She grabbed ahold of his hand.

"You okay?" She asked, looking at him sideways. *I feel like there's something you're not telling me.*

"You worry too much." And he put his hands up to cup the sides of her head, pulling her to him. He could feel the warming surge, a soft buzz as his forehead pressed against hers. He stopped, holding his breath, looking into her eyes. He allowed his thoughts to remain open for the moment. She smiled between the cradle of his hold and nodded. But before he released her, he kissed her gently on the forehead with one final thought, *I love you,* and then he shut her out reserving the last part, *but those three words will never be enough.* And letting her go, he turned to walk out keeping his eyes closed until all he could see was the path leading away from her.

Common Ground

Heli pressed past the men and women hard at work. The standing glass pit was already lit, a beacon to draw the entire community together soon. Everyone to speak of seemed to be in high-gear preparation off to some job, fixing a problem, or managing one another in a slew of organized chaos.

The apothecary was lit up behind thin white linen walls of the makeshift space where Emeal stored all of the herbal and medicinal wares that the Frey depended on. Heli knew this might be his only opportunity to find out what was behind Cue's speech, and although he didn't know Emeal well, they shared one single unspoken regard. Terra.

He stepped around the edge of the tent-like shelter and reached for the open flap to enter. Just as he approached, Emeal emerged with her hands full of an assortment of powdery substances arranged neatly in pilings on a tray. Preparing them must have had her at the pestle all day.

He jolted back mid-step, startling her, and she jumped in unison, holding fast to the platter laid across her forearms so that only a dusting fell to the ground. Heli looked down at the tray. "Flavor for the feast tomorrow night?" he asked.

"Ah...no, not this." She looked down to inspect her wares. "Can I help you with something, Heli?" She spoke dismissively, barely whispering his name and looking around as if she had forgotten something.

"I hope so. That speech Cue gave earlier, it must have been important?" Heli asked.

"Very important." She looked up.

"You have a way with crowds," he pressed.

"I wasn't up there on that podium," she said, looking at him as if she had just brought him into focus.

"You certainly played your part," Heli continued.

"My part?" Her eyes narrowed on him.

"I've seen it. In Dous." He prompted, "It's how you place your short order from the universe and make things happen. You're like him, somehow, aren't you?"

"Cue has made much more progress with you than I thought."

Heli paused and glanced around. "I would've assumed he kept you up to speed on everything."

She looked past him for a brief moment, swallowing hard. The light that had left her eyes returned with a quick inhale. "We are all very busy and I am sure he would have briefed me sooner or later."

"What was with the trance?" Heli asked. He watched her features twist.

"It's not what you think. I'll admit, I held them in a state of focal attention, but everything Cue said spoke to their own inner desires. No magic, no force of will. I only use it as a tool to get their attention and in that way it allows them to move forward together."

"Look, you may think that by doing this you can drag these people along and somehow prepare them for the future you have in mind, but what you're doing is only another source of control, which is what I assumed you were up against," Heli said.

"Certainly, but of course you would never understand." She shifted, attempting to hold on to the tray. "You've only been here a few days, long enough to see how we've adjusted, but you were never a part of the struggle."

Heli reached out to offer a hand, but the glare she shot him had him thinking twice so he backed away.

She squinted. "Is there anything else I can help you with? I have important work to do. If you're quite...through," she spoke, and turned her head to look out in the direction of the gathering space. He could see the scar up close now. It trailed nearly halfway down her face, a shimmering line along her cheekbone.

"He did that to you, didn't he?" Heli softened his expression looking over the damage.

She shot her eyes back toward him. "It is not your business to pry into things you don't understand, young man."

"It was before he knew how to control it, wasn't it?" Heli continued.

"It was an accident." She returned his challenging stare, angling to sashay her way around him, and as she did, she brushed his shoulder. He reached up to grip her upper arm and she froze, looking down at his hand. Heli calmly whispered, "Then you understand why I'm asking. I can't afford the same mistake." He slowly unhinged his grip.

She didn't move, but turned her eyes to meet his. "Careful, you may not wish to upset your friends." And as suddenly as he had released his fingers' grip on her he turned around to see Terra, Dous, and Mianna headed toward them.

You, getting chummy with Emeal? What are you up to? Terra stopped in front of him and the question rose silently in her thoughts.

She had her hands full. Thought I could help.

Emeal spoke to break the silence. "Well, we look forward to seeing the three of you as our honored guests at the ceremony. I must be going. Mianna, your father would like you to seat them at his table for the meal tomorrow night. We'll see you all at sundown for a lighter fare this evening." She threw one last glance at Heli as she turned to head up the incline toward the square.

"Not much in the way of leisure time here," Dous said as they all watched Emeal go.

"It's not all work and no play." Mianna smiled.

"I don't know, all I've seen you do since we arrived here is hustle your tail off. That, on top of carting me all over the place," Dous said.

"We're busy for a good reason, and personally I'd rather be carting you around than play a part in all this."

She smiled out at the congested mass of people then back at the three of them.

"Entertaining you all is a welcome change actually. This is a special time and you are special visitors," she continued. "We want everything to be perfect." She paused, edging in closer to the three of them. "In fact, I'm not supposed to give away the surprise, but my father is planning on hosting a very special ceremony in your honor tomorrow night." Mianna's eyes lit up in the dusty light.

"A ceremony?" Heli asked.

"I don't know exactly, but I think it might have something to do with solidifying your inclusion here," she whispered and her head darted around again.

"Official acceptance into the Frey?" Dous asked.

"I think so." She nodded, smiling. "I'd venture to guess that they'll offer you the mark."

"I'm not letting anyone put a brand me," Heli said.

"Well that's if they even think you're worthy." Mianna's tone was tart.

"We accept, if they offer," Dous replied and his eyes jumped from Mianna to Heli as he sent Heli a thought. *Show a little respect.*

Heli pressed his lips together working hard to keep his mind and mouth closed.

"We would be honored," Terra said, smiling.

Heli nodded silently and tried to form a smile.

Mianna smiled in return. "Then tomorrow, before the main event, there's something I'd like to show you."

Heli felt Terra's hand on his and her projecting, *Play nice, just smile and nod—we're going!*

Chasm

"This is how you get your kicks? We're not jumping in there. Are we?" Heli looked down into the dark abyss of the blackest hole in the earth he'd ever seen. A small spring of fresh runoff seemed to shrink and disappear over the smooth rock tongue leading into it. The mouth of the curving belly of rock dipped down into a window-sized chute and a cooling hiss of mist lingered at the opening.

You asked if we had any fun here," Mianna said. She looked at Dous, who was staring anxiously down into the void.

"Zuke's not gonna fit in there," he said.

"You won't need Zuke for this ride. We come out on the water and then one of us can take the switchback up to retrieve him," Mianna said.

"And these?" Heli asked, pulling at the taut fabric of the slick black cutting edge Hodgesuit Mianna had given them. "I know it's your little hobby to dice these rags up but when you asked if you could make some adjustments to one of ours, I thought you might do something cool like make a mood suit or something," Heli said.

"A mood suit?" Dous laughed. "I don't think 'sour' would be a good color on you," he joked.

"For crying out loud, at least give me something to wear that doesn't cut off my circulation. I feel like I've been squeezed into a rubber hose." Heli pulled at his collar.

"I know they're not perfect. These are just hybrid prototypes and I have to make due with what's on hand at the lab, but there's always room for improvement. Hopefully you're not allergic to latex. It's a liquid lining I added. The suits are already fitted with flexible Lycra fibers, but by lining your suits I could make it more of a custom fit, not only increasing durability but sealing it for use in the water."

"I don't know, I think it's a good look on you." Terra lifted an eyebrow to Heli.

"Is it me or did you grease these things up?" Heli said and ran his hands down the front of the suit. He caught Terra looking at Dous, the two of them ineffectively trying to hide their smiles. "What are you two laughing at? You both look like a pair of tar bubbles yourselves." He suddenly noticed how the suit clung tight to every curve of Terra's body.

"It does seem to have a certain waxiness to it." Dous mimicked Heli by running his hands up and down the legs of his suit.

"That's the infused lubricant I added to the sealer. It'll allow for extra speed and protection from abrasion on the ride down. The entire experience is enhanced by the garment," Mianna said.

Dous sat listening to her while his tongue seemed to be caught in this throat. He cleared it and said, "This isn't your first time? You've done this before?"

"I've taken a few trial runs," Mianna answered.

"Well, at least you can rest assure that she's experienced." Heli smiled at Dous. Dous seemed to choke suddenly on an empty pocket of air and leaned back on Zuke, open mouthed and speechless.

Terra stared at Heli. *I can't believe you. You are absolutely shameless.*

Oh, come on, I'm just having a little fun. That's what we're here for, right? Besides I only said what he was thinking. His shields were down.

Thoughts aren't the same as saying it out loud. Give him a break, Terra projected. They both watched Dous scan the ground like he'd give anything to find a bug to squash.

Mianna hesitated, watching them in their silent conversation. "I always test the suits for quality control. These were designed for this and they ride well." Then she pointed out toward the dark hollow depression. "The chute's been here since the fault-line shift a century ago. It feeds into one of the natural underground mineral springs on the outer banks of the quarry."

"Well at least we know we'll have a soft landing." Dous had somehow regained his composure.

"I'm not as concerned by the water landing as I am by the idea of being swallowed by a chasm in the earth," Heli admitted.

"You're afraid?" Mianna challenged.

"You bet your rubber Hodgies I am. Any sane person would be. I don't know very many people who would readily jump into a pitch-black hole in the ground and smile about it." Heli rolled his eyes.

"Here, try the lumilights." Mianna reached to pinch something along the collar of Dous's suit. He suddenly transformed into a brilliant glow of violet delirium.

"Whoa!" he exclaimed as his eyes widened on the suit he wore.

Mianna turned away from Dous and spoke to Heli. "Look, I know you don't trust me so here's an opportunity to show you I'm on your side."

"I don't think risking our necks so you can prove something here even with all these bells and whistles is going to convince us," Heli said.

Mianna proceeded to walk around behind each of them. She came to Heli first and he felt a feathery pressure against his neck just as a warm illumination surrounded him. Mianna reached up behind her own neck and her suit began to glow the same lambent purple they each cast.

"This is crazy," Dous said.

"That's why we're doing it." A fire was lit in Mianna's eyes that scared Heli more than their looming plunge.

"I'll hold your hand." Terra giggled and moved to stand next to Heli.

"You think this is funny?" Heli said, puffing up his chest and turning toward her.

"It's just a slide. She just wants to show us a little fun. I'm sure she wouldn't go through all of this if it wasn't relatively safe," Terra said.

Heli looked at Mianna. "And this pool of water, on the other side, you happen to know how deep it runs?" His hands were shaking now.

"It cuts under deeper than I can dive holding my breath," Mianna answered.

"Oh, that makes me feel so much better," Heli said, and even his own sarcasm couldn't quell the queasy undercurrent of dread he was experiencing.

"We'll jump together." Terra reached up to take hold of Heli's hand.

He pulled away. "You might not want to touch me right now, and I cannot believe you want to do this. Do you all have a death wish or something?" Heli looked to Terra first and then at Dous. His focus veered back toward the hole.

Terra repositioned herself closer to the opening, crossing her arms in front of her glowing form. "I know you, and you're not going to just sit back and watch me jump down there alone. You'll come after me." The contest in her eyes was gone in the same instant he saw her face slacken, and with an incremental step backwards, she dropped out of sight.

Heli choked on his next intake of air, feeling the violent tug on his lungs and a combination of fear and excitement edging on nausea. He only looked up at Dous and Mianna for a brief instant before the shock wore off and he dove in feet first after her.

***

Racing through a portal of pitch black, Heli's heart beat like a hummingbird's, the palpitations a hundred beats per second pounding bruises onto his chest. The sensation coupled with falling was supported with the lightest contact on the rock's smooth surface. It held him in the jet stream of pouring water on the seemingly endless downpour. He thought he could hear Terra's screams ahead of him, realizing he was uncontrollably letting loose a few whoops of his own. Every sound was being swallowed up by speed and what felt like eons in a never-ending cascading plummet downward.

All of it ended as abruptly as it had begun. In the time it took for him to register the piercing pinpoint of light from Terra's suit ahead of him, he was expelled out of the chute like a cannon ball, falling through mid-air. The sudden asphyxiation from the water's icy cold fingers pressed him down deeper with the plunge. He emerged from the surface of the watery net to exhale shaking the wet mop of hair hanging in his eyes just as Terra's thoughts pressed in with urgency: *Move!*

He caught the frantic tone in her order and quickly began to cut his way through the water with both arms slicing and kicking, his legs pushing him forward toward her voice. He looked out through the fuzzy stream of water still dripping over his eyes as another bursting splash came from behind. Dous had hit the surface, catapulted down below the dark water, and then his glowing form emerged, bobbing up through the ripples.

He quickly swam in a full arm sprint toward them and again the sputtering splash of Mianna's body split the water's wavy form, rocking them all slightly.

"Oh my god! That was insane!" Dous yelled. He was half laughing, half screaming as he blindly paddled his way toward Mianna. She emerged with her eyes still closed. In the low glow of the lumilights Heli could see her grinning from ear to ear.

"Everyone still in one piece?" she asked, a bit breathless.

"That was amazing!" Terra laughed.

Heli couldn't find the words. As pitch black as the depths of the water they floated in, his mind was a blank wash. It pelted him from the inside out, an unrelenting surge of adrenaline that exploded under his chest, and he felt warmth in his cheeks broadening across his face until he became aware that he too was smiling. Losing all control, he began to laugh out loud and as the lightness took over and the others joined in on the delirium, he felt them—tears of pure joy running down his cheeks.

As if she could read more than his mind, Terra took a hold of Heli's shoulders to press him down under the settling waves with all her might, sending them both under the water and out of sight. Blinded by the force of emotion, he felt the surge and her lips meeting his.

Resurfacing only moments later with Terra's arms wrapped around him while he treaded the water to keep them both afloat, he heard her sputter. "Then its official, we'll have another go?"

***

"I have to admit, that was pure entertainment," Dous said.

Heli looked up at the sky, darkening now with the last strokes of light along the horizon. "More like some wild initiation." He had never seen sky like this. From where they all lay sprawled out on the ground he could see the layers of orange and blue that lit up the edge of a newfangled skyline. He traced the watery glaze of the dusky edge until his eyes came back around to meet his friends.

"We should get going," Mianna said. Her gaze met Heli's as he joined her in rising up, brushing off the dust from his Hodgesuit and offering a hand out to Terra.

"Thank you for showing us this," Terra said.

"It's the least I could do." She reached down to aid in moving Dous onto Zuke. Heli moved in to offer a helping hand.

"Well I for one am starving after all that. I could eat a barn right now." Dous hobbled onto the seat with the aid of his escorts.

"You could eat a barn any day of the week." Heli shook his head.

I See It

Mianna led them to their table. Cue was already seated. He smiled as they approached and stood to greet them, extending a hand to offer them each a seat.

Heli held back awkwardly, waiting.

Terra probed and gently tapped the seat beside her. *Planning on joining us?*

As he did Terra leaned in to whisper, "Did you get a glimpse of that bird?"

Heli looked up to the sky. "Where?"

"Not in the air," she laughed, "on the table over there."

He scanned the tables in front of them locating the one she was referring to surrounded by piles of food that piles of people were bringing out in armfuls.

He shivered when he saw it: a massive mound of a plucked and roasted bird carcass, the largest he had ever seen, sat bulging over the edges of the platter.

"We eat that?" Heli asked.

"Must be a regenerated species of some kind. Dous told me that they were once a favored delicacy for important feasts in the past. Some kind of relic," Terra said.

"Well I can see why it ended up on a platter. I bet it never left the ground. That thing is enormous."

The sights and sounds all had him feeling a bit out of place and yet he found himself licking his lips when a basket of bread was delivered by a young girl. She planted it in front of him and stopped, studying him. By his own estimations and the toothless gap between her teeth, Heli thought she couldn't be more than four or five years old. The tone of her skin stood out, a creamy froth of mahogany. She was obviously not a product of The Blend.

"Thank you," Heli said.

She leaned in and spoke softly. "I see it." A bigger smile snuck out between her rosy bronzed lips and she hid her face behind a cupped hand.

"You see what?" Heli played along.

"Your light," she whispered.

Heli moved back, to see that they were the only ones privy to the conversation. At the moment Terra seemed engrossed with something Cue was discussing with Mianna and Dous.

"A light?" he asked conspiratorially. Her whispering was contagious.

"Ma mam says you lit up the world for us." Then a smile split her lips and he could see the gap between her teeth again. She seemed to be more of a representation of this light herself at the moment. She turned, and Heli watched the glow fade as her eyes caught the stern glower of a woman off in the distance. She quickly scooted off in that direction.

"You have a fan." Terra turned and leaned in toward Heli.

He shook his head. "She brought me bread." He continued to look after the small girl as her mother reached down to take her hand.

Terra's hand met his under the table. "Sweet."

Heli sat quietly in the moment taking in the sight of the people filing the seats.

The laughter filled the air and the breeze flowed through him like a sieve, leaving him purified. In that moment he knew he could withstand any possible future knowing that the little girl's words were meant for him.

***

Cue stood, instantly signaling a hush from the crowd. "Thank you all for joining us here tonight. I especially want to thank our honored guests for coming and entertaining the possibility that they might perhaps make their stay more permanent." He turned to look directly at Heli. "Tonight, we would like to welcome you into the Frey, no longer as mere guests, but as our dear comrades and citizens. We invite you to call this place your home."

Heli looked over to Dous and Terra, their gaze dead set on the crowd. *Well this is awkward.*

I think we should say something, Terra thought.

In this 'we' you mean me? Heli asked.

Terra frowned, pushing her seat back to stand. She stood for a moment in the estranged silence. "We wish to thank you for your hospitality and for welcoming us like family." Heli could see her hands trembling as she set them down on the table in front of her.

He stood to join her. Their eyes met. *I'll stand by you, not on you. Your words, remember?*

She cleared her throat. "All of you, the good people here, have treated us with nothing but kindness and courtesy. We're humbled by your faith in us and we willingly accept your invitation."

Cue stood and reached to take her left hand. "Will you accept the mark as a gift from our loyal citizens? Wearing it will secure our commitment to you, the Cor." He paused to look at Heli and then Dous, and then continued meaningfully, "as we embark on the next phase of this journey together?"

Heli started to project a thought before Terra's answer, *I don't think—,* but he was shaken from his thoughts as he looked out into the crowd and saw the little girl who had spoken to him earlier that night. Something about the hope in her eyes, the solid regard she offered him in that brief, tender moment, and he felt helpless to enter into a debate. *I don't think we can say no.*

A smile lit up Terra's entire face, and Dous joined in with his thoughts, *So, we're all in?*

All or nothing, Heli projected.

"We accept," she answered, and with her hand still cupped in Cue's, he raised it up victoriously. He nodded toward Emeal, who was seated nearby, "Please bring the prepared slates."

She exited and returned quickly with a tray. Familiar filings of colorful powders caked the tray, the same tray she had been carrying when Heli bumped into her at the apothecary.

Cue spoke again. "Please join us all by the fire." He moved around the table while Mianna signaled that they follow him with a swing of her arm and together they moved out toward the center square, a procession of the Frey's citizens leading from behind.

As they reached the top of the mound nearer and nearer to the burning sconce, Cue turned and whispered so only Heli could hear. "I've realized what will keep the Prana under control. All you need to think of is your future and theirs." Just as the words slipped into his ear, Heli felt a light tugging on his leg from the opposite side. It was the little girl from earlier that evening. She winked at him with both eyes and he suddenly felt enlightened.

Cue spoke, "As with your birth order, your induction will follow the same cycle." Emeal set down the tray on the podium mound where Cue had given his speech. She mixed the assortment of powders in a center pedestal bowl. A young boy brought a small flask of fluid and handed it to Mianna, who assisted Emeal. Wisps of the substance began to float above the vessel in a swirling arc of powdered steam as she poured, bright colors dissolving into the black, tarry mixture she stirred. Mianna handed Emeal a brush that she dipped into the contents of the container. She held it out in front of her to assess its tip. "You apply the mark yourself to the left hand between the thumb and forefinger." She held out her own mark in reference to these instructions, then handed the tool to Dous.

He scanned the crowd of onlookers, eyes wide open. Mianna instructed, "The circle will remain open, but let the mark define you. With the strand, you give it purpose. One solid stroke."

Dous let out a cool breath and took the brush with some hesitation. Before he began, he looked up at Heli. *Here goes nothing.* He marked his left hand.

What only took a few seconds had the crowd cheering, hooting, and hollering and Dous's chest puffed up as he stared down at his most recent rendering. Mianna smiled at him and looked at her father, who nodded. She gently whispered something in his ear and then she was suddenly wheeling him off away from them.

"Where are they going?" Heli asked.

Cue smiled, quickly responding over the drowning noise of the crowd. "Mianna has prepared a special gift for your friend. They'll be back. Your turn."

Heli gripped Terra's hand. *We're really going through with this?*

Her eyes cloaked any reservation. *Yes, we are.*

Cue reached and this time he took hold of one of each of their hands in unison. "The two of you share an uncommon bond. One that defies any other. We wish to acknowledge that here tonight among friends. Do you both arrive here voluntarily to enter into this communion?" Cue waited for their reply. Heli looked out, surveying the crowd. It was a community of euphoric rejoice, bonded by the certainty of their decision projecting back. Even he felt swept up in it.

All he had to do was take one look at Terra to know her answer. They spoke in unison. "We do." Cue moved to guide their hands from his and into one another's. "You will each make your mark on one another with promissory ties."

Emeal gave Cue two brushes, tipped with fresh black resin. He handed them to Terra and Heli. Terra looked down at Heli's hand in hers and traced a beautiful arc on his left hand. A chill ran up his arm as the cold, wet touch of the brush lingered in his senses. He held his breath watching her admire it before lifting her eyes to him. *Your turn.*

Heli took his time, precisely observing how the curves of the muscles of her hand made the perfect canvas for such a distinction. The brush felt as if it were guiding him, not the other way around. He smiled pleased as he finished the rendering.

Then Cue took from Emeal two of the beaded neckpieces Heli had seen adorning other members of the Frey. One was a string of turquoise and golden beads and the other was held in stark contrast with black, white, and blood orange. Cue proceeded to wrap them around their clasped and newly marked hands.

"Are you willing now and always to affirm your standing with one another as our newest members of the Frey?" Cue's voice was firm.

Heli looked at Terra again and she nodded and spoke for them. "We do."

Cue continued, "This ceremony, in ways unseen, will greatly strengthen your union. And as you recall your words and intentions tonight, let them guide you and support you. Before the many witnesses tonight, are you ready to confirm this most sacred of dedications?"

Heli was surprised by the formality of this part of the ceremony, yet the hand he held was so warm in his. He looked at Terra and felt a new kinship, alight with optimism that they were willingly entering into this commitment to the Frey together, the place they could now begin to call home.

"We do." Heli spoke this time as he swallowed back an old nagging thought. He looked out beyond the plethora of eyes still watching them and could see Dous's strained features aimed back at them from a distance.

"And so the binding is made." Cue wrapped the cords into a final loop over their wrists.

With Cue's head still bowed low over their clasped hands, Dous's voice came through projecting urgent thoughts: *Do you have any idea what you just did?*

Heli saw Dous break away from Mianna's reach and bolt through the crowd toward them. Those in his path darted to the side to escape being run down.

We need to talk. Now! Heli yanked Terra out from Cue's watchful hands. They pushed through the surge of confusion and congratulatory raps from the people as they passed.

As they angled down through the parting of the crowd Heli overheard Emeal ask Cue, "Where are they going?"

But it was his answer almost out of earshot that caused Heli's stomach to lurch. "Let them be. It's done."

Heli found himself panting as they all careened to a stop on the hill overlooking the coverts and Dous swiveled around to face them.

"Mianna distracted me." Dous shook his head between his hands like he was trying to remove some entrapment device from it.

"What do you mean she distracted you? From what? Where were you?" Heli asked.

Heli watched as Dous reached to grip his hand, turning it around. "Those words toward the end of the ceremony, I remember them from one of the historical hall cubes in anthropology. They originate from an ancient binding ritual. Are you both marked?"

He looked at Terra, panic stricken.

"What do you mean are we both marked? We marked each other!" Heli barked.

Terra held out her hand for Dous to see.

"Oh no, why would they do this?" He put his head in his hands pulling at the tight curls.

"Why would they do what?" Terra asked. Heli could hardly speak as Dous's words were finally taking shape in his mind.

"Enter you two into a sacred betrothal. Like as in matrimonial. That was a marriage ceremony." Dous let the words roll out in one exhausted breath.

"Excuse me? We did not just get . . ." Heli looked at Terra, who was near tears, her hands clasped in front of her.

Dous bobbed his head, finishing Heli's thought. *Hitched.*

Ceremonial Rights

"So outside of the Frey and the ceremony, who says this is even official?" Heli could hear his own breath in the silence that surrounded him in their covert. He kept it steady and rhythmic to stay calm. He looked down to see the dark line in an arc on his left hand while he gripped the edge of the cushioned seat.

"Look, all I know is that you confirmed your commitment in front of witnesses and an officiant. Those words Cue had you reciting were directed toward only one end, vows for a life with one another. Whether you choose to accept it or not doesn't really matter in the eyes of all those people. They see it as official," Dous said.

"You think there's more behind this? Like some sort of agenda?" Terra asked Dous. She spoke so softly. Heli could hardly register her exact words. She had shut him out from her thoughts.

"And I thought I was the paranoid one. I think we all might be overreacting a bit." Heli could see how Terra was glaring at him from under heavy lashes, her jaw set firm and silent.

"Then tell me, what would the two of you reciting words that I am certain qualify as official 'wedding' vows have to do with a simple induction into the Frey? I mean, I realize that our grandparents might be the last generation to care, but I am not just being paranoid. That was for real. And yeah, I suspect that there is something behind it," Dous said.

"Well, what do we do about it?" Heli asked. "It can't be impossible to undo."

"I don't think you're hearing me. This isn't about some regulatory action you have to uphold. Sure, you can renounce that it ever happened. It's the simple fact that it happened at all," Dous said.

Terra turned away trying to hide her tears.

"I think we all just need some time to figure things out. We're not going to resolve this tonight. We sleep on it, gather our wits and in the morning deal with the next steps." Heli looked at Terra. She had completely angled herself away from the conversation.

You okay? She remained unresponsive—completely out of his reach.

"I'm such an idiot." Dous's words of deprecation only added to the strain they were all under. "Mianna had to know about this. And her little diversion caught me off guard, but then she slipped up, spilling the beans about how the marks would make official what you have together. I'm just sorry I wasn't there in time to put a stop to it."

"If this is anyone's fault, it's ours. Blindsided yes, but we did this," Heli said.

"It is my fault. I became so wrapped up in the idea that Mianna actually liked me that I stopped paying attention to what really mattered," Dous said.

"She does like you," Heli said.

"Yeah, right. Once a scapegoat, always a scapegoat. And since when did you find it in your heart to stick up for her, especially after this mess!"

Heli looked at Terra again and this time he saw the tears that were trailing down her cheeks, her eyes squeezing together firmly to release them.

"Mianna's got some serious explaining to do," Dous said.

"Then you should go talk to her." Heli suggested, aiming his gaze at Terra again. *We could use some time alone anyway.*

Dous made his way back toward the door. Heli heard Zuke's brake clamp down. "I guess there are worse things they could've done to you." He pressed the exit mount as the door opened and he rolled out.

Heli could feel the pressure of the air building up around them as soon as they were shut inside alone together, crippling him from speaking. Just as he settled into the silence Terra spoke. "Is it so bad? Like Dous said? The thought of this happening? You and Dous talk about it like it's the end of the world." Her voice sent a soft painful reminder of Cue's warning.

"I happen to know firsthand what it would be like if it were the end of the world, and this," he nodded his head, "is a beginning. I just don't know where to go with it."

Terra looked up at him, her eyes pleading. "I know this is crazy and we still have a lot to learn about each other, but when I agreed to those things, I was answering honestly, with my whole heart, and I can't deny that…" She paused to swallow with another release of tears. "I don't want you to regret that we—" She stopped.

Heli could feel the heat and the buzzing coming to surface all over, but there was no threat now that he knew what to do. He slid down the barrier of pillows between them, moving them aside one at a time but wanting nothing more than to tear away at the distance. When he reached her, he slowly let his hand fall on her waist to draw her to him. She was still crying and he knew her tears had been the miracle elixir quenching the fire growing inside of him.

He whispered into her neck, "No regrets. Just pictured it differently."

"You've thought about it?" Her red tear-stained face lifted to peer back at him.

"I have, and I do…often. I'll confess, and I don't confess much, I've played it over in my head a hundred times. But it was never like that. It was ours." He shifted as they both moved onto their knees to face one another, taking both of her hands, and cupping them in his. "This is how I pictured it. Just us, alone and scared, but clear on the fact that we were moving on to something bigger than we've ever known. We don't need a ceremony to make what we have official." He could feel the nerves jetting around in his body as he spoke. "In my version my stomach always did a flip at this part." He pulled her in so close that he could feel her warm breath on his chin. "And I'd kiss you up and down your neck." He brushed her neck with soft kisses, each one making him forget to come up for air.

With little soft sounds escaping her lips, her next words came out low and airy. "Then what?"

"Then there was nothing else to be done for it," Heli whispered. Her arms were wrapped neatly around his neck as he scooped up her legs to carry her up the stairs beyond the alcove of cushions toward her room.

She whispered back, "And we crossed the threshold together."

He held his forehead firmly against hers. "And we never looked back."

Aftershock

Heli woke entangled in a nest of blankets and bedding. For a moment he was unsure of where he was, blinking back the sleep that had built up and the numbing haze of waking in an unfamiliar place. He rubbed his eyes and Terra moved next to him. She clutched the blankets that were wrapped around them, nuzzling up into the curve of his arm. He held his breath, suddenly solidly aware of where he was.

Good morning. She stretched alongside him like a cat releasing him and then wrapping her arms around him again.

Morning, stumbled out in his thoughts. He looked out the open veranda doors; the soft light from the sun peaking just above the horizon was their only witness. She shivered and he reached to pull up the sheet that was drawn down below her elbow, while he moved his hand slowly, sliding it up along her bare skin. He could see the mark on his own hand. Everything flashed back in an instant, the ceremony, their talk, and what came later. While he gazed at it, he could see the dark inlaid stroke, a permanency in stark contrast to his fair skin.

"You're quiet," Terra said, but she didn't move.

"Yeah." He reached down, searching to find her left hand that was curled up against her bare chest gripping her heart. "Can I see it?" He drew her hand up. He had done a fine job on the impression and for a moment as he looked into the circular frame he felt as if he were getting a glimpse into the looking glass of their past, present, and a future. He had yet to comprehend what it all meant but holding her in his arms he could see in every way how these rings defined them.

He pulled her hand to his mouth and kissed it.

"You hungry?" he asked.

"Famished." She sat up. He could tell she was nervous. He lay frozen, watching her slowly edge her way out of the bed to move toward the wardrobe. She looked back over her shoulder with one of the sheets wrapped around her and smiled. "Am I going to breakfast alone?" He reached out to grab her, pulling her back to him, nibbling on her shoulder. "I'll follow you anywhere, but not just yet."

***

"I never heard Dous come back last night," Heli said as they walked together hand in hand toward the center square mound.

"Mmm? I guess I wasn't paying much attention." She kept her gaze ahead of them but he could see the curl to her lips.

"They don't have any guest coverts," Heli said.

"Well, I'm sure we'll find out soon enough. We're heading toward the food. He can't be too far off— Oh!" she cut off suddenly.

"You okay?" Heli stopped alongside her, rubbing his hand up and down her arm.

"Yeah, dizzy spell. Running on empty I guess." She shook her head and the breath she let out sounded more like a *foof* as they picked up the pace again. She held Heli's hand a little tighter.

They entered the eatery. Many others were already settled. All eyes shifted as if a spotlight followed them. Heli could see the undeniable assumptions in their stares. He steered Terra back toward an empty table.

Why are they all looking at us like that? Terra projected.

People smiled and nodded as they passed. *Must've gotten more sleep than we did last night.*

Finally, able to see through the threads of people, Heli spotted Dous sitting next to Mianna at one of the far banquet tables.

As they approached, Heli released Terra's hand and Dous looked up with his mouth wide open in mid-sentence. Mianna looked away.

Heli projected a thought. *Should my ears be burning?*

Dous shifted in his seat like he couldn't quite find a comfortable position. *No, we were just talking about last night. I mean...*He pinched up his face, scratching his head, and spoke aloud this time, "Wanna join us?"

Heli noticed there were two chairs left at their table and how they were each situated on either side of them. Terra had already begun moving around to sit by Mianna, so he pulled out the chair next to Dous.

As Terra was about to sit, Heli overheard Mianna say, "Oh, we can move down if you two want to sit together."

"We're fine," Terra said.

Awkwardly Mianna continued, "Oh, okay?" She looked confusedly between them, then back to Dous.

Mianna's next words cleared some of the tension away from the elephant clearly standing in the eatery. "Okay, so Dous told me about Synthanutrients. That's what they call them, right?" She looked between them.

"More like a travesty to nutritional provisions. This right here," Dous held up a piece of fruit with its peeling still on, "is an experience."

Heli was a bit put off by watching Dous's display of appreciation, biting into the thick rind and licking his lips free from the juices that ran loose in a gushy trail down his chin. Mianna brought up a cloth to wipe away the mess. Heli watched how she doted over him. They were like a ridiculous old couple set in their ways already. Tired, hungry, and getting grouchier by the minute, Heli asked, "So it looks like you two worked things out?"

"Yeah," Dous said through a mouthful, coughing up a bit, "and Cue wants to talk to us after breakfast."

"Really? Well, that's convenient. I'd like to talk to him too. And who do we have to thank for setting up that rendezvous?" Heli glanced at Mianna.

"Well—" Dous started.

Mianna interrupted, "Heli, I'm sorry you didn't know what the ceremony meant for the two of you. I assumed that my father would have told you after all of the time you've been spending together."

"Your little diversion was well timed," Heli said.

Easy Heli, Dous thought. Heli looked up at him, feeling an overwhelming sense of lost loyalties.

"What other kinds of tricks do you have up your sleeve?" Heli murmured.

"I was only—"

Dous stopped her. "Wait!" Dous took a deep breath. He slowly pushed Zuke back from the table. He pressed forward with both hands on the edge, raising himself to stand. Heli moved in quickly to brace him and Dous let go of the edge, waving a hand to swat Heli away. He was standing on his own.

"How in the world?" Heli spit out.

"Remember how I told you about the suit that Mianna was working on? Well I'm wearing it." A wave of anticipation moved across Dous's features.

Heli looked Dous up and down and lifted a hand to touch it. He noted the way it moved like pliable metal, yet naturally, befitting a moveable, breathable standard garment, but it was somehow more. Much more.

"She had it ready for me to try on last night. Her father gave her permission to give it to me right after the marking," he said.

Is that the story she fed you? Heli let the thought fly.

She's done it. What no one else could. She's given me legs. I have to believe in this. I have to believe in her. Dous lowered back down to sit on Zuke again.

The chatter surrounded them once more.

"We didn't see you come back last night," Heli said, feeling a relentless urge to keep digging.

"We stayed up late talking. She wanted to show me how it works and make a few adjustments. Cue invited me to stay in their covert if that's what you're worried about." Dous paused. "You don't hear me asking where you slept last night."

A sound escaped Terra's mouth and Heli let the thought spill out, *That's not fair.*

You want to know what's not fair? That the two most important people in my life just got hitched and I somehow missed it. A hot breath escaped him. *I know it's not your fault, but you can't blame her either.*

Fine. Heli looked from Dous to Mianna. "Where's your father?"

***

"Welcome back, Dous." Cue reached out two hands, shaking one of Dous's firmly.

You two seem chummy, Heli thought, and Dous lifted his head away, shutting him out.

"Thanks for meeting with us. We understand how busy you are," Dous said politely.

"Heli," Cue nodded, "and Terra. Thank you for coming. I believe I owe you both some explanation."

"Mianna said you wished to speak with us. There's only one thing we need to discuss." Heli cleared his throat.

"I'm sure you're referring to the ceremony last night." Cue nodded.

"You…" Heli started.

"Married us," Terra finished for him.

"Well, yes, it was what some would observe as a legitimate union," Cue said.

"Some? Everyone here looks at us like we're up for auction," Heli said.

"How could you do that without telling us?" Terra looked at him and then looked at Heli, unreadable pain in her eyes.

"It was necessary," Cue responded.

"Necessary?" Heli asked. He could feel his hands swelling with heat.

"You don't understand what is at stake." Cue shook his head. "You couldn't, and I couldn't tell you before . . ." He paused. "Before it was…made official."

"Made official?" Dous asked.

Cue stood tall, but his mannerisms were taking on an unfamiliar disarray. "Their union, it's been made official. The resin in their imprint was made to ensure us of that.

"Wait a minute, are you insinuating that they…consummated this thing?" Dous turned and looked at Heli, then his eyes flew to Terra, the blood rushing to her cheeks in an instant. A short, shocked breath escaped him.

Terra paled again looking back at him.

"Wait, you're saying there something in the resin that affected what happened last night?" Heli felt his tongue go dry in an instant while he stared back at Cue. "You drugged us?"

Terra reached for him, but he moved away quickly, unsure of his own stability.

"Not a drug. Natural inducements," Cue said.

Heli closed his eyes tightly, clenching his fists to hold back the rage. He could hear his own voice shaking. "I would qualify anything that might influence someone's mind and body as a drug, especially if it didn't come by our own volition."

"How could you?" Terra looked at Cue with tears streaming down her cheeks.

"This is Emeal's handy work, isn't it?" Heli held out his hand. "She mixed the resin. And the two of you knew all along. You were planning this! That's why you brought us here! It wasn't to protect us, or help us," Heli flared.

Both Terra and Dous took a step back from him.

"You played us?" Dous said, and he looked at Mianna. Although he was wearing the suit that kept him standing, he had a firm grip on Zuke's armrest like he might need to sit down at any moment.

"Don't worry," Heli nodded, "she had nothing to do with this. You've been playing all of us." Heli stared at Cue and then back to Mianna.

She herself wore a look that seemed to rest between horror and relief. Her head was cast down and she lifted it to look solemnly at her father.

"And what about Emeal? She's your ready accomplice. Does she owe you some kind of favor? Anything to do with your dead wife?"

Cue held up a hand, cutting Heli off, and Mianna squealed, covering her mouth.

"That's enough!" Cue's voice was stern and he turned to Mianna. "Go find Emeal. Bring her here. She should take part in this conversation."

Mianna looked at him, her eyes twisted with the betrayal she must have felt, but she turned quickly obeying his command.

"Please, sit down?" His hand stretched out along the foyer and out to the circlet of couches.

"Okay, I'd like a word or two with her myself," Heli said, aiming to take Terra's hand, but she slid past him. He and Cue followed her down the short flight of stairs into the sunken space.

Dous stopped at the top. Heli turned back and Dous's brow furrowed. *You need a hand?* Heli projected.

I'm fine. Dous didn't look up, taking each step with focused care.

Terra sat on one end with her arms crossed. Heli made his way over to her. She didn't release the tight fold she had wrapped herself up in when he approached. He squeezed in beside her, reaching to seize her hand. *What's wrong?* He could feel the tension in her loose grip.

Not now, she sent.

"My apologies for no fire. We conserve all we can during the day," Cue said.

"You're all very good at that," Heli noted and went on, "preserving what you can behind the facade of transparent walls."

The uncomfortable moment was interrupted by a cool breeze as the door opened and Emeal entered. Mianna scooted in from close behind.

Mianna quickly made her way down to join them and sat between her father and Dous. Emeal took her time, gliding toward them. She stopped at the top of the alcove looking down on all of them regally.

"Cue," she said, "I understand you're in need of my assistance?"

"They're here for some answers," Cue said.

"Of course, where shall we start?" she offered and stepped down the stairs to stand next to Cue.

"From the beginning, by all means." Heli resisted the urge to stand and challenge her face to face.

She struck Heli as someone much like himself.

"In everything we know, wrought by our common histories, we share a similar story in connection to IDEA," she said.

"What happened between the three of you?" Terra whispered, and Heli turned to look at her. Her face was sallow and pale and under the umbrella of her golden lashes her eyes met Emeal's with complaisance.

Emeal reached and touched her scar and suddenly her hardened stance faded. She shifted to settle down into the couch next to Cue, her eyes dropping to the mark on her hand. "Thryn, as you've learned, was our third." Emeal cleared her throat and looked at Cue.

Cue turned to Mianna. "I apologize for any pain this conversation may bring you, but I think it's time for you to hear it as well." He nodded dutifully. "Your mother arrived at IDEA at a precarious time in our development. The bond between the three of us had not been secured yet."

Emeal continued for him, placing her hand on his knee. "Your father fell in love with your mother Arah almost in the instant they met. I read it in his eyes when he first saw her. Thryn sensed it too."

"You could read one another's emotions?" Terra asked.

We tell them nothing about us, Heli's thoughts spilled.

"We've always been able to see things beyond what the surface shows in our emotions, particularly the things we shared within our growing bond," Emeal said.

Emeal looked up at Mianna. "Thryn was a complicated sort. She hadn't come out with it yet, but her feelings for Cue bled like an open wound into our minds, feelings that they both knew he couldn't rightfully share. It caused a fracturing that none of us were prepared for."

Cue stretched a hand out and placed it on his daughter's leg. "Your mother wrapped a knot around my heart so secure that I made little room for anyone else. And unfortunately, the tragedy in loving her was what later put the mission at risk," he said.

Dous looked confused and asked, "But you went into the Strata, knowing the bond wasn't secure? Why take that chance?"

Emeal answered, "We were the first. No one at IDEA knew or understood the critical nature of these bonds."

"There was a certain shame in knowing I couldn't share her feelings. Thryn shut us out completely," Cue admitted. "Our biggest mistake was thinking we could go in with our pride intact, but our conscience beaten."

Emeal cleared her throat. "What appeared to have succeeded initially, turned out to be a disaster of complexities that IDEA almost didn't recover from. Around that same time Jacque was expelled from the program and Tracy took his place."

"What did Jacque have to do with it?" Heli asked.

"I believe he may have known where things stood between Thryn and me," Cue said.

"And he didn't try to stop you?" Terra asked.

"He was dealing with his own battle." Cue spread his hands on his lap. "He'd been pining away after Thryn for months."

"He cared for her?" Terra asked.

"In whatever manner is possible for a man like him," Cue added.

"But she knew better than to give him the time of day, right?" Dous asked.

"Jacque was rather benign in the beginning. The quiet sort. I never would have pegged him for the man he is today. Nearly unrecognizable," Cue said.

Emeal spoke again. "Thryn was vulnerable and he took full advantage of that fact. In every way avoiding us, she took to spending time with him. She'd shut us out completely. And I'm sure on some level he knew we weren't ready."

"Did she ever return his feelings?" Dous asked.

"No, what they shared never developed beyond a friendship, but as she began to depend on him more and more I think he remained hopeful that they could be something more between them. Poor Thryn had reached a point of desperation in giving him even a glimmer of that false hope," Emeal said.

"It's the primary reason we opted for the ceremony to honor what was secure between you before witnesses. Something Emeal, Thryn, and I could never fulfill. Our lives since that time have been spent in an effort toward making amends," Cue admitted.

"Glad we could serve to appease your guilt trip," Heli said.

"Do you object to your commitment to Terra?" Cue said, masterfully spinning it around.

Heli noticed how Terra straightened up waiting for his answer.

"Absolutely not." He looked her straight in the eye. "It's just, I mean," he paused and looked back at Cue, "are we living in another millennium here? Because I've only heard of this kind of arrangement in historical hall cubes and those were some seriously archaic notions." Heli looked over again at Terra. Her lips were drawn in a tight line. Her thoughts were sealed.

"They're a bit young for this, wouldn't you agree?" Dous added.

Cue rolled his eyes over toward Emeal and she spoke for him. "You bring up an interesting question. I forget that you haven't been briefed on your entire history."

"By the way, I can totally see through this good cop, bad cop thing you're doing." Heli looked back and forth between Cue and Emeal.

Emeal's eyes widened on him and she shook her head. "As with precaution and timeline obligations, there were measures taken to ensure that you were ready for this stage of your progression," she explained.

"More secrets to toe the line you mean?" Heli flew back in his seat and slapped himself hard against the soft pillows. "Why am I not surprised?" He looked up at Cue.

"Okay, I think we're all clear on the fact that time was of the essence, but what is it you're getting at?" Dous asked.

"How old are you?" Cue asked Dous directly.

"Just turned eighteen?" Dous sounded unsure.

"Wrong," Emeal said. "You're actually three revolutions beyond what you know as your chronological age, which means you're—"

"Twenty-one!" Dous blinked and shook his head.

Heli interrupted, "I can do the math but so help me god if you throw one more red herring out . . ." Heli took a deep breath, feeling the familiar kindling in his fingertips.

"Your true age was kept secret, even from you, in order to ensure your safety in hiding as you matured," Cue added.

"That's what my mom was always going on about." Dous seized the conversation suddenly. "She used to always ask me how old I would be if I didn't know how old I was. She'd say the same thing every year on my birthday. It never made much sense to me. I didn't realize it was really just some twisted inside joke."

"That's not the point!" Heli could feel the fury rising as he looked at Cue. "You tricked us and no matter what your excuses are to rationalize it, we lose more faith with every minute that we're left in the dark."

"We made certain that you were of the prime age for this union by today's and any other day's standards and—"

"No! You made certain that you had control! I would say that getting married is as personal a choice as possible in our lifetime and you took that from us." Heli could feel his voice tighten and his breathing relax when he turned to look at Terra, who had visible tears streaking her face. He paused for a moment contemplating his next words. "I love her and I'd go through it all again if it means we're together," Terra looked at him again, "but this is a decision we wanted to make on our own."

"We lost three years?" Dous asked and his head was swaying back and forth. Heli could hear him anxiously pressing through with a thought. *I don't know if I can take any more.*

"If only you could think of it more as a net gain," Emeal said.

Terra's face went flush, ripe with red, and her voice was spiked with rage. "You people can't just keep screwing with us like this! Every time we settle in, we get comfortable, and start trusting, everything gets turned all around!"

"We meant no harm by any of you, we only meant to honor you," Cue said.

"What kind of twisted message does lying to us offer?" Heli whispered.

Emeal returned to the subject. "Your developmental progress was key in eliciting particular emotional responses. And as much as your environmental stimuli aided in your readiness for what IDEA had in store for the three of you, what happened between the two of you has placed a seal on it."

"For who? You two? The Frey? This godforsaken mission?" Heli nodded his head up and down. "Well, mission accomplished."

Terra closed her eyes, turning redder by the moment.

"Heli, we're sorry you feel that you were coerced into this situation but we know it was right in accordance with the prophecy," Cue said.

"Do our lives or what we want even count? Or are we just pawns in this game?" Heli asked.

Dous spoke. "I'm actually really glad someone finally brought that up. It's as if everything from day one has had us all literally spinning our wheels around this prophecy. There's never been much explanation beyond what's been spoon-fed to us. I mean we know why we were created. We know what we were sent to accomplish in the Strata, but what about now, today, and tomorrow?"

"From this point on, we don't even know." Cue looked at Heli.

"There's obviously more to it than that," Heli said.

"For those of us who've lived in the shadows of the prophecy, having dedicated our lives to assure not only your safety but to grant your secure union, we know that the time has finally come for us to move out with our message," Cue said.

"And there's only one thing that could possibly stand in our way," Emeal added.

"The Regulation." Dous nodded.

"No, they'll have no power among the masses when this gets out," Cue continued, "but if Jacque finds a way to access any of you, it's over and we're back to square one."

"Well, that's not gonna happen. He knows how we feel about him and that we'd never go back into the Strata willingly," Dous said.

Heli could hear his own pulse beatboxing in his ears. He pressed in to send Terra a thought—*I'll never let him near you again*—but he knew they were powerless promises, affirming nothing.

She didn't respond and turned her head away from him.

"I know what I have to do." Heli pressed his lips together. "You need to show me how I can get access to him." He looked at Cue.

"Heli, please!" Terra spoke sharply.

"No! This, I can do!" he spit back, and he watched her shrink behind a void of understanding.

Heli tore his eyes away from her and spoke to Cue. "If you really want to make amends then help me put an end to this."

Upholding Consequences

Heli sat with Dous along the bank of the ditch that fed into the quarry. He scanned the limestone wall mounts.

"We haven't spoken in two days." Heli picked at a seam on his Hodgesuit. Although it was no longer necessary, wearing the suit gave him a sense of security.

"You can't keep putting this off. You need to talk to her," Dous said.

Heli scratched his temple. "If I thought there was any way around it, I'd change course in a heartbeat. You know that. But this may be the only opportunity we have to make things right."

"But Jacque doesn't care what this does to us," Dous said.

"You, of all people, know where my priorities lie, and they won't always line up perfectly with what we all want. The stakes keep rising and I can't just sit around and gamble with what might happen if I don't resolve this. You said it before, and Terra agreed, the people of the Frey could be in danger. We made a commitment to them." He held up his marked hand. "And I've accepted my role in that. I have to do this while I can."

Creases of concern showed in Dous's eyes. "Yeah, but at the very least you owe it to her to have the conversation and try to reason with her. I'm worried about her. I've never seen her like this. Emeal and Mianna can barely get a word out of her, other than a response to basic needs. It's like this whole thing has taken over. She sleeps all the time, she hardly eats anything but sips of tea and tidbits and even that has to be coaxed down. She's sick over it."

"She's angry with me. She'll get through it. It isn't as if I haven't tried. I nearly spent the night at her door last night." Heli rolled his neck feeling a painful crick. "Knocking, pleading, and groveling; I've tried it all." A short sigh escaped him. "And I've gotten nothing but a partner in silence." He took a deep breath. "I'll keep trying."

Heli aimed his attention away from the heavy subject. "Does that wall seem to look greener to you?"

Dous laughed. "They must be seeding it out again. Mianna mentioned something about it. Emeal's beyond delighted." His eyebrows lifted. "Their yields have nearly doubled in the last week. You should see the garden. Too bad I'm not superstitious or I would think this decision of yours is good for the crop."

He looked up at the bright sky surrounding them. Not a hint of cloud cover, only leaps and bounds of blue.

"I'm sure it has something to do with the shift. Everything is bouncing back."

Dous nodded. "I know you're set on this decision and I know why, but I'm not the one you should be explaining it to. She's been locked up in that room ever since then. It's not good for her. It's not good for any of us."

"Cue and I are almost there. I meet with him one more time this afternoon. He thinks I'm ready," Heli said.

"You want my blessing? Go talk to her." Dous nodded.

"I suck at this stuff," Heli admitted.

Dous turned and clocked him on the shoulder with a light punch. "Suck it up, buddy. You're a ball and chains man now. You better get used to it."

***

Heli stood waiting for Cue in the tower where they had conducted most of Heli's training. Arriving early, the empty screens were like sleeping eyes. Yet in the quiet he couldn't help but feel as if they were watching him and studying him. He contemplated what it would take to bring the shining onyx faces surrounding him to life the way Cue could. A wanderlust of temptation took over and he reached out to touch the face of one of the glass surfaces. Nothing happened. Nudging him in the dark was his recall of the time when he had placed his hands on the interactive table in the Query Room at IDEA and it had flickered with a dusting of energy. This was all before they knew. Before he had any understanding of the Prana. He closed his eyes tight imagining how he felt then as if reliving that contentious time might ignite something. Simmering inside of him was the helplessness, the loss of control, and currently the emptiness in his hands that hadn't felt the warmth of another human being in days. He opened his eyes and the entire room suddenly flooded with light, projections piling out in a chaotic surge of images and data.

I did it! Heli's elation faded the moment he realized there was no one to share it with. His thoughts scrambled momentarily by the sound of someone climbing the stairs. He turned expecting to see Cue. An involuntarily spasm of surprise escaped him when he saw Mianna's small form emerge from the entryway.

"My father won't be able to—" She stopped and gazed around the illuminated space, the glow of the screens reflecting off her wide-open gaze around the room.

"I uh—" Heli started.

"You've worked it out on your own." She nodded to one of the screens. "You're really going through with this?"

"I'm working my way up to it," Heli answered.

"What about Terra?" Mianna asked.

"We'll survive this," Heli said.

"She needs you." Mianna's voice was soft but the acoustics in the curved space sent her words straight to his heart.

"I'm not turning back from this," he said.

"You don't have to go through with this. What you intend to do with this man Jacque;" Mianna dropped her head, shaking it, "if you don't come back from this, I don't think she'd survive that." Mianna lifted her head, but kept her eyes wandering from one screen to another.

"I have to do this. It's the only way we have any chance of having a future together," he said softly. He watched her close her eyes against the light. "If something does go wrong," he swallowed, "they'll need you."

Lifting her head, her words trailed out in a tempered whisper. "Of course."

She hesitated for a moment, then she turned and headed toward the entryway, and stopped. "But I go with you."

"Um, where on earth did you get that idea?" Heli said. A long pause hung between them before she answered.

"I messed things up. Plans have changed," she said.

"Whatever it is you think you may have done, I don't think your father would be too keen on you attending this reunion," Heli said.

"I…I provided him with a suit," she confessed.

"Provided who?" Heli asked.

"Jacque," she said, and looked up to face him this time.

"You what?" The surge of energy Heli felt from the news caused the screens surrounding them to flicker.

"It was all before I met any of you. He promised me a way out in exchange for help with a project he was working on. I didn't know who I was dealing with. When the original com-trip came through for my father in the lab, I happened to be there to answer it. The man on the other line probed me further and asked what kind of work I did for the cause. He seemed to be so informed that I assumed he was collaborating with my father." She stopped and leaned against one of the shining screens.

"You didn't give him information about the location of the Frey, did you?" Heli asked.

"No, I'm not that dense, but he knows more than he should. I shared some of the details of what I do with the suits. He sounded interested. He wanted to know more. No one ever showed an interest in what I did before, not even my father. It felt good to have someone paying attention for once. We were in contact many more times after that. He sent me the schematics for a prototype of what he wanted. I assumed this kind of Hodgesuit would be useful for atmospheric industry protective uniforms. From the materials I had available, it seemed plausible that I could put together a suit to serve his purpose," she said.

"How in the world did you do it? I mean whatever it's made of would have to be essentially impenetrable," Heli said.

"It comes down to a general understanding of scientific principles and basic chemistry. Not to mention the fact that I'm somewhat of a rock hound. I already had access to the raw materials I needed from extractions in the quarry. The lab provided me with a space to see it through," she said.

"What on earth would you have available here that could withstand the force of this?" He placed a hand against one of the screens and Mianna jumped away as it jolted with a charge that encircled them with light. The surge led to a complete blackout other than the low light provided by the auxiliary backlighting.

"Mica. It's extracted right here from the quarry in raw form. It's fireproof, infusible, and incombustible, withstanding extremely high temperatures and we just happen to have it available in overabundant tailings piles left behind," she added.

"Mica? That flaky stuff you find on rocks?" Heli asked.

"Actually, it's a group of sheet minerals as a component of rock. It took some time to collect the technological data for its potential use, yet even with its impurities and structural imperfections the electrical application was ideal. What with it having a unique combination of dielectric strength and capacitance stability." Mianna paused, eyeing Heli closely in the dimmed light. "Sorry, I'm kind of a nerd about this stuff."

"I can see why you and Dous get along. What else should I know?" he asked.

"Well, it's labor and time intensive but with what I couldn't do by hand, the lab provided me with wares to go through the process of cutting, sorting, and processing it from its crude form to the quality of commercial grade material I could use in the fibers interwoven into the design."

"How do you know it works?" Heli asked.

"I tested it. I have the results back at the lab. It wasn't until after I had the initial mockup of the Hodgesuit completed for testing that Jacque initiated contact one last time and confirmed that I was the one for the job." Mianna's gaze dropped from him and she stared at the floor. "He became more persistant and he wanted it sent out via com-courier immediately. I hadn't thought to ask many questions outside of the project until then. It definitely ruffled some feathers when I mentioned how I might like to share the news with my father. That's when I started questioning who I was dealing with."

Heli stood, startled, and asked, "How does it work?"

"The design and technology in the material have a very specified function. For the suit to be reengineered and effective against the level of energy the Prana can induce it requires a conductivity sequence using nanotechnology controlled by hardware I've embedded in the suit. And this is what also makes it fallible," she ended.

"A scientific loophole," Heli said.

"Something like that. I didn't know why he wanted it developed, but once I understood your plans for him, I knew I must inform my father and tell you," she said.

"Well this does change things quite a bit," he said.

"Then let me help you."

"Help me? So far you've been nothing but trouble and now you're telling me that you've created a suit that can protect Jacque from the only means I had to deal with him and that there's little chance we'll ever find a way around it?" Heli took a step toward her. She shrank back as the light surrounding them resurged.

"I'm sorry!" Her eyes cast low. Heli moved back.

"What are we gonna do now?" He shook his head. "I can't go in there knowing he's prepared for our little surprise when he's wearing that thing."

"That's why I have to go. I'm the only one who knows how to dismantle it. This can still work, but you need to let me go with you," she pleaded.

He looked up at her. "That would mean I have to trust you? How do I know this isn't just another setup or deterrent?

"There's more," she said.

"What more could you add to this nightmare?" Heli asked, shaking his hands from the fists he had been holding. With a guarded urgency her eyes flew up to meet his. "She's pregnant."

"Excuse me?" He choked on the words and everything suddenly went haywire around them and he thought he heard a fuse blow, leaving them standing in the dark.

"Emeal is sure of it now," she confessed.

"Wa...wait, I...I don't get it. Are you messing with me? Is this about keeping me here?" He could hardly breathe. It hit him like the force of a heavy wind, what Dous had mentioned about the crops and the abundance from the recent yield. Heli now knew Terra's connection could have something to do with this and he knew what she said was true. His own pulse beat with the undeniable truth. "How do you know for sure?" Heli could feel that grumbling in his own voice as he forced the words out.

"It's a simple test. Emeal runs the midwifery rounds here. She's certain," Mianna answered.

"Emeal knows? When was anyone going to tell me?" Heli whispered.

"Emeal wanted to tell you both together before you left. I'm no good at this, I'm sorry," she said.

"Does Dous know about any of this?" Heli asked.

"No. I thought you should be the first to know and perhaps it would be better if you told him."

Staring into the dark as his eyes adjusted, he took a deep breath. "Does she know?"

"I think so. We haven't talked directly, but I highly doubt she doesn't suspect something."

Heli could see clear shapes forming and he looked at Mianna as her eyes softened. "I swear on my own life and the others here in the Frey that I will do anything I have to do to make this right."

"No, you'll swear on all our lives. Then, you give me a reason to believe you," Heli said. She nodded and turned to make her exit.

***

Please, let me come in. Don't shut me out like this, Heli thought through the haze of the unyielding witching hour of the night. He sat propped up against her door like all the nights before, only this time he had something new, something more to hold him there.

We need to talk. It's been over a week and we're nearly ready. I can't leave until I know you'll be okay. I know you're upset and I understand why. He lifted his hand, and his eyes were drawn to the discernible mark on it as he traced a line down the door with his forefinger. *I can do this, I know I can. I've been able to control it now for the last few days.*

He heard a slight shuffling behind the barrier of the door and he could feel how close she was now. *I need to do this for you, for all of us. If we never face him and end this, everything that's happened is in vain.*

Then he heard the sound of her soft pained whisper as her voice carried through the solid door separating them. "How would you feel if the tables were turned?"

He stood up, speaking to the door. "That's why I need to go, so that we never have to face that possibility and we can move forward with this together."

You know then? she projected.

He leaned against the door. "Yes, I know everything."

Then you should know why I won't let you in. Because if I get near you…I might forget why it's so important to convince you to stay. Her thoughts were drowning in his mind. He pressed his forehead against the door and closed his eyes. She was there now. Conducting a sensory overload, he could feel through every cell in his body and he imagined her breath seeping through, mingling with his own. Drawing one last flush of air into his lungs to take her in, he backed away. *I have to go. I love you.* And as if looking back would turn him to stone, he forced one foot in front of the other, hearing her soft crying dissolve in the distance, knowing this might be their last good-bye.

***

"You talked to her?" Dous asked as Heli approached him. He was settled in by the fire already lit for the evening. Heli didn't answer.

"I guess that's a yes? So, when do we launch?" Dous asked. Heli looked up at him. He still hadn't grown accustomed to seeing his friend standing at eye level and he squinted at him.

"There is no 'we' this time." Heli shook his head and watched Dous's mouth twitch and turn into a frown.

"I knew you'd say that, but—"

"No buts, I don't know how far the Pranic transmission can go and I don't want anyone I care about anywhere near that place when I let loose.

Besides, someone needs to stay here and keep an eye on things."

"Why do you get to have all the fun? I could stow away in the back compartment. With your newly assessed shock factor and my new moves." Dous's arms flew around in a circle in some kind of butchered martial arts move. "We'd be unstoppable."

Heli rolled his eyes and smiled, assuming Mianna hadn't had the opportunity to throw in the little twist that would have Dous petitioning her role in the operation.

"But seriously, how are you planning on getting in there?" Dous asked.

"Cue has a plan. You seen Mianna lately?"

"No, she's been MIA all day. I'm sure this is hard for her too, with Cue going," Dous said.

"Well, you're probably the best person to be there for her. You should go try to find her." Heli held back from any other thoughts.

"You want me," Dous pointed to himself, "to go find Mianna? Now you're starting to worry me?"

"I don't know, she's starting to grow on me a little I guess, and I realize how much she means to you and Terra," Heli admitted.

Dous cocked an eye at him. "Turning soft on me?"

"Look, I don't mean to get off the subject here, but there's a little something I should tell you before I go," Heli said.

Dous's eyes opened wider. "Sounds like more of a *big* something."

"Well I guess I'll just come out with it then. Terra is . . ." Heli paused, "we're sort of . . ." he held his breath, "we're going to be parents."

Dous stared back speechless with his mouth wide open.

"Say something." Heli ran his hands through his matted hair. "Come on, say anything."

"Oh . . ..my...god," was all he said.

"Yeah, that about says it all." Heli licked his lips.

"Whoa! I'm just...Whoa!" Dous shrugged.

Heli cleared his throat. "I know."

"You mean she's like, actually, going to have a baby?" Dous said.

Heli took another deep breath. "Yes, I believe that's precisely what will happen."

"Oh man, I get it now." Heli watched Dous's face change while a huge smile spread across his face. "She's not sick, she's..." He shook his head.

"You okay?" Heli asked.

"I'm great! I'm completely, surprisingly amazing right now. Do you know what this means? I'm technically an uncle." Dous pointed to his chest.

Heli drew up a hand. "Simmer down. This is new to all of us. The dust is still blowing. We only recently found out how old we really are. In fact, Terra's even more worked up about me leaving now. I'm going to need you to be there for her."

"Of course, but we'll all be there for her. That includes you," Dous said.

"Seriously, if something happens I'm gonna need you to be there for them," Heli said.

"Why don't you ever look at the jug and see it half full? Nothing is going to happen to you. I wouldn't say it if I didn't believe it with all my heart. You're coming back. There's no way I'd let you miss out on this and you know what happens when I put in my bid to the universe?" Dous cocked an eyebrow.

"I don't make promises anymore and neither should you. There's too much that's out of our hands," Heli said and closed his eyes.

Dous spoke and Heli felt the jolt of his words pry his eyes back open. "Mianna says that you have a sure thing in this operation. Cue must think it'll be a swift job. Whatever he's got up his sleeve, it must be good for them to be that confident."

Heli knew he might regret holding his secret with Mianna back. "You two make a good team. She belongs in your life as much as we do."

"Stop talking like this is some kind of last rights and what's with all the mushy stuff about me and Mianna? Having a kid crossed your wires or something?" Dous said.

"Look, I know I'm a hard nut to crack sometimes and you and Terra do a pretty good job reminding me of that. But I think it's time to give credit where credit's due," Heli said.

"She does have a way with people." Dous smiled.

"She has a way with you," Heli said.

"Okay? Are we going there again?" Dous shifted his shoulders uncomfortably.

"Don't tell me it hasn't dawned on you?" Heli asked in return.

"Well, sure, but it was before all this." Dous gestured toward his upright body. "I had a good excuse to keep her around. There wasn't any pressure," Dous said.

"Pressure?" Heli scratched his head. "Tell me, when she's gone, or when she leaves your sight, what's the first thing that pops into your head?"

Dous looked up at the sky, bringing his head back down. "I think...lunch?"

"Seriously?" Heli asked.

"No." Dous shook his hands at the sides of his head. "I don't know, I think...I wonder what she's doing, when she'll show up again." Dous stood looking past Heli.

"There, that wasn't so painful, was it?" Heli said.

"I guess it's a little bit like anticipating the next meal," Dous joked.

What? Heli thought.

"I mean, it's the best analogy I can think of. When she leaves, it's like this particular flavor lingers. It's not like sweet or bitter, you know, it's better than that. Potent, and it sticks on the palate." Dous stood taller with a certain satisfaction.

"Well this is a first. Never in my life have I heard anyone compare their experience with a girl to food," Heli said.

"Hey, what part of the meal would you say Terra is?" Dous asked.

"Good lord."

Dous stared at him and Heli answered, "I guess if she were anything representative of food I'd say she's an aperitif."

"Mmm…what's that? Must be good?" Dous asked.

"Forget it. How in the world did we get this far off the subject? I tell you I'm having a kid and you somehow turn this around to a conversation about how women are like food." Heli bent down to pick up his bag. "Cue wants me to meet him for a final analysis tonight and then we're heading out early tomorrow morning. If you see her, just tell her . . ." Heli paused. "You can probably explain it better than I can."

"I know, I got it—you love her, you're risking your neck for her, and if it were necessary you'd jump into a pit of deadly venomous spiders for her, yadda yadda yadda." Dous stopped when Heli held up a hand.

"I take that back. Just give her a hug, or maybe a fist bump. Just don't say anything." Heli turned to leave and from behind him he heard Dous speak.

"It's gonna all work out. It has to. If anyone can do this, it's you."

Heli turned back around to face his friend. "Glad to know somebody believes in me," Heli said. His chest tightened.

"She's just scared. That's all. We almost lost you once before. It's a lot to ask of a person to face up to that again." Dous lifted his head with the comment.

"This is who we are now. It's why we're here," Heli said.

"I guess so, but now you have another good reason to stick around," Dous said.

"I know, and that reason, above all else, is why I have to go." Heli looked down at his marked hand and for the first time felt he understood its meaning.

"Then go get the job done," Dous said, "and ask for forgiveness later."

Heli took a few steps closer to his friend. "You know, you're the first friend I ever had." He watched as Dous's eyes bulged out, staring wildly back at him.

"Don't worry, I'm not going to hug you or anything, just want you to know that I . . ." Heli stalled. "I'll see you soon."

Dous waved a hand as Heli moved down the embankment and out of sight.

Deviation

"Able to get all those loose ends tied up?" Cue spoke before Heli had even emerged to join him on the platform of the tower. The area was already ablaze with light from the monitors and Heli was short of breath from the climb, having taken upward strides two steps at a time.

"I think I can safely say that they're loosely tied," Heli said breathlessly.

"Hmm?" Cue reached toward one of the screens, pinch pulling a line of code to stretch it out in a linear sequence in front of him. Seemingly preoccupied, he finally looked up with a wakeful jolt, coming out of his stream of focus.

"We leave at first light," Cue said and returned to scanning the operations.

"Any chance I might be able to crash at your covert tonight?" Heli asked.

"That may not bode well with those loose ends," Cue remarked, looking from the screens to focus on Heli again.

"Yeah, that…well, I can't stay there tonight," Heli said sharply.

"All relationships have challenges. And yours is an untested one. You both know everything that's at stake now," Cue said.

"Yeah, and we completely disagree on how this should be handled and she won't talk to me," Heli confided. "We've hardly breached the subject of the baby."

"Emeal updated me," Cue said.

"This doesn't seem to be shocking news to you. What do you make of all of it?" Heli asked. If Cue was as uncomfortable with this conversation as Heli was, he didn't show it.

"I know a little something about these things, if that's what you're asking." Cue turned to look at him.

"I was hoping to iron things out before I go off on a mission I might never return from," Heli said.

"I'll ask you again and this will be the last time. Do you regret that it happened?" Cue looked at Heli with a cautious eye.

"No." He felt his answer sink in. "I just…I mean, I knew we were headed in this direction, only I didn't expect it so soon. Don't get me wrong, it—" Heli stopped, short of breath. Why was he sharing so much, so openly?

"Your union was made with proper officiating and you're both of prime age. There should be no amount of guilt. What happened between you was only natural and in line with your own biorhythms at this stage in your development," Cue said.

Heli couldn't help but cringe. "Why do you have to make it sound so sterile and scientific. It's a little more complicated than that."

"I'm only trying to help you see the validity of your situation," Cue said.

"Validity? Yeah, that could have helped in pleading my case in the aftermath." Heli paused. "Why do I keep having to ask myself if I'm doing the right thing?"

He looked up at Cue again and noticed the way he studied him. "What? Why are you looking at me like that?"

Cue stared at him harder, like he was trying to see things that were still out of focus. He blinked. "It's nothing. Why don't you go retrieve your things and I'll see you back at the covert?"

Heli looked down at his feet, their exchange and his thoughts urging him to stay, but he turned instead and headed down the stairs. Some things were better left unspoken.

***

A faint light whispered out from Terra's patio, casting a glow on the mounded clay tiles lining the earth-entrenched structure. Heli lifted his chin to the breeze to jolt awake his senses. The door was wide open in its sleeve, just the way she liked it. He stopped, considering what he was about to do. The soft light beckoned him from the short distance and there were no barriers between them now. Only the ones they had put up against one another.

He held little restraint as he approached the door, feeling assuredly like the intruder he was. He placed his bets on each and every move that could give him away before he could reach her. He stood frozen at the door frame. The only thing standing between them now was the silent waving of the linen curtain in the breeze. A low light escaped from Terra's CS card on the bedside wall mount and it took a moment for his eyes to adjust. He stood over the hammock staring down in shock. *Empty.* The ball of nerves clenched even tighter in his belly as he scanned the room.

With his sight fully adjusted and his anxiety brimming he could tell that she wasn't in the room at all, which sent a bolt of confusion through him. In the commotion of the thrill and the dread, he raced to the panel to swipe the door open and tap the light of a wall sconce into the center room. Hope filled him, expecting to see her waiting for him on the central couch. Another plummeting rise and fall of confusion came when he saw that the entire main floor covert was empty as well. He stood in the low light, seeing a gray mashup of patterns of plush pillows and solid fixtures around the room, but nothing that showed evidence of Terra being there.

He ran back toward the door opposite of Terra's room. He knocked twice, hard. He heard a rustling and a sharp choke, then a groan. The door slid open and Heli looked down to see Dous on Zuke. Dous rubbed his eyes and spoke with a groggy voice, "Hey, what's going on? You're taking off early?" A loud yawn escaped his lips and he sat up straighter, looking at Heli curiously.

"Terra's not in her room!" Heli spoke louder than he meant to.

"What?" The question trailed out with another yawn. "Give me a minute." Dous closed his eyes again, opening them and briefly lifting his eyebrows. "She's gotta be in there. Mianna stopped by earlier and they talked for a while before we all hit the sack."

Dous crossed his arms in a waking embrace and Heli cuffed him on the tricep to get his attention. "Ouch!"

"She's not there! I went in from the patio. It was open. Her room's empty!" Heli flared.

Dous's arms fell into his lap and he peered up at Heli, more focused now. "What do you mean, she's not there?"

"Like zip, zilch, poof, disappeared. I wanted to see her one last time before I left. I saw the door open and I snuck in. She's gone," Heli said.

Dous pulled his head back sharply. "Well that was a bad idea. I know I told you to talk to her but you don't show up unannounced in the middle of the night. Maybe she read your mind and decided to sleep somewhere else. She was with Mianna, maybe she ended up over there."

"Not this late and in her condition. I don't think she'd go to these lengths to avoid me. I know her. She'd lock herself up inside if that was her plan." Heli could hear his voice shrinking." Sorry, it just doesn't make any sense." Dous's voice softened and he looked at Heli.

"We need to go find Mianna. Something's not right, I can feel it," Heli said, and in his desperation, he shifted to position himself behind Dous, wheeling Zuke toward the main door.

"Wait, I need my suit!" Dous yelled, craning his neck around, nearly falling off Zuke's mount in mid motion.

"I'll grab it!" Heli jumped back and ran into Dous's room. He tore open the wardrobe and sifted through the Hodgesuits until he recognized the cool, smooth metallic gleam of the one he was looking for. He grabbed it and ran back out behind Dous to push him on. "Here," Heli tossed it into Dous's lap, "you can change later."

***

"You made it. I was beginning to worry." Cue stood in the door of his covert looking at Heli and then at Dous. "Mianna's asleep. You can see her tomorrow."

"He's not here to see her." Heli pushed Zuke forward through the door, forcing Cue out of the way.

"What's going on?" Cue stood aside.

"Terra's gone," Heli said.

"What do you mean gone?" Cue shifted his eyes back and forth between the young men.

"I went to see her. I had to see her before . . ." Heli hesitated.

Dous finished for him. "He wanted a proper good-bye."

"She wasn't there," Heli said.

From Cue's expression, Heli could see the lines tighten in new waves of concern spreading across his features. "I'll wake Mianna."

He walked over to one of the doors set in along the back wall of the covert and entered without knocking. The lights never came on before Mianna emerged with her father. She hugged herself in the thin coverlet she wore. Heli noticed Dous's face light up at the sight of her.

"What's going on?" Mianna asked and her head popped up a bit as soon as she saw Dous next to Heli. "Hi." She smiled and Dous replied with a short "Hey."

"You were the last one with Terra tonight?" Heli asked.

"Yes." Her voice was all but a whisper. "I went to talk to Dous." She looked at Heli and then her glance swerved to land on Dous. He nodded. "We talked. I brought her some broth that Emeal had made to settle her stomach."

"When you left, did she give you any indication that she might go out, for a walk or something?" Heli asked.

"No, we talked for a short while after that. She said she was exhausted and she asked if I would bring her more tomorrow morning with her tea," Mianna said. "Why? What's wrong?" Then she looked down toward Dous in his chair. He was shirtless and still clinging to the suit.

He stared up at her squirming self-consciously. "I'll go get changed."

Mianna looked back over at her father. "She's not in her room?"

"That would appear to be the case," Cue said.

"But that doesn't make any sense. She wouldn't go out in her condition," Mianna said.

Cue quickly turned away from his daughter and looked at Heli. "I'll need to go fetch Emeal and we can get some people out along the perimeter to start looking for her. In the meantime, you three stay together and we'll meet up in the center square after we've checked the areas surrounding the Frey."

"Have you tried her CS card?" Mianna's eyes popped open on Heli.

"It's still laying on the rechargeable inter-feed mat by her bed. She didn't take it with her wherever she went," Heli said.

"She'd never leave without her card. Emeal specifically told her to keep it close at all times so that if anything happened with the baby we could get to her quickly." Mianna said and looked at Heli as if they were thinking the same thing and he watched her face drain to a pasty white. "Oh no."

"Oh no what?" Heli moved in closer. "Tell me," he urged.

"I remember something. When I was leaving, there were a couple of outsiders by the ditch. I didn't think anything of it at first. We get people coming in and out all the time, occasionally at this time of night. But I remember watching them and how they hung back as I moved on."

"Did you get a good look at them?" Heli took a step in toward her.

"No, I told you it was dark and the fire had been extinguished for the night," she answered, and her eyes narrowed.

"You think these two might have something to do with her disappearance?" Heli flared and he felt his fists burning at his sides.

"I don't know, but it certainly caught my attention. They were watching me," she said.

"And you didn't think to confront them?" Heli asked.

"I'm sorry, I'm not one to be so suspicious." She looked back at him.

Dous was coming out of one of the rooms wearing the suit and standing again. "So, what's the plan?" He paused looking at the two of them. "Everthing okay?"

Heli pointed at Mianna. "No! Everything is not okay! Terra's missing and your girlfriend here says she noticed some strangers lurking around our covert earlier tonight and now she's accusing me of being paranoid!"

"I've been gone like two minutes and you already want to take her head off?" Dous said. "Take it easy. Blaming this on her isn't going to get us anywhere. What do we know that we can use?"

"Well, we know Terra is no longer where we all assumed she was. We know she's not feeling well and that two potential strangers know more about what's going on than we do. And all I know is that this whole thing is taking me over the edge." Heli ended his tirade.

"Well then, we start there," Dous said.

Just then, both Emeal and Cue came bursting through the covert entrance and a thin man wearing a heavy tunic followed them.

"This is Peter. He's one of our nighttime watch citizens. He claims to have seen something that might give us more information about Terra's whereabouts," Cue said.

The man tapped his foot nervously as he spoke and his voice had a stammering nasal quality to it that made Heli wince. "The pair, I spotted them near the perimeter tonight, not unlike others we see round these parts. Got a good look at 'em too, but I assumed they were poachers from outside."

Cue responded with further explanation. "We often get movers from the outskirts sneaking in to take advantage of the bounty the Frey can provide."

"Movers?" Dous asked.

"Poor sods aiming to feed their family, more than likely on the run from Regulators," Cue clarified.

"From what I seen they was a tall man and a woman." Peter's less sophisticated dialect caught Heli's ear.

Cue asked, "Were you able to intercept them or offer them refuge?"

"Na, they never let out from the shadows along the edge. Appeared to be leavin' so I let 'em be. I did keep my eye on the load they were carrying and then they disappeared," he answered.

"When you say load, would that be a sack-of-potatoes-sized load or something larger, like a person?" Heli asked.

"Well, I assumed a large bounty, vegetables from the garden or something. The one the size of an ox carried the load in both arms up front." He stumbled as he went on, "Pos...sibly the size of a person."

Cue looked at him firmly this time. "Come on, we need you to think. Where did you see them exit with the bundle?"

"I guess he could have been carrying someone, someone small, but I can't be sure. They pushed on through the brush along the north rim. Sorry I let this one slip, sir." The timid man lowered his head to look at the floor.

"Thank you for your report. It does give us something to go on. Sorry to take you away from your post." Cue nodded.

The wiry little man bowed and turned to walk out when a thought popped into Heli's mind. "You say the man was as big as an ox? Bigger than, say, Cue here?"

"Yes, he was memorable that way. At first, I wondered how it might be two women as the big one wore a strange tail of hair down his back," Peter answered.

Heli heard Dous's thoughts before he could project his own: *Justin.*

***

"Why on earth would Justin sneak in here unannounced and kidnap Terra?" Dous spit out.

"Well if it was Justin, then who was the woman with him?" Heli asked.

They both stood now thinking, side by side, and it suddenly dawned on Heli. "I'm going. Tonight."

"Then this isn't going to be the solo trip you intended." Dous's gaze was level with Cue's.

Cue interjected, "Wait a minute, the situation with his development of the Prana is very volatile."

"I really don't care. I'm going. Terra's in danger and so is her baby. As of now, all deals are off. If Terra's there, our only agenda is to find her and bring her back. Together," Dous said.

"Neither one of you is operating with an ounce of reason. Decisions made on this basis can be very dangerous," Cue said.

"No decision ever worth making didn't come with high stakes," Heli said.

"I don't think you understand me. We have to stick to the plan or we run the risk that he'll find a way to get what he wants from all three of you. Once we enter those gates, all bets are off." Cue positioned himself with crossed arms in front of them.

"You're probably right, but Terra's abduction just bumped up the ante and I'm not about to tell anyone who cares about her that they can't play a part in her retrieval and that includes her." Heli pointed to Mianna.

"What? Absolutely not!" Cue insisted.

Mianna let out an incomprehensible plea in revolt.

"She's not going anywhere near that place!" He took a step closer. The heat between them in the updraft had both Dous and Mianna each taking a step back.

"She told you about the suit, right?" Heli asked.

Cue's head dropped in defeat and he sucked in a deep breath.

"You've been trying to figure out a way around this too. And I can only guess you were about ready to call the whole thing off," Heli said. Cue looked sternly at his daughter.

"Why provoke these things?" Cue looked at Mianna.

Mianna circled around the boys and moved to her father's side, taking his hand into hers.

"This is my mess. If you've taught me anything, it's that it's my job to clean it up."

"She's right and we've been working on a destabilizer for the Hodgesuit. She's figured it out," Heli said.

"What?" Dous asked.

"That's why you haven't seen much of her lately. She's been a little busy," Heli confessed.

Dous looked at her as she angled back around to reach for his hand, but he wouldn't take it.

"She is the only one who understands the suits. The one Jacque wears protects him from the Prana, it could be our only barrier to reaching Terra," Heli said.

Mianna begged, "Father, I have to do this. I know I can dismantle it!"

Cue squeezed his mouth into a tight line. "If I live to regret this…" He looked up at her. Heli watched her shoulders relax as she ran into her father's arms.

Cue squeezed her tightly against him. "We leave within the hour. You'll all need to rest up along the way."

"We don't need an hour. We're ready whenever you are," Heli said, looking over at Dous, who nodded in agreement.

"I just need a minute to grab some things from the lab." Mianna pushed out of her father's embrace.

She stopped in front of Dous. "I'm sorry I didn't tell you."

"I'll go with you to the lab and help you gather what you need," Dous offered.

Mianna nodded and Dous followed her out. He looked back over his shoulder at Heli.

Heli projected a thought, *You can blame this one on me.*

Prime Objective

"He'll be expecting us," Cue said.

"Good, and I've got the perfect housewarming gift," Heli replied, flitting his fingers and smiling. They were all crammed into the hovercraft sitting closely on one side of the curved seats.

"You're going to need to rein that in until we can get an assessment on all of the other factors. Namely, our objective will be to recover Terra. This operation will be about keeping your head." Cue eyed him.

"You really think I don't know where my priorities lie?" Heli challenged.

"Okay then, I'll go over this one more time. Dous gets in, meets us at the front after we've disabled the security system, we find Terra, and we get out as quickly as possible. No loose strings—together, and only as a means of defense do you resort to anything outside of that." Cue looked at Heli and turned to give a firm glance toward Mianna.

She lifted her chin to look at him, a look that said *I'm a big girl now* and then shied away.

Heli addressed her. "You have what we need in case an opportunity does arrive?"

"I do," she answered and withdrew a small pouch. It was no bigger than the palm of her hand. She dangled it in front of them. It looked like one of the biostamp sensors that had covered his chest after waking from his bout with the Chronovirus.

"How close will you have to get?" Dous asked.

Mianna looked down at her lap. "The connectivity in the hardware on the suit is in the collar. Most of the threading is hidden in the pockets of the seams. The conduits trail down among the fibers throughout the weave. This malware apparatus and what basically makes it possible to hack into the system will need to be positioned along the back of the neckline. It'll only provide temporary disabling."

"How temporary are we talking about?" Heli asked.

"Once the adhesive is applied, it contains sensory information only readable by the enhancement software embedded in the nano-fibers of the suit. You'll have about an hour tops before the hardwired malware-bytes in the design are able to identify and expel anything that may have been compromised."

Heli shook his head and peered out the window of the hovercraft they rode in, flicking a finger on the edge of the pane as they flew over the thick mesh of green below. "Your smart suit better pass this test."

Dous spoke on an exhale, "Should we even discuss a plan as to how we get this disabler on him?" His concern was clear as he stared at Mianna.

"She'll have to do it," Heli said.

Mianna spoke. "I'm the only one who knows these things inside and out. It's very technical in its application. It must be done with precision. A slip of the wrist, sleight of hand and it's disabled."

"When it's done, if we have to resort to it," Heli glanced at Cue, "we'll only have a small window of time for you all to move on out," Heli remarked.

"You all comfortable relying on that little do-dad?" Dous asked and looked at Cue.

"If I can apply it right, he'll never know what happened. Besides, if all goes as planned I don't have to lift a finger." Mianna reached a hand to touch Dous on the leg. "This little do-dad is our insurance and I owe it to Terra to do my part."

"This isn't some magic show. You don't get a courtesy rehearsal." Dous faltered and turned once again to Cue. "You're not worried about her getting close to him?"

Cue nodded. "It's done, there's no turning back. You all brought her in and I won't take her out at this point. Heli's right. We might need her."

Mianna smiled.

"It's not so much what *we* do that I'm worried about," Dous said. "He's always three steps ahead of us. Everything he does. We all know what this is about. He wants us back. And here we go jumping right into his hands again without a solid plan and little chance that this will even work?"

"And that is why we will need you to do your part to ensure that this does go according to plan," Cue said, looking directly at Dous.

"It's as solid as we get. We don't have time to sit around and discuss the alternatives. He's got Terra. Besides, he isn't invincible." Heli looked at Mianna.

Cue blinked. "Our prime objective is obviously to find Terra and if, and only if an opportunity arises, do we take advantage and wipe Jacque out of the equation."

"Okay, let's get on with the plan," Heli said.

"We'll need to review the specs of the grounds so we can go over the entry plan." Cue pulled a nano-bar projection device out of his pocket, pressing the signal and sending the projection hovering out between them instantly. Heli felt a certain calm wash over him with the familiar 3-D projection as if he were already inside.

He could see the tips of the triple-pitched tent-like rooftop blanketing the Query Room and the canopy of treetops from a birds-eye view, lifelike in the satellite spectrum collage. He thought he could even spot the willow tree where he had first tasted a sampling of the Prana in sharing his first kiss with Terra. These areas marked some of the most significant moments of his life. Even where the Strata was situated, out beyond the garden boundaries along the edge of the grounds, he felt a primal urge to jump into the projection. The homing pattern Tracy had explained that was to aid in their transition when they first arrived at IDEA was resurfacing as they drew closer. He could feel its pull, a magnet to his center.

"We're almost there," Cue said. He resituated himself in his seat, coming forward to stare harder at the projection. "What is this here? I don't remember it from when I was there," he asked.

Heli moved in to get a better look. "I think that's the irrigation drainage ditch. I've seen where it lets out beyond the periphery."

"Where does it lead? Is it enclosed?" Cue asked.

"I think there is some kind of cover-port over where it feeds out into the runoff," Heli answered.

"Then this is our access point," Cue said.

"You mean waltzing in through front doors wasn't part of the plan?" Dous was the only one who seemed to find the comment funny and still had a smile on his face. When he looked at Cue the corners of his lips dropped and he cleared his throat.

"Actually, that's precisely the plan for the three of us. After you get through there, we'll be awaiting your escort through the front entry doors." Cue offered a smile mirroring the one that had faded from Dous's face.

"Me?" Dous adjusted the front of his Hodgesuit.

"You're comfortable in the water and we need someone who can enter without disturbing the sensors that surround this place," Cue said. "You're the only one who has the capacity to do something like this."

"You mean something this absurd? And how am I supposed to accomplish this?" Dous asked.

"You'll go in and you can operate beyond the radar detection simply by willing it," Cue answered.

"Geez! Why haven't I been 'willing' a chocolate sundae to appear every night?" Dous said.

"It doesn't exactly work like that. You have keen sensors within you that work with necessity on a grander scale than your simple desire for dessert. I'm afraid a need for chocolate is not universally shared, but perhaps when we all return from this I can accommodate you." Cue winked.

"And what exactly are we doing while he's risking his neck in there?" Heli asked.

"We will be doing our part to disarm the security system." Cue looked at Heli.

Heli shook his head. "I'm ready for that?"

"I wouldn't be taking you in to face him if I didn't think you were ready. And I'll be there to assist," Cue said.

"You seem pretty confident about this. What about that whole thing with how I was absorbing your energy when you were reading my levels?" Heli asked.

"You leave that part up to me. I'll have you primed and ready right on cue," he said and laughed.

"So just before dawn?" Mianna asked.

"Before dawn," Cue confirmed. "It'll be some time before we arrive. I suggest you all get what little rest you can. This is shaping up to be a long night." He rested his head back against the top of the seat and closed his eyes.

Slurry

"What is this stuff?" Dous asked, standing knee deep in a trough of unidentifiable sludge. The full moon shone down on them, unveiled from under a blanket of cloud cover.

"It's the irrigation tail water. It's likely filtered through a treatment sieve up above," Cue said, eyeing the gurgling mass of watery discharge.

"You want me to go in there?" Dous asked.

"Keep your mouth closed," Heli warned.

Dous looked at him, nodding once behind a hardened stare. "Seriously, not funny."

"You see that pour spout draining out from below the water's surface?" Cue pointed to an opening just above the pool where the lip of the drainage pipe opened. It looked like the tongue of Poseidon himself.

"You want me to go through there? Are you kidding? How big is that hole?" Dous asked.

"About three feet in diameter. Rough estimate," Cue answered, bending at the knees to kneel down closer to the earth. He eyed the opening head on.

Dous looked down at his mid-section and cupped his hands around the waist of his Hodgesuit. He shivered despite the oddly warmer air of pre-dawn. "Can this suit get wet?"

"Completely submersible," Mianna answered.

"I can swim in this one? How come you never told me?" Dous asked.

"I designed it for you. Of course, it's made for the water." She winked.

"Agh! Feels sticky out here," Heli complained.

"Humidity." Cue stood from his crouched position by the water's edge. "Another sign of the atmosphere complying with the shift." He smiled up at the sky, pinching and rubbing his fingers together.

"I don't know about this." Facing the opening, Dous closed his eyes, and slid one foot down into the water. "There's gotta be another way in?"

"We don't have time to look for another point of entry," Cue said, looking back down at Dous, who was by now ankle deep in the water.

Heli side-stepped Cue, putting a hand out to stop his approach. He turned to face Dous. "There's no other way to get to her. It has to be done from the inside. You're the only one who can do this." Heli could see a trailing shadow of doubt behind the moonlight in Dous's eyes.

Dous looked back at the shallow water and took a few more steps toward the port hole, then he looked up. He was now knee deep in the murk. "What if I can't find her?" He shot a glance at Mianna, who stood in the backdrop a few feet away from the action.

She wandered in closer and peered down into the pool he stood in and then she looked directly at him. As she spoke his eyes opened wide on her. "You need to do this. It has to be you." She aimed her gaze directly on Dous. She removed her sandals one at time and dipped one foot and then the other into the shallow water without the protection of Hodgewear. Her bare legs flashed white against the shimmering surface. Pulling up on her skirt-line as she approached him, she moved up close enough that their noses nearly touched. The bold look she had in her eyes faded the moment she reached out her hand to take hold of his. Leaning in she kissed him softly on the lips. Heli heard Dous's thoughts before he had time to block them. *Whoa!*

Heli kept his eyes averted. The distinguishable hush could mean only one thing. He scanned to see where Cue stood. Obviously from the way Cue's eyes narrowed in on them, he hadn't expected this either.

Heli picked up a rock and skipped it out toward the two lovebirds, splashing spitting droplets up against their legs. Mianna pulled back. Dous looked like a fish still trying to move upstream with his lips pursed and his eyes closed.

Heli coughed. "Better get going."

Dous held up his pointer finger in the air and opened his eyes again. "I need a second here." He breathed in deeply as if he were trying to savor something in the moist air. Mianna stood close, still holding his other hand. She was looking at him, her curious eyes waiting.

Say something. Heli sent out the thought to Dous.

He watched Dous simply squeeze Mianna's hand before releasing it, ignoring Heli's command. He turned to face the pour spout, only standing for a second with his back turned on them, before he crouched down and dove forward. The only evidence that he was on the move was when he pressed through the mouth of the opening, jamming the artery of flowing water for the moment. When all he could see were Dous's feet sliding through the port hole and out of sight Heli received one final thought. *Tell her I'll come back to her.*

***

Heli stood, not knowing what to say, relieved when Cue broke the silence. "Time to move." His voice was gruff and the long moments after Dous's exit lingered on uncomfortably.

Heli picked up speed in an effort to keep up with Cue's solid stride. He finally caught up with him. "So how is it exactly that we take this thing down?"

Cue's silence met Heli with no answer while his attention was set on the high periphery wall. Mianna fell a short distance behind them, and her little shuffle caught Heli's attention. He looked back. She had her arms wrapped tightly around herself and must have tripped on a rock or something in the dark. Heli slowed down, dropping back. "You okay?" He offered an awkward hand and then withdrew it when he could see she wouldn't take it.

"I'm fine," she answered. Her head bent down and her eyes trailed to the ground as she stepped more gingerly.

"That was a...impressive. He certainly needed a little convincing," Heli said.

"It wasn't a performance, if that's what you're getting at. I do actually care about him you know," she said.

"I know, and he wouldn't come out with it after that kiss, but Dous wanted you to know that he's coming back...to you." Heli caught his foot on a rock and faltered.

"He didn't say anything after." She stared ahead.

"We can read each other's thoughts, you know." Heli clenched his jaw, cursing himself for needing to justify Dous's actions by sharing their secret.

Her head shot up and she stared at him more intently.

"He could've shielded me from it, but he didn't. Thoughts don't lie," Heli said.

She shook her head looking at her father who walked ahead of them. "Has he ever kissed anyone before?"

"Somehow I doubt it." Heli knew he was grappling for anything to ease the tension. She was laughing with her next words. "He could use some practice." She sent Heli a side glance and he groaned.

"We're as close as two dudes can get, but I think that's gonna have to be someone else's department." Heli allowed himself to smile.

Cue slowed suddenly. He threw a hand out to signal the pause and silence. He was scanning the trellised walls. The hedged brackets of foliage that covered the barrier left little pocket views of the grounds inside. Heli leaned in, to peer through the outgrowth. He could see very little, but of what he could see, there was a soft hum of light cast over the side garden area. The landscape lighting offered an inviting warmth. A fairyland mirage hovered around the familiar sight and Heli could feel his insides responding to its lure.

"Why are we stopping?" Heli whispered.

"This'll be our rally point," Cue answered, keeping his voice low.

"Now what?" Heli asked.

"Mianna, I want you to head to the front that way." He pointed. "Stay close to the walls and we should have the cameras disabled by the time you reach the entrance to reconnect with Dous." He looked at her and she nodded, shifting to move around Heli.

"You're sending her alone? Shouldn't we stay together?" Heli asked.

"I don't want her within a hundred feet from this when we go live with the Prana." Cue's eyes traveled up the high precipice of the wall.

"Okay, so we dismantle the system and then what? They're bound to notice," Heli said.

"That's irrelevant once we make our way inside. He's expecting us, but not like this. We use it to our advantage—and buy some time," Cue answered.

"How can you say it's irrelevant?" Heli asked. He was confused, "Jacque doesn't pull any punches. Once he gets wind that we're here, if he doesn't already know, he'll make us wish we'd never come."

"Then we get in fast, do what we have to do and get out as quickly as possible," Cue said.

"That's just it! I'm not sure I'll know what to do once we're in there," Heli confided.

"If there's anything I know about you it's that you'll do well to trust your instincts," Cue said.

"I'm here making a decision that could do us all irreparable harm if we don't get it right. It's hard to put faith in that." Heli put a hand on the wall.

"All you have is faith then. Without it, it's all a wash and we're empty inside. You'll do well to remember that," Cue said.

"Empty?" Heli challenged.

"When you choose what's right, above what's wrong, no matter what the consequences, all decisions become simple," he answered. "Do you think I look forward to re-entering those gates? Returning to . . ." Cue paused and shook his head. "Forget it. I know you understand. It's time to get on with this."

Heli watched him move forward to place his hands against the wall, seemingly assessing the conductivity. The mark on Cue's hand stood out staring back at Heli like a third eye calling his attention. He looked down at his own marked hand, a reminder of the many reasons that brought him back.

"Place your hands on the wall," Cue commanded.

Before following his instructions Heli asked, "What happened here? To you and Emeal? To Thryn?"

Cue brought his hands down.

"We're wasting valuable time," Cue said.

"I need to know," Heli said.

From the way Cue stared at him, Heli became concerned that he might be considering clocking him one to get the Prana rolling. But instead his hard eyes softened. "I left to protect my family." His eyes closed and he hung his head. "There were certain expectations that went beyond our Cor bond. Things became much more pressing. Thryn and I, our relationship became complicated."

"Mianna's mother, Arah?" Heli asked.

"It...it was my fault Thryn went back in." Cue's voice caught.

"I thought you were only operating on the assumption that she'd gone back in," Heli said.

"No." He shook his head and dropped his hand. "We watched her go in, Emeal and I. Emeal tried to go in after her. I stopped her." His marked hand came up reflexively to meet his cheek.

"The scar on her face?" Heli asked. He could imagine the scene, one of pain and chaos.

"There was no turning back after that. We would risk our own lives if we went back in to retrieve her.

Emeal was injured. I doubt she would've survived the journey," Cue admitted.

"You let her go." Heli tried to sound sympathetic. The thought of abandoning either one of his friends to the Strata had him shaking his head to clear it.

"I would've done anything to keep those who I cared most about safe. She of all people understood that. So, yes, I let her go." There was a pause in his voice as if he were about to say something more before he side-stepped Heli and motioned for them to proceed.

"We need to move on to this now. The closer Mianna gets toward the entry of the compound with visuo-cams still at work, the more risk we run of being discovered," he said.

Cue and Heli both placed their hands along the fence, a grounding source for how they would disable the prying eyes of IDEA. Heli could smell the heat they were producing before he could feel it. He concentrated on the face of the man responsible for all of this and hate swelled in him. He could feel the sizzle of the power draining, pouring back into him. If everything went as planned Mianna would be reunited with Dous at the front entry, leaving it open as an access point, and together they would retreat in the opposite direction from where Heli and Cue were attempting to dismantle the security system.

Dous, is Mianna with you? Heli projected, working to reach his friend.

There was no reply.

Dous, we're approaching the doors. We need confirmation that all visuos are down. Dead silence.

"I can't get through. Dous isn't responding," Heli said and he leaned up against the wall. Cue stood back from his position.

"What are you talking about?" asked Cue.

"We can sort of talk to each other in here." Heli tapped his head. "It's similar to the way you and Emeal can read each other's emotions," Heli said.

"That would have been helpful to know." Cue sounded frustrated.

"Hey, you have your secrets, I have mine," Heli said.

"Okay then, what's happening?" Cue asked.

"I'm open to both of them right now, but I can't seem to reach either of them. Or . . ." He paused and stared up the flat face of the wall suddenly feeling a desperate rising against the barrier. "They can't reach me for some reason."

"Maybe they're too far away," Cue said.

Heli shook his head. "It's not like a radio signal where distance matters. We can opt to hear each other when we want to from anywhere. I'm getting nothing. It's like some kind of firewall between us or something." Heli tightened his grip on the sprouting tendrils of vines growing along the porous screen. It gave him little to hold on to. He pressed his head against the wall to concentrate.

Terra hadn't been open to him since their conversation earlier that night, before she disappeared. An emptiness he was all too familiar with from his past sat in the pit of his belly. Severe hunger for their connection was crippling his ability to think straight. He could feel the heat...a searing, roaring blaze welling up from his center once again, moving out.

"Hold on, Heli!" Cue's voice was stern.

Heli shook his head. He closed his eyes in an attempt to get control. "I...I don't know if I can!" He clenched his teeth, forcing it back.

Stop! We're coming to open the doors! Dous's thoughts came slamming into his head.

Heli threw himself back from the wall. "There! It's Dous! I can hear him. He wants me to stop."

"What?" Cue moved off.

What's going on? What happened? Why couldn't I reach you? Heli spit out his thoughts.

We have to abort the plan. He's threatening to hurt them. Dous's thoughts propelled back.

What's wrong? Where are you? Heli projected.

He knows we're inside. We— His thoughts were cut off suddenly.

"Oh god, we gotta get in there!" Heli ran toward the front doors.

Cue called after him, "Is everyone okay?"

"I don't know how he did it, but Jacque knows we're here!" Heli yelled as he ran in a full sprint.

"What do you mean?" Cue barked as he ran to catch up.

"It's over! We just need to get in there!" Heli screamed.

***

Heli slowed his pace as he approached the two heavy doors, standing guard with steely sheets of metal. He felt a strange kinship with these doors, as if they might sweep open in greeting to signify his return, but there was no show of an invitation even when the doors did finally open. Mianna scooted out first, her eyes bloodshot and puffy from tears and she ran into her father's arms. Heli looked in past the scene of their reunion into the darkened foyer where a tall figure stood waiting. Heli recognized the still form. Justin stood back with his head bent low.

"Where are they?" Heli asked. He kept his hands pinned to his sides staring at Justin.

"You'll need to talk to Jacque first," he said, offering Heli a curt nod. "Come in, I'll take you to him."

Heli stepped over the threshold and looked behind him. Cue stood back. His untrusting eyes darted between Heli and his daughter and then they rested on Justin. "It's been a long time, old friend."

"Yes. I'm sorry it isn't on better terms. I'll show you to the Query Room where Jacque is waiting," Justin said.

Heli aimed cautiously. "First we need confirmation that they're all right."

"Dous is with Terra," Mianna said with her head still pressed against her father's chest, shielded by his embrace.

"You saw them? They're okay?" Heli asked.

"They're okay now." Her voice was shaking. "He knocked Dous unconscious after he tried to reach you." Her seething eyes set on Justin.

"You knocked him out? At least now we know whose side you're on," Heli said.

"He's his own moderator. At least that's what he tried to convince me once," Cue muttered in anger.

"Enough. Jacque will speak with you all first and then I'll take you to them," Justin replied.

Heli took a step toward Justin, who reflexively took two steps back, rubbing the scars on his hand. Heli looked back at Cue and Mianna, who appeared to be ostensibly aware of what it meant to be crossing the threshold of this space. They followed Heli while he stayed close behind Justin and they traveled through the ground floor corridor out toward the garden area.

As they approached, the garden entry doors, they opened automatically. Warmth tumbled in as they moved out. A fragrant buttery citrus aroma filled Heli's lungs and he couldn't stop himself from taking a deep breath to hold it, savoring the familiar sights and scents. The others walked along beside him.

"Things have certainly changed around here," Cue said as his eyes traveled up scanning the path.

"Tracy's work," Heli said.

"She made some valuable adjustments," Justin said.

Cue looked at him. "You haven't changed a bit. Your loyalties still following the tide wherever it may flow in this place."

Justin looked at him but kept silent.

As they walked, Heli could see the pitched skyline of the rooftop to the Query Room where he, Terra, and Dous had spent much of their time while in training. And at the head of the table, defiling his memories, stood Jacque behind the podium, his lips pressed tightly together, eye to eye with Heli. Heli slowed his pace, staying back while the others followed suit. Jacque swallowed, his protruding Adam's apple rolling in a tight bulge.

"You brought your friends." His attention shifted to Cue, who stood by Heli's side. Jacque wore the protective suit and Heli shot a glance over toward Mianna. She nodded to him in silent commiseration.

All of Jacque's attention returned to Heli. "So, back for more, are we?"

"You know why we're here," Heli said.

"Oh yes, that. But tell me, why the surprise visit when this little homecoming could have been so much more fulfilling had I known you were coming? I will admit, I've been expecting you." Jacque ran his hand down the arm of the suit.

Mianna began to inch her way in closer toward Jacque, millimeter by millimeter before he turned to look at her, suddenly aware of her proximity.

"That will be close enough, young lady. If time and math serve me correctly I would muster to guess that you're one of his." His thick accent seemed heavy in his throat as his eyes fell back on Cue.

"My daughter, yes," Cue spoke with reservation.

"Audacious like her mother. And how, by the way, is Arah?" Jacque asked in the sadistic manner of driving the knife in to turn it.

"You know full well how she faired after what we did to her. She lived out the remains of her life free of this nightmare." Cue's voice shook.

"Science and progress. A necessary evil at times." He drew out the statement and turned to look at Heli again.

"Well, now that we've all had proper introductions. It's all very convenient the way this has turned out," Jacque said.

"Where are they?" Heli asked. His fingers tingled. He shook them, needing to control himself until the opportunity came. Mianna had inched her way further and closer to Jacque than Heli felt comfortable with and he looked back at Cue, who was wringing out his hands. She made incremental strides, hardly noticeable. Heli worked to keep Jacque's attention.

"How did you know we were here?" Heli asked.

"Not so fast. This little operation of yours isn't going to be as easy as you thought." Jacque turned his head to stare forcibly at Mianna, who had gained more than a foot in her approach in the last few seconds. He eyed her now but addressed Cue. "You should have let us take care of this mistake when she took up less space." His eyes jumped over the distance between himself and the few feet left between them.

"I wasn't going to let you touch my family," Cue spoke through clenched teeth.

"But you let us have him." Jacque aimed a charming smile toward Heli.

Heli looked at Cue. He watched as Cue appeared to age ten years in one exhale.

Jacque let loose a cackle that made Heli's skin crawl. "Ah! All of these secrets we keep. You haven't told him, have you?"

"What secrets?" Mianna's eyes flew back and forth between Cue and Heli.

"Oh dear, now I've upset you all with talk of pedigree. But in my lifetime, I've learned that honesty is the best policy when it comes to family matters. What did you think, that by not telling them, you could stave off that old *like father, like son* innuendo and protect him from making the same mistakes you did?"

Heli felt the rush of light and heat welling up uncontrollably.

He searched the area and his eyes fell on Mianna, whose face mirrored his own in sudden shocked realization. A relationship he never knew existed until now was having the effect he desperately needed at the moment.

Jacque whispered, "Tracy must have left that little detail out of your training. Or better yet, I seem to recall in some of the files on record that it was you," he half pointed in a motion to Cue, "who advised her not to tell him during his time here?" His eyes were tight slits now staring at Cue.

"You bastard," Cue wheezed.

Then Jacque piped up, moving the subject along. "Well I for one am thoroughly enjoying this lovely reunion, but it has certainly served to distract you from other pressing issues." Jacque held his gaze on Heli.

"You win. We're all here. What more do you want from us?" Heli asked.

"I want to see you beg." His simpering voice penetrated as he stared at Heli, "And when someone wishes to trespass onto these grounds unannounced I will treat them like the intruders they are."

"Please." Heli closed his eyes. "Where are they? You obviously want us here for your own reasons. I'll do whatever you want me to do, I just need to see them."

"Yes, you do." Jacque's lip curled up decisively.

"Is Dous still with her?" Mianna asked.

"Don't worry your pretty little blue head about him. That reminds me, that suit he wears. He must be familiar with a friend of mine." He looked to all three of them in turn.

"You didn't remove it, did you?" Mianna squirmed, backing away from him and holding her hand to her gut like someone had sucker-punched her.

"I only need to borrow it for a bit. No need to worry, I gave him something suitable to put on in the meantime. He won't be without it for long. He's no good to me if he's immobilized. Besides, you're all here now and it would be rude if I didn't invite you to stay and treat you with the hospitality you're all so accustomed to in that place of yours. What do you call it? The Frey?" Heli put out a hand to stop Mianna from moving closer.

Instead Cue pressed in. "You've located it?" Tears welled up, giving away any attempt of a bluff.

"You didn't think you could hide your little utopian treasure forever?" Jacque squinted at Cue.

Cue blinked frantically as if he were experiencing some kind of excruciating pain.

"We're all better off without places like that crowding our preserved open spaces. Fortunately for all of you, you won't be there for the AGR greeting party. No, instead, you'll join me as my honored guests to enjoy the show." He grinned. "Right in the nick of time." He nodded his head appreciatively and flicked a floating icon open to a familiar image. Heli looked back and forth between Cue and Mianna, who each stared at the image before them, horrorstruck.

The visuo-cam of the Frey's landscape showed a decisively serene repose in dawn's early glow. The timber borders and gravely knolls spread across the scene. A tingling heat channeled down through Heli's hands just as a lead-weighted sinking feeling caught him. He couldn't take his eyes off the barrier. Along the entire ridge-line shadows danced in the distance. A flicker of movement faded in and out, nearly indiscernible. Suddenly the brush exploded and they emerged, multiplying like a horde of roaches stampeding in the distance. Mianna gasped and Heli jumped while his eyes only left the screen for a moment. When he looked back at the hovering projection, he noticed the familiar emblematic uniform of the AG Regulation flash across the screen on one of the foot men. They were headed straight toward the epicenter of the sleeping populace. Swift as the rushing gale of an oncoming storm, the purpose of this operation was clear in the eyes of the enlisted who flashed across the screen as they marched forward. Each of them wore recognizable Regulation grade artillery strapped across their chests. The decisive weaponry they wore signaled a clear takedown. Heli closed his eyes and heard Cue whisper, "Dear God."

"Not even that will save them," Jacque said.

Heli somehow managed to speak, releasing the pressure as he fought his way through the agonizing vision. "All those people?" And the face of the child, the little girl who had seen him for who he was, flashed through his mind.

"Those people? And here I thought they were 'your' people." Jacque grabbed Mianna's hand, pulling it up with a quick jerk to reveal her marking. "You wear this, like your...sister here, whose loyalties are to them," Jacque nodded toward Cue and took his eyes off Mianna, "yet you sacrificed all of them to return here to rescue your friend. I think there might be hope for you yet."

Jacque pinched the screen with his free hand and the image of the Frey disappeared just as the first sound of a scream rang through the backdrop.

Heli saw a flash in Mianna's eyes. He signaled to her with a nod. She yanked her hand to free it from Jacque's clasp in a tangle of fury and rage. Her hand met his shoulder and neckline as if she were struggling to press away and his elbow flew out, swinging up and hitting her hard directly in the jaw. She stumbled back away from him holding her hand to her lip as it bled. It was as agile a movement as Heli had ever witnessed and she quickly moved as far away from his clutches as she could to find her father's protective arms outstretched toward her. Cue held her tightly against him, but she looked at Heli. The message from her stark stare came crystal clear. She had done her part; on his mark, when the time came, he would finish it.

Rectified

"They're both okay, right?" Heli asked, lowering his voice toward Justin. Justin slowed down allowing them to fall behind a good distance from Jacque who walked a distance ahead of them on the garden path.

Just as they reached the edge of the formal gardens where illusive hedges signaled their exit Justin responded, "Dous will be fine. I'm trained in de-escalation."

"You knocked him out cold."

"Just a standard sleeper hold. The trick is how to apply pressure to bring someone down without leading to permanent injury."

"Why are you helping him?" Heli nodded toward Jacque.

"I do nothing outside of the cause. It's never been about him," he said.

"He sacrificed all those innocent people to the Regulation. You stood by and let it happen. As far as I'm concerned anyone who's allied with that is an enemy to the cause." Heli said.

Justin stopped and clenched his jaw uttering his next words under his breath, "There are things you still don't understand." He shook his head and looked Heli in the eye. "My role in this along with Mr. Cruise…we don't blame you for what you see on the surface."

"On the surface all I see are two tight lipped cronies who are servants to a cause I'll never comprehend."

Justin dropped his head. "Would call Terra's mother an enemy too?" Justin asked.

"What on earth does she have to do with anything?" Heli asked.

"She was the one who accompanied me in retrieving Terra. Would you ever question her reasons for serving him?"

"Well, no. Terra's her daughter. Her reasons are clear."

"Has it ever occurred to you that there might be good reason for why the grain of sand is kept hidden inside the oyster?"

"So what? We're diving for pearls here?"

"Wisdom like pearls takes time and penance to cultivate." Justin peered up at the camera lens above them as they walked.

Heli squinted his eyes against the bleeding sun's rays.

Justin whispered, "Jacque gave Terra's mother good reason to come and let's just say that this," he held up his injured hand "would be the least of my worries if I hadn't helped bring Terra back."

"I'm sorry...that I hurt you. I didn't know how to control it then."

Justin whispered, "And now you do?"

"I've learned how to manage it or I couldn't have made it through to this point."

"Well good. It might interest you to know that Terra's mother is here primarily to help care for her."

Justin went on, "Jacque came back as we assumed he would. He was suspicious from the beginning that there was more to your disappearance than what we had reported. We told him that you had convinced the others to retreat and go into hiding and that you all disappeared one night."

"Sounds about right. He obviously didn't buy it, did he?" Heli asked.

"When he recovered the data files from the days before your exit, he questioned why thee were no audio or visio-files recording your retreat. Threats were made." Heli could see the muscles in Justin's temples roll along his jawline. "He had us run some diagnostics on the results from your entry into the Strata. That's when we detected something in Terra's system—a foreign sensitivity. We were able to track it through the trace minerals you all still carry in your systems from prior entry into the Strata. It's how we were able to locate the Frey after the anomaly produced itself in Terra's body." He paused and slowed even more.

"Mr. Cruise and I only happened to come across it when we were rebooting the system to access information for Jacque. Once it was affirmed that something was wrong, it was our obligation to bring her here for treatment. Mr. Cruise suggested that Terra's mother be brought in. The only reason she became involved was to aid in Terra's recovery," he said.

"What do you know about her condition?" Heli asked. His head began swimming and the ground suddenly felt unstable.

"We ran more tests. We've ruled out any critical dangers such as the Chronovirus. Jacque's been vying to run more tests, but we've all been so wrapped up in your surprise visit," Justin said, and Heli dropped his shoulders letting out a short breath.

He realized suddenly that they had arrived at the entry of the large terrarium patio he knew so well. As they entered Heli looked up and could see the midday stages of light that hovered around a ceiling of blue sky.

Jacque stopped and turned around to face them. He eyed them suspiciously. Justin took a few steps away from Heli. "Before we take this any further you and I need to have a little chat." Jacque looked at Heli. "Justin, you may lead on." Jacque stood blocking the entrance to Terra's old quarters. He was looking at Heli's marked hand.

"I can see how you value tradition in that mark you wear of theirs," Jacque said.

"It's not just theirs, it was meant for us," Heli responded.

"Getting a bit big headed now, aren't we? So is this the swell of pride that must have gotten in the way of you asking for the appropriate permission for my daughter's hand?" Jacque said. "And don't even get me going on what happened after that."

"It's none of your business!" Heli raged. The simmering heat was working its way up. *Not yet.* He closed his eyes and imagined Terra as she would move through the poses of her daily Sun Salutations and his thoughts moved with her.

"Actually, seeing how 'this business' would explain why I could locate the three of you and how it is the sole reason she was brought here, I think that makes it my business." Jacque stood with his arms crossed.

"What do you mean?" Heli snapped to, withdrawing some of his anger, suddenly feeling on trial.

"For someone so keen on keeping up with everything, you sure do miss a lot. Oh, but you're smarter than that and you assumed I wouldn't find out," Jacque said.

Heli shook his head, ramblings of every sort boggling his mind to keep him from falling to pieces. "Quit playing games with me!"

"This is no game. And it's not so simple. We were as perplexed as you at first. Those idiots had no idea. A foreign sensitivity in her system?" Jacque shook his head and paused, looking at Heli as if waiting for the light bulb to turn on. "And this is why it has become every bit a part of my business when I finally discovered that my own blood line has been tainted by yours."

The driving torque of his words had Heli shuffling to keep from losing his balance.

"Now that's the look from you I've been waiting for," Jacque said.

Heli stood silently. He lifted his chin considering the opportunity. *Too close.* And in the midst of his indecision, her thoughts came reaching in. *Heli? Are you there?*

"Bravo, lad! I'd have tossed you one of those old timer's cigars, but I'm fairly certain that this is a smoke-free environment." Jacque looked at him, still standing in his way.

"Heli shook his head and heard her thoughts cut in again. *You're here, I can feel it. Where are you?* Her thoughts were alive and beating into his mind.

Heli didn't want to shut her out, but he needed to concentrate. "How can you be so sure? I mean, it's only been a couple of days." Heli slid his hand through his hair.

"Oh, there are ways. I ran a few diagnostics of my own with the help of her mother. Very useful, that one," Jacque said.

Heli closed down. He shut his mind and his mouth.

"Now, I think you're ready to see her." Jacque moved aside to allow Heli to enter the patio suite.

Reunited

Heli had a difficult time keeping his head up. A virtual noose tugged on him, bringing him to a lowly place in his mind. He was running out of time, but he had to see her.

I'm here. He sent.

He remembered the last time they had been together in this space, the night before they left. The room was still encased in screens of glossy evergreen foliage in splashes of burgundy, orange, and red. It had been designed for her and he could feel the thrum of every breath she had taken in the air that surrounded him in the protruding leaves.

Heli approached the corner where the taut hammock hung and peered over the edge to look upon Terra for the first time in days. In the instant that he saw her all of the numbness that had settled into his chest burst and it was all he could do not to shatter into pieces himself.

"It's really you." She sat up from her cradled form and looked at him.

"Yes," he said cautiously.

But I'm not the reason you came. Her thoughts flew with the flash of her gaze that fell away.

I'm here for you. He swallowed.

She closed her eyes against him and shook her head.

Heli moved closer.

Her eyes opened and raised to his. "How can I trust that?"

All it ever was since the moment I first saw you in that room, those ember eyes dancing in the firelight. It was always you. Without hesitation he moved toward her and wrapped his arms around her. She felt warm and alive against him. He drew his face into the crux of her neck. No words, without thoughts, in as quiet a space as she would allow, while together they adjusted to being filled up wholly again. The surge of adrenaline returned and feeling her breath on his shoulder cooled the vibrations in his pounding heart. He waited patiently, holding on for dear life, knowing she was weeping. She lifted a hand covered in bright discs of hovering sensors. She arched back and wiped away a tear that traveled down his own cheek. Lolling his head into her soft fingertips he attempted to somehow brace himself.

I came as soon as I could. He paused.

You're here now. Just don't let go. He took both of her hands in his and looked down on the hand where her mark stood stark among the neon lights that traced her veins.

"They have you lit up like a Holo-tarmac." He brought up her hand to kiss it gently.

"They're checking on everything. Every little thing." She shook her head and looked up as her attention shifted over his shoulder. Heli turned, sensing the approach of someone behind him.

"Well, you made good time." The woman's voice was smooth, a peace-loving tone he hadn't expected and that he wasn't sure he deserved.

"I don't believe we've been properly introduced." She smiled and reached out a hand to meet his. Her grip was firm. He felt as if he were standing with his feet covered in wet sand and the tide was drawing out to pull at him and tip him over.

"Hello," Heli said. He remembered their first encounter—vividly. She had looked at him with those same soul-filled amber eyes he knew so well.

He spoke to her politely. "Thank you for coming here for Terra while she . . ." He stumbled on his words, feeling the sweat build up along the nape of his neck.

"We're just happy you came." She took her other hand and patted the top of his and turned her attention to Terra. "I think I'll go and gather some of the rose hip berries and herbs we talked about from the garden to use in some tea for you. I'll leave you two alone." She withdrew her hand humming a soothing melody as she walked out.

Terra closed her eyes to the rhythm of her mother's croon and Heli stood by mystified by how it worked to calm him too. He was so tired. He hadn't even thought about how sleep deprived he was. He could see now that Terra seemed to be in a daze of exhaustion herself, settled in the cradle of the hammock. Heli carefully edged his way back to sit on the cot-like seat near the panel-screened partition in the room. He would wait until he knew she was asleep, but sleep had him before his head even hit the padding.

***

Heli gasped, coming out of a dream-studded fog. Everything felt heavy and he was damp all over. He could feel the swell of the blood reentering his muscles. He panicked with the jolt. How long had he been asleep? He took his time standing up. Adjusting to his foggy vision, he could see that Terra was still unconscious. A familiar voice rang out.

"I thought you were a goner for a while there." Dous stood leaning up against the partition next to him.

"How long have I been here?" Heli asked.

"Must have been quite a power-nap I think. I just ran into Terra's mom on my way in. She said you were here and from what I could ascertain, you were still conscious when she saw you." Dous laughed.

"You're okay. You got your suit back." Relief escaped Heli. "Your head all right?" Heli leaned in to get a look at Dous's head of dark curls that seemed more spring-loaded at the moment.

"I'll be all right. Quite a knot to bring down, but nothing an anti-inflammatory press can't alleviate." Dous changed the subject. "You sleep like a rock, you know that? I couldn't even get into your head while you were down."

"Oh my god, what time is it?" Heli looked over at Terra's sleeping form.

Heli sent the quick thought, already moving out. *The tripwire is set. I need to take him out now! I don't have much time!*

Well, speaking of good timing. He asked me to come 'retrieve' you for a meeting he's called in the Query Room. Dous picked up the pace to keep up with Heli.

Perfect. The prey calling on the predator, Heli projected.

His thoughts were cut off by Terra's mother, who rounded the corner with her hands clutching two burlap bags of her samplings from the garden.

"Hello again." She wiped her soiled hands along the side of her Hodgesuit before extending one toward Dous.

"Hello, Ms. Sial." Dous quickly shook her hand.

"You can call me Corinne," she said.

"She's still sleeping," Heli said, and Corinne's eyes traveled over toward Terra's quarters. A silken smile took over her face.

"We have to go. I'm sorry. I hate to leave her," Heli said.

"She'll understand." She began pulling out the wares from the knapsacks as Heli and Dous darted out together.

Branded

"We must have arrived ahead of schedule," Dous said as they entered the Query Room.

Heli let out a long exhale. "No, it's just like him to make us wait." *Especially when every second matters.*

"He's a busy man. Doing his villainous best to take over the world. That can't be an easy job, you know," Dous joked.

Heli actually found it in himself to laugh. He looked around and his eyes settled on the familiar table mount.

"Check this out." Heli placed his hands on the clear surface of the interactive tabletop. It surged with light immediately when he touched it this time. Hovering icons shimmered in front of them.

"Whoa! Some serious juice you got running through those veins!" Dous cried out, turning his head to look at the hovering mass of information.

Heli shrugged. "Shall we see what might be keeping him?"

Heli signaled for Dous to open the visuo icons surrounding the area. In a matter of moments, they found what they were looking for.

"What's he up to with Cue?" Dous asked.

Heli tapped the audio bit.

"You're about out of time, my friend. You know you both can't take up the same space for very long now that he's become aware of the conditions. The simple fact that you share the same genetic makeup goes against all of nature's laws. I do appreciate the irony though. This was your bright idea at one time, a product of the laws stemming from your own great cause." Jacque's words were cool in the pixelated image hovering before them. Heli tensed, watching the interaction.

Cue held his form. He straightened up, but then arched forward, convulsing violently. Heli and Dous watched with horror as Cue regained his posture, only then to suffer ricocheting thrusts of what looked like the assault of an invisible perpetrator. Cue's face was pinched and he groaned in agonizing pain. His movements ebbed back again to offer him some sort of short-lived relief. He clung to a railing against the wall as if he could anticipate the next wave of suffering.

"We made a deal and I stood by it." Cue cringed, succumbing to another blow and destabilizing quickly.

"Our agreement ended the moment Thryn went in." Jacque pointed an accusing finger toward him.

"And you would allow all of them to follow suit to go back in there to suit your own ends!" Cue raged. His voice caught and slowed, "I couldn't have affected her choice. She never would've stayed with you. She opted for an eternity in that wormhole knowing it was the only place you'd never be able to reach her." Mercifully the words were out before another seizing cramp set in nearly cutting him in half by the way his back arched in revolt. It took him to the ground.

"You do look terrible. I guess the jewels of nature are not always the best accessory. I must say, I appreciate the assistance though. She even has her cruel way with her own disciples. I won't even have to lift a finger." Jacque moved in closer to peck at Cue's huddled form with a gouging finger. "Pathetic. Let this be your punishment for defiling her image."

Heli searched the panels, frantically scanning the coordinates above the visuo-file. Dous stood by struck dumb, unmoving.

"You knew what this would do. You were the one who told him and set it into motion!" Cue coughed on the mucus and blood spilled out the edge of his mouth. Heli knew his lungs were failing him, filling up with fluid.

"I guess if it makes you feel better to shoot the messenger. Go right ahead, I also believe you called me a bastard earlier. Brilliant bastard would be more like it," Jacque mocked and looked down to where Cue had recently spit up blood. "Careful, I just had that floor cleaned."

Helpless and searching for what could be done at this instant, Heli knew they were running out of time.

"Where the hell are they? He's dying in there!" Heli could hardly control himself. He looked at Dous and firmly sent a thought. *You need to get out of here now!*

Cue spoke with another retching jolt. "You would stand by...and watch this?" He cursed under his breath and held his abdomen.

Heli could see Dous still standing there frozen. He sent one more urgent and final thought. *Go! Now!*

Dous took off running away from him.

The voices kept pounding in. He didn't know what to do. His head was whirling in a space out of reach. He was losing all control.

Jacque's voice pierced through the muck and mire of the screen. "I delight in it. You and that product of you are the only things standing in my way. Besides, it's out of my hands now."

Heli watched as Cue opened his mouth to speak, doubling over in pain with one hand extended out, inarticulate and pleading.

Heli's heart was pounding so fast that he couldn't even register the level of energy he must have been producing. The visuo projection began to spit the flashing haze of the image, fading in and out. Heli watched as Jacque hovered over Cue the way a wild animal might eye a tiny moving insect, its hunger set in on the imminent final deadly pounce. "This is beyond you or me. There, there now. Let it come. It's time to let go." Jacque bent over Cue's twisted body only a few inches away. Cue rolled over slightly, propping himself against the wall to face his tormentor. Heli could see how close to death he was and he could feel it like the closing off of a torqued spigot to his own lungs.

Jacque was close enough to Cue's ear that Heli could hardly extrapolate the words he uttered. "And now it's time for you to finally come through with your end of the bargain. Go be with your beloved Arah forever." Heli watched as the image faded. Only a flash of Cue's hand rising as if to caress Jacque's face played on the screen and the image blinked out.

Emboldened

You saw it? Do you think he's alive? Dous kicked at the grass under their feet on the path leading back into the Query Room.

I can't imagine anyone going through all that and being okay. We've gotta find Mianna, Heli sent.

This is bad. I don't know, but my gut... Dous paused.

You live by your gut. What do you think? Heli probed.

Dous looked at him. *Just the thought of what he's capable of. I seriously doubt that having Cue here, interfering with his plans, ever sat well in his eyes.*

Heli's mind was riddling. *Mianna disabled the suit. I have to go find him. I don't have much time to act. It might already be too late.*

Are you sure you want to chance this? Dous asked.

I'll know what to do when the time comes. Just promise me that when I give you the signal you'll do what I tell you and get the hell out.

Dous's face fell. *What if something goes wrong? What if you miss the window and the suit starts working again? We're already cutting it way too close.*

None of that matters if you get hurt in the process. I don't do this unless you promise me you'll get out of the way when the time comes, Heli sent.

A projection floating over the table mount caught Dous's attention. He moved around Heli to get closer. "These look like blueprints. Not sure to what, but . . ." Dous squinted into the light. "See that white cluster in there?" He pointed to a clump of what looked to be little swirling bursts of fire crackers. "Like a billion solar systems."

Heli suddenly saw it too. He couldn't tear his eyes away from it until he heard the voice he had been waiting for.

"Find something interesting in there?" Jacque had entered from the side and now stood on the other side of the table watching them.

"Quite the curiosity burning in those eyes." He looked at Heli.

"Where's Cue?" Heli asked.

"I can always count on you to cut right to the chase." Jacque lifted his left eye where there should have been an eyebrow. All that remained was the rosy sheen of a fresh injury.

"What happened to you?" Heli asked.

Jacque reached up and tenderly touched the area. "Old wounds resurfacing."

"We saw you, with him. What have you done?" Heli demanded.

"Here we go." Jacque stood still as a statue. "I came prepared, you know."

"Prepared?" Heli asked.

"I needed insurance. You must take me for a fool if you think I didn't know what really brought you back to this place." Jacque looked Heli over quickly and then his focus jumped to Dous.

Heli taunted, "You look like one of those extinct hairless mole rats. I've heard that can happen when the right amount of electricity goes coursing through a person's veins. Cue got to you didn't he? One more jolt like that . . ."

Jacque's face turned a ruddy shade of red.

"Something wrong with the suit?" Heli asked. "Tell me what you've done to Cue! Or I don't give you time to answer." Heli's throat burned with the heat.

"I've done nothing. I didn't so much as lay a hand on him, as you say you saw with your own eyes." Jacque's own hands trembled. "At least not until the very end."

"He's dead then?" Dous whispered.

"That, right there," Jacque pointed to the image still hovering over the table, "took scientists over a decade to deliver. Once they had a greater understanding of our orientation in the universe they were able to create the first map to actual scale. Look carefully. Can you see how it breathes?"

Heli could see it, alive, pulsing to expand and shrink in real time.

"If you're looking to blame someone for the death of your friend, you need only to go as far as a mirror. The universe only makes room for one. And as you can see, your precious laws of nature aren't designed to be that flexible," Jacque said.

Heli let down a bit when Dous blurted, "Wait I...I don't understand. Are you saying this is some kind of doppelgänger nightmare?"

"Heli and Cue shared an unfortunate interdependency—a non-mutualistic one. One in which dual awareness is the recipe for disaster. "He knew about this and that's why he never told you," Jacque said.

"Stalling with these distractions won't save you." Heli could hear his own teeth grinding together as he rose to stand. "He kept this from me for a good reason. You're the one who delivered the news that would kill him." A bitter nausea drained down into his gut as he lifted his head. "I only blame you for that!"

There was little distance between them and the barricade of the table.

Dous, it's time for you to go, Heli projected, keeping his eyes on Jacque.

He could see in his periphery how Dous turned and looked at him quickly, and then moved to retreat. As soon as he met the entry his pace picked up a bit.

Jacque shifted incrementally. "You can't outrun me, old man." Heli said and stood firm.

"Getting rid of me will not end this!" The desperation in his voice rose. "I'm the only link you have to the outside world and to those who would rather see you dead than anywhere beyond these gates."

Heli hesitated. "Don't worry, I promise I won't watch you suffer the way you did with Cue. I'll make this quick," Heli said.

"How kind of you." Jacque's bold voice returned. "But I doubt you'll enjoy it as much as I did."

Heat rose in the pit of Heli's stomach. He clenched his fists in a tight ball, feeling the fire searing through his fingertips. "No more talking," he fumed in all but a whisper. The impaling resurgence exploded through him and suddenly he felt himself pulled on a catapult of rage as he thrust himself on top of Jacque.

Time slowed as his hands made contact with Jacque's neck. All the hate, all of the sorrow settled in his trembling fingers as they found their rightful place around Jacque's throat. Together they toppled onto the table, obliterating the cluster of stars that had hovered there moments before. And like a flicker in the distance before the surge of the full blast, Heli was suddenly aware of another's presence in the caustic space.

Terra's mother Corinne stood like a statue in the doorway with her eyes set on them. A flash of fear crossed her face before she let go of a wild shriek. The jolt lifted her a few feet off the ground and tossed her against the stone seating where she lay sprawled in the corner like a bag of beans. Horror oozed from her scream and echoed through Heli's boiling blood. All of his attention was torn from the contorted face of his foe to the gruesome reality that she too had gone down with the hit. The scene before him unfolded like his terrible nightmares. Her head hung loosely with her body slumped against the stone. She was unconscious, *or dead?*

He quickly removed his hands from Jacque's neck, pushing himself off the motionless body beneath him. *What was she doing here?* He had never thought to warn her to stay away like the others. Standing in numb disbelief, he couldn't disassociate from the scene before him. He looked back and forth between his two victims and a realization pierced through him as he dropped his eyes to look at his hands, splaying them out in front of him. He could suddenly imagine the blood welling up in pools to saturate them. A low groan came from nearby. He held his breath in desperation, hoping that the sound was coming from the right person. His eyes darted around to Terra's mother's limp body. He wanted to run to her, check her pulse, look for signs of life, but he was rooted in the horrific reality of what he had just done. Solid molten shackles of guilt held him still and in silence until he heard his name being called in the distance.

Delusion

"She withstood quite a jolt, but I believe we have her stable now." Justin squinted down at Corinne's still form. No words could cushion this blow. Heli had little memory of this particular room in the infirmary but he knew it was where he'd been treated after contracting the Chronovirus. The constant din of machinery and monitors offered up a stream of white noise melodious to his beaten spirit. It reminded him that Corinne still showed signs of life and that there was still hope.

"What do you think did more damage, the shock or the fall?" Dous asked. He joined Heli and placed a solid hand on his shoulder while they both waited for Justin's response.

"There are certainly markers of a concussion, but I think we all know what would have caused the greater damage," Justin said.

Under the weight of his own duress, Heli cursed himself silently. He could hear his own thoughts projecting out, aiming to rationalize what he had done. Terra was already under enough stress and he knew it would only make things worse if she had this to deal with.

"She's suffered a jolt of somewhere close to a billion volts of electricity—that's comparable to being struck by lightning in the old days before the Synthasphere came up. Directly or indirectly, it's a miracle she survived at all." Justin peered back at Heli and although he couldn't see through the impassive stare and Justin's dour features, it felt like stinging slaps across his cheek.

"He survived. Why wouldn't she?" Dous asked, sounding hopeful as he glanced between Heli and Justin.

"I tried. I thought I was ready…a clean sweep. She just showed up out of nowhere. I tried to pull back, but it was too late." Heli shook his head and closed his eyes.

We should tell her before it's too late. Dous's thoughts were soft.

Heli was suddenly reminded of another pressing issue. "Have you told Mianna about Cue?" He watched Dous's face grow long and he nodded his head.

"She wanted to be alone for a while," he said.

"Hasn't there been enough damage for one day!" Heli pounded his fist on the wall next to him.

"This isn't your fault," Dous tried.

"Her mother is unconscious by my hand!" Heli held up the hand that had recently put a mark on the wall. "She flat-out begged me not to go through with it. It is my fault." Heli squeezed back tears.

"How long could she be like this?" Dous turned to Justin.

"She's in a resuscitative state. My greatest concern at this point is her heart. Could be days, months, I don't know. The damage is considerable, and by a miracle she could pull through. But I warn you, if she does make it through, she'll need ongoing care."

There would be no reversing the slow drops of tortured time Heli would have to endure. He looked at Dous. *Please, let me figure this out. I promise I'll tell Terra. I just can't do it yet.*

I know you're trying to protect her, but no one is going to be able to protect you from the fallout when she discovers you kept this from her, Dous projected.

"I can't run the risk of what this might do to her or the baby," Heli responded.

"I agree." Justin's nose flared with the sentiment as he looked at Dous. "It could very well be dangerous for both Terra and the child if she has to deal with this on top of everything else."

"See, I'm not alone here. Even he thinks this should wait," Heli said.

"Okay, but when it's time to tell her, you better let her know I fought for this," Dous said.

"What about Jacque? He's still alive. What are we going to do about him?" Heli felt recharged, suddenly envisioning how he looked forward to pulling the plug on this loose end himself.

Justin dropped his head. "All of this," he looked around at the myriad of glowing life lines feeding medication to Terra's mother and the extensive equipment surrounding them, "requires resources from the outside. I'm afraid that without Jacque and his connections, we don't have the capacity to keep this up and running."

Heli closed his eyes and reopened them to stare up at the ceiling. "He's halfway to hell, and we're still being trussed around on his line. And all I've done is secured the knot."

"You didn't know she was there," Dous said.

Justin spoke, "It doesn't matter. What's done is done."

Heli twisted his neck, feeling the tight knots pop. "But it does matter." Heli pressed his marked hand against his chest. "And I'll live the rest of my life with the fact that not only is Cue dead because of my mere existence, but that the mother of the woman I love and the grandmother of my unborn child may not be far behind. And you're right, what's done is done." Heli bit his lip, drawing it out painfully from his teeth. "Now it's my job to finish it."

Dous looked at Heli pleadingly. "We don't fix this, we face it. Together. And if cowering to him saves her life and the baby's, we don't have a choice."

Heli stood hopeless. "I'll never be able to remedy this." And he pushed his way through them toward the exit, his pace quickening as he ran the other direction out onto the path. All he could hear beyond the throbbing in his head and the sound of his own pounding feet was the thought in his isolated mind. *Coward!*

Disarmament

"This place has a basement? I never saw markers of anything below the first level on the blueprints." Heli glanced at Justin as they walked together down a narrow hallway.

"Mr. Cruise and I agreed that it would be best to keep his location confidential, in case you got any more bright ideas. It's less of the secure vault it once was, but has served its purpose," Justin said.

"At least now he's closer to where he belongs. That being hell," Heli said.

"We no longer use the area. Pretty much isolated to storage these days. We were able to hold him in one of the small units while we decide what to do with him. I assume you want some say in this decision," Justin said.

"After the mess I've made, how can you be so sympathetic?" Heli asked.

Justin stopped as they approached the door to where Jacque was being held. "You need to know that I don't blame you for any of this the way you seem to be so keen on blaming yourself."

"Didn't you know that there's a certain level of satisfaction in self-deprecation? And how is it that he's better off than her? He had a direct hit," Heli asked as they approached a door and Justin stopped.

"He wears the scars. It spreads like a blooming orchid up his neck and down his back, and the injury was significant." Justin paused and looked down at his own injured hand. The healed fern-like patterns ran up his forearm from his experience with the Prana. "But as with any direct contact injury of this nature, Corinne provided a shared conduction source. It's likely the only reason either one of them survived at all," Justin said.

"Tell me the truth. Do you think she'll survive this?" Heli asked.

"The truth is that there was significant capillary damage from what she experienced in the ground current injury. It's especially volatile for her heart and vasculature system at this point. Only time will tell," Justin replied.

"What do we do with him?" Heli's hand gestures out the door toward the hall to the infirmary where Jacque waits in shackles. "I'm only asking because I think you know what I'd like to do to him. I bet you've even got him trussed up in that suit again in working order, don't you? And that brings me to an even more important question. I still can't tell whose side you're on," Heli said.

"Quality assurance has always been a part of my job. And the short answer? I'll always be on the 'right' side. No matter what I do, or who you think I work for, my only priority is to serve IDEA's original mission and affirm the prophecy. There's much more at stake here than you or I will ever know," Justin confirmed.

Justin reached to swipe the sensor and Heli grabbed his arm to stop him. "Just promise me that when the time comes, you'll let me deal with him on my own terms?"

"As long as you can promise me that you'll keep your head for now." Justin twisted his hand out of Heli's grip.

"I suppose, being that I've already made a deal with the devil," Heli said, gesturing toward the door. Justin swiped his free hand across the panel for an instantaneous scan of his palm and the lock disengaged.

***

Heli slipped in after Justin before the door receded back into its sleeve, closing them in the tight cubical space. He looked across the small confines of the chamber. The rank odors of stale sweat and thin air traveled up his nostrils and he took a step back. Jacque lifted his head to look at Heli. He shifted to sit up straighter and Heli could see the strain required for the minor adjustment.

"Let the games begin," Heli whispered.

"We have to quit meeting like this. It isn't quite how I envisioned our working together." Jacque's voice was ragged.

"There'll be no 'together' between you and me, ever," Heli said.

"This is hardly how negotiations are accomplished," Jacque responded, suddenly rooster-breasted and head held high. Heli stood over him and for the first time since the attack, he felt a thread of confidence return.

"Are you blind? Have you not noticed the four walls surrounding you? You're our prisoner now," Heli challenged.

"Yes, and I've been meaning to ask about these accommodations. Quite the formalities when you'll be letting me go," Jacque countered.

"You're delusional." Heli laughed.

"Actually, I'm feeling quite unflappable at this point." He looked up and stared hard into Heli's eyes. Heli's smile faded. "Unfortunate what's happened to Corinne," Jacque said. He spoke of her as if he were referring to something as mundane as the weather.

Heli stood in silent shock as the moments trickled out into a blinding eternity.

"You told him?" Heli turned to look at Justin.

Jacque responded before Justin could. "I called on Terra's mother to join us for our little chat. Haven't you learned anything? I know what you came here to do. And I knew you'd come after me as soon as we were left alone. That little maggot spawn of Cue's made quite an adjustment to the suit." Each word spit out like shrapnel through a clenched jaw and he continued, "But as I told you before, I've always believed in having a sound insurance policy. Unfortunately for her she couldn't have been more punctual, otherwise we might have avoided this whole mess altogether."

"I am through negotiating with you!" Heli felt his voice rising.

"Oh yes, but I'm not through with you yet," Jacque said. In Terra's condition I'm sure this news about her mother has been more than enough for her to bear." Jacque studied him before continuing, "Hmm…based on the look on your face I would wager to guess that you haven't had the nerve to tell her, have you? I completely understand. It would devastate her to know what you've done. And knowing this I think you also understand that I am the only one in a position to help clean up this mess you've made." Jacque looked over at Justin, who stood mute by the exit. "By the way," Jacque's voice almost chirped, "thank you for seeing to it that the suit is in working order again."

Justin groaned, squeezing his mouth shut in a tight line.

"I'll need your word that Corinne will be taken care of." Heli lifted his head.

"As I can see you've had proper consultation," Jacque tipped his head toward Justin. "So happy to see you've finally come to your senses. Especially now that you realize that I'm the only one with the means and access to the resources to respond to her treatment. Would there be anything else for the good of the order?" Jacque was too agreeable.

"Terra can't know what happened. At least, not until I'm ready to tell her myself. As far as she knows nothing has changed. You're still in charge." Heli could feel his bargaining chips fly.

"I like the sound of that, but I have one more counteroffer before we close this deal." Jacque winked. "I do all of this for you and you and your friends return to the Strata to retrieve something for me," Jacque said.

"Are you crazy? We are not risking our lives in that thing again to achieve some Regulation plot," Heli sputtered.

"Not for the Regulation. This expedition is more personal." Jacque's features suddenly softened.

"What is it you're after in there?" Heli asked.

Jacque's eyes narrowed on him. "I'm not as heartless as you may think. What I aim to bring back is something I've realized that I no longer wish to live without." He paused. "Cue had his secrets, but I have no doubts that he kept you up to speed with the details of the others involved."

"He did," Heli answered.

"Then perhaps you can understand the motivation behind this recovery effort," Jacque said.

"This is an actual person and not a 'thing' we're talking about? Just needing to clarify since you seem to be all too certain that our target wants to be rescued," Heli said.

"She doesn't belong in there," Jacque said.

"Thryn went in on her own accord," Heli clarified.

"Cue gave up on her!" Jacque sharpened his tone. "She's the last vestige of anything worthwhile from a lifetime of service to this program and you will free her from that cage of time rot if it's the last thing you do!"

"You actually think it's possible to find her in there?" Heli asked.

Jacque leaned in, his eyes steady and focused on Heli. "Only one way to find out."

"How do you know it's even possible to bring her back? And your benefactors, the Regulation, they'll want more," Heli said.

"Yes, that's likely true, if I were stupid enough to involve them. They'll be none the wiser and Thryn will be back where she belongs. And later, if I decide to negotiate conditions with them, it will be on my terms. Their sole focus right now is to weed out any opposition who carry knowledge of the shift and I just handed them the jackpot. They have no cause to question me. And later when this all dies down there will be much to take advantage of with the state of replenished resources."

"You mean control of those resources despite how plentiful they might be. You'd be pulling the wool over everyone's eyes." Heli stared back.

"Ah, the grand history of a copious mankind—blind to their own abundance and masters of their own delusion. Nothing new to the good people of this planet," Jacque offered.

"There's only one little problem with your plan. Terra can't go into the Strata while she's carrying the baby," Heli said.

"There are means to put an end to such problems?" Jacque lifted his eyebrows.

"If you think we would even consider—" Heli stood up.

"Calm down. I'm only offering viable options," Jacque said.

"That will never be an option." Tendrils of searing anger frayed Heli's composure. "And you better hope that suit is one hundred percent functional if you ever say anything like that to me again. I'll go tell her everything now myself if it means that."

"Just when I thought we were beginning to understand one another." Jacque took a deep breath. "Allow me to remind you of your position now that we've entered into negotiations. That little ticking time bomb Terra carries is going to go off whether you're ready or not. And you, Terra and Dous will be prepared for entry into the Strata in short order time of three months."

"That's crazy! You're willing to place your bets on the life of your own grandchild? They can't go in there. It's too dangerous and—" Heli shook his head.

"She won't be carrying the child when she enters," Jacque said.

"Deal's off!" Heli's body jolted as he prepared to pounce. He looked at his hands, imagining how they must be glowing with heat ready to combust. *How could he get around that suit?*

Jacque went on, "The child doesn't have to die."

"She's hardly into her first trimester! How is that even possible?" Heli asked.

"You comply with my request and I assure you that the child will live. A win-win of sorts."

Heli sat back down. "Nothing with you is a winning proposition."

"When will you learn? You know I have the means to force your hand if necessary and because I know you won't risk the life of your unborn child I am confident that we'll come to an agreement." Jacque's eyes widened on him. "Or, as I mentioned before I can eliminate the problem altogether. The Regulation knows how valuable I am to their efforts. I can't just disappear off the radar. They are mandated to respond. Three days of no contact is all it would take for them to signal the release of the trace minerals already in Terra's bloodstream and suddenly your most viable options are irrelevant." He paused. "And the child dies."

Retroaction

I don't really have a choice. Everything's out on the chopping block, even risking the life of his own grandchild. Heli projected.

He's completely sadistic. Dous sat pale faced.

"No kidding. You just now realized that?" Heli asked aloud.

"There's some serious controversy surrounding these trial gestational studies," Dous began.

"I've read about it. It was only developed like a decade ago? And minimal trial testing was successful with human subjects. I guess things could have improved since then, but I highly doubt it's foolproof at this stage."

I know, but what other options do we have? Let her mother die? Take the chance that he sends us in while Terra's still pregnant? I can't let that happen. As transparent as Heli felt his thoughts might be, he felt more security in keeping this conversation private.

Yeah, but do you really know what you're deciding on? With the use of this rapid growth hormone the gestational period is narrowed to one single trimester. Growing a baby is hard enough in natural time, but reduce that time to one-third, it's absurd. Dous glanced at Heli.

I don't want to keep discussing this without Terra, Heli sent. *I have to talk to her. This isn't my decision alone.*

The man is shameless. More humanity in your pinky finger than he's ever had, Dous projected.

"I don't know, right now...this little digit could do some serious damage." Heli held up his hand and wiggled his pinky finger.

"She's strong. She can handle this." Dous looked at him directly.

"I know, that's what's killing me. I've never given either of you the credit that you deserve. And right now, I'm the only one who can't seem to handle things," Heli said, training his eyes back on the ground.

I had him in my grip. He was a dead man. I should have been paying more attention. Heli shared the thought.

Dous leaned in. "You did your best. No more, no less. You have to quit punishing yourself."

Heli opened his eyes wide on his friend. "My best was a complete hack job. And now Cue's dead, Terra's mother isn't too far behind, and I've gotta get used to the fact that I'm going to be a father in less than three months."

"Okay, I take it all back. It isn't that you punish yourself, you just have to quit feeling sorry for yourself." Dous looked down at his legs. His hands slapped his thighs. "I never thought this was possible, me standing here looking at you eye to eye. Let me tell you something—I'm relying on a Hodgesuit to hold me up, keep me standing, but if it all disappeared tomorrow, do you think I'd quit? Give up? There are plenty of excuses I could live by to keep me down. Difference is, I still wouldn't let any of it hold me back and I won't allow you to do this to yourself. You have to go face up to what you have now, today. And for god's sake, stop whining about it."

Heli set his head back amazed. "Whining? I don't whine."

"Oh, I would certainly qualify the crapload you keep feeding yourself as an unspecified level of whining." Dous shook his head.

"Okay," Heli said. "I'll try to talk to her."

***

"Thanks for bringing my tea." She sat up straighter. Heli carefully adjusted to sit by her in the hammock. He handed her the cup of tea, still steaming, and she took a sip.

"How can you stand that swill?" Heli asked.

A little laugh escaped her. "Have you even tried it?" She pressed the tumbler up to his face.

"I'm a super-smeller. All I need is one whiff to know if something is worth an ounce of my taste buds. No, thank you," he said pressing the cup away.

"A super-smeller?" Terra crinkled her nose. "Then that would explain your aversion to some of the other concoctions Cruise puts together." She smiled. "That's okay, more for me I guess. I don't even really know what exactly is in it." She stared down into the cup.

"One of Cruise's secret recipes, but I'm practically addicted."

"Well if Cruise had anything to do with it, I'm sure it's tailored just for you." Heli leaned back and she carefully lay back to join him, cradling the cup in her hands.

You can stay if you want," Terra whispered.

"I will," Heli said, and kissed the top of her head.

"I haven't been sleeping well lately. I wish I knew what was keeping my mother so busy that she can't even check in," she said.

Wrapped up in his arms Heli could feel the heavy drag of her exhaustion and he considered what amount of damage he could stave off in exchange for one night's naive bliss.

He pressed his head back against the padded quilt, feeling its taut lining. This waiting game only worked to put off what had to be resolved. "There's something I need to talk to you about." She craned her head up to look at him. Her eyes were alarmingly beautiful as she stared back at him in the gamboge hue of the evening. When he blinked, he held his eyes closed against hers.

"Okay," she said.

When he reopened his eyes, she was staring at him in such a way, with such anticipation, all he wanted to do was pull her close and kiss her and let the nightmare of what he was preparing to tell her melt away. "Your mother," he paused to clear his throat, "she hasn't been away because she was too busy to see you. She'd never leave you this long. You know that." He nodded and she nodded back slowly.

"What are you . . ." She stalled and sucked in a small pull of air. "Something's happened to her. Oh god, did Jacque do something?" Her voice pinched in a higher octave. "Tell me!"

Heli felt a gasping release of the masquerade before he allowed the words to form. "I...It was me. This is my fault."

Terra pressed back against the curves of the lining, edging away from him. "What do you mean it was your fault?"

"She came in while Jacque and I—" Heli felt his voice crack and he pressed his lips together not sure if he could go on, and then the floodgates opened. "I went after him. I had my hands around his throat and I was going to end this like I promised." He shook his head.

"She showed up out of the blue, and the Prana…I couldn't stop it at that point."

Terra had already moved to the opposite end of the hammock and was staring back at him. Her eyes were those of a stranger's. Deep and desolate and coursing through him was a dread he had never known.

"You didn't come back for me. You came back for your own selfish pride. Get out," she sputtered through tears. "Get out!" she shrieked, and threw the cup of tea, smashing it on the tile floor. Heli bolted upright. "Get out! Get out! Get out!" Her voice was rigid and hoarse and she pounded him with her fists as he shielded himself from the repeated blows. The ground had been more forgiving as he came down hard on his knees. He was able to reposition himself to stand. Involuntarily wincing in pain, he bent over for a moment, feeling the pulse of her sobs spilling out through the room.

There was no help for it. He couldn't even look back at her. He began hobbling out, gaining speed into a quick shuffle, until finally he exploded in a full-out sprint, running down the only path that would accept him. To run forever would have been a kinder torture, and when his muscles finally began to seize on him he pushed even harder. Through the green, memories whisked by from a time when mistakes were forgivable—a time when he was whole. His calves were shredded with a burning he felt all over. As he slowed to catch his breath, sizzling tears streamed down his hot cheeks and a final wheeze allowed him to gain only sips of air through buried sobs set to drown him.

***

We both knew this was coming. Dous sat next to Heli.

I know, but it feels like…death. Heli threw his head back to look at a canvas of cerulean sky. He was still perched on the ground not ready to get up and face what the adjustment would mean. His legs surged with overuse and even though his breath had resumed a more distinct rhythm, he fought to catch it.

"Then I'm glad I found you when I did since this might be your last rights." Dous rolled his eyes. "You're not dying. You need to get up. We should go check on Corinne, see if there's been any improvement."

"What's the use? She's probably not going to make it and then Terra will have even greater cause to hate me forever," Heli whispered.

"I'm actually proud of you." Dous looked at him. Heli still sat on the ground and looked up at his friend.

"Proud?" Heli asked. "What is there to be proud of?"

"You did what you needed to do. You came through without putting yourself first. I'd say that takes some growing up."

"This hell we're stuck in makes me a bonafide adult?" Heli tossed his head and locks of hair stung his sweaty cheeks.

"No, it makes you a man," Dous said and stood up.

"In all honesty, I wanted to keep running." Heli moved onto his knees and Dous reached down to help him up.

"Glad your legs gave out on you then." Dous raised his eyebrows and smiled a little as Heli looked up.

"How did I get so lucky?" Heli asked, drawing himself up with the helping hand.

"Hm?" Dous looked at Heli more intently.

"I mean, I could've been bonded for life with two people I couldn't stand, or even worse two people that couldn't stand me," Heli said.

"Well that would have pretty much sucked," Dous said.

"I guess some of us are just charmed that way." Heli smiled his half smile.

"Why, I think a real-live bromance might be blossoming here," Dous responded.

Heli nodded. "Well, I'd pretty much put up with anything at this point if you can manage to deal with me."

Heli looked down at himself. His Hodgesuit was torn in places and his fingers ran over one of the tattered fringes as he batted away the dirt. "Now how'd I manage that?"

Dous twisted his lips. "I know someone who can fix that. Come on."

At the Heart

Laid out on the cot, Corinne looked to be in a peaceful sleep, her lids closed with a feathery slit between them. Heli studied the pale, sallow tone of her face. In his exile, Heli knew that if he couldn't be with Terra then the next best thing for him to do was to focus on her mother. He stared at Corinne's still form. Yellow and violet tubes wove around her body and were fed through her mouth and nose. The bright colors served as a reminder of what vital sustenance they were providing. And for the first time ever in his life something close to a prayer emerged through his thoughts. *Please. I know I can't fix this alone. Without Terra I know I'm less of who I should be. And she needs her mother. Please.* He stood still with his feet set evenly while emotions cascaded down over him. Even the air surrounding him felt lighter in the exchange and for the first time in days, he felt removed from the place of despair he had come to know so well. His chest filled up as he took his next breath and a profound solace took over.

She was still alive and although her skin showed little of its normal olive glow, she looked like she was just resting peacefully. There were no telling marks from what he could see, no visible reminder of the incident. And Mr. Cruise had added to the relief when he reported that her vitals were strong and that they would be able to remove the ports soon so she could breathe on her own.

"Once the cardiac monitor is inserted, it'll be programmed to continuously assess her heart's activity. She'll likely experience fainting spells for a time after she's woken and we'll need to keep track of the potential symptoms of cardiac arrest," Mr. Cruise said as Heli and Dous stood by her cot.

"So many sensors," Dous said, observing the light show adorning her body from head to toe. "Is all of this really necessary?"

"Well, we're making every effort, and Jacque's called out every available resource as promised. Just taking full advantage of this while we can," Mr. Cruise said.

At least he's coming through with his end of the bargain. Dous's thoughts edged in.

Heli changed the subject and turned to Mr. Cruise. "What's your first name?"

"I don't see what this has to do with Corinne's recovery," the stout little stump of a man replied.

"I mean we're all on a first-name basis with Justin, so what's with the formality?" Heli probed further.

"I reserve that information for certain isolated people in my life," he said.

"And we don't make the cut?" Dous asked.

Cruise stood and glared at both of them. His eyes said a number of things.

"Well, I just wanted to formally say thank you." Heli extended a hand.

Mr. Cruise cautiously edged his hand across Corinne's still form, finally taking Heli's in his grip, holding on longer than was necessary. When their hands did finally separate, Heli observed how the little man watched him differently now.

"I don't know what you have to thank me for," he said, looking between Dous and Heli.

"For your role in all of this. For taking care of all of them." Heli looked down toward Corinne.

"Not to mention your gift of the grub," Dous added, patting his stomach. "You give new meaning to the word food these days."

He nodded silently in a manner of acceptance and as he turned to leave, he paused in the door frame with his back turned to them. "Mickey. You can call me Mickey."

***

Heli's eyes scanned the horizon while the sun spilled its light over the dawn's shadowy trail. The edge of the grass-covered hill shimmered with the increasing light of dawn. Heli sat alone on the mound where he and Terra had spent many of their evenings stargazing. He heard a shuffle in the silent paralysis of the morning. He looked back over his shoulder as Mianna approached.

She kneeled down without a word and stared out at the sky.

"I've been worried about you," she said.

"You're worried about me? Why? It's not like you don't have enough to deal with on your own." Heli angled his head to look at her.

"We've both suffered great loss recently," she said and swallowed hard. "And if I thought my father and the Frey was all I had I'd be a complete wreck." She dropped her head and let the tears fall. For the first time since he had last touched Terra Heli felt the urge to reach out, but he didn't move.

"My father...your father, he was proud of you," she said.

"Not much to be proud of these days." Heli's throat clenched.

"You did the right thing telling her the truth. If I had known there was time before—" she stopped, leaned in, and collapsed into Heli's arms, letting it all out in a wail Heli could feel coursing right through his spine.

He sat frozen for a time, his arms wrapped awkwardly around her.

When she sat up and pushed away, she looked at him. Her eyes were wide and shining, bluer than his own. She smiled at him and placed her hand on his shoulder. "He kept so many secrets from me, but you're one I'm glad I came to know."

"I'm sorry about everything," Heli said. "I wish that there could have been another way."

"He knew what it meant to bring you here. He was willing to run the risk if it meant he could help you. You know I never understood until now why he was so obsessed with your progress." She bit her lip again and closed her eyes to release more tears.

"My surrogate father, the man who raised me, we weren't close. Ever. But with Cue there had always been something there. I never connected with the family I was raised by. I didn't even experience the true meaning of family until I met Terra and Dous," Heli admitted.

"I've been on my own for a long time. Friends never came easy, but I think on some level just knowing that we're related helps to explain things about myself," she said.

"We're probably more alike than either one of us would like to admit," Heli offered.

Mianna stared at him. "Terra…she'll forgive you for this. I'm sure of it."

"Well it's all out of my hands now." He shook both of them in front of him.

"I'll talk to her. You just concentrate on getting her mother through this." Mianna stood up slowly, still smiling down at him. "You're not alone in this."

Quickening

Heli felt his strength renewed after his time with Mianna and her assurances that Terra would forgive him. The one delusion he didn't carry along with him was the fact that she would never forget. He looked down at his hand, lightly rubbing his thumb over the curve of the circle. He stood just outside Terra's alcove, gathering his courage. The silence provided relief while his thoughts began to spill.

If there's one thing you've taught me, it's been that you're worth the wait. I'll wait, until you're ready. I did this to us. I put a mark on what we have. I can't change what happened, and I can't erase the pain it's caused, but I never meant to hurt her or disappoint you. Heli waited a few seconds. *I've been watching over her. Things have stabilized. There's every hope that she's going to pull through this. She'll still have a long way to go, but...*He slid down the wall with his back against the partition to sit on the hard floor tiles.

Her thoughts suddenly came slipping through. *I know it was an accident. Mianna explained everything to me. And I don't mean to punish you forever, but somehow everything we do leads us apart. I don't know how we build anything back up from that.*

Heli shook his head, projecting behind lonely tears. *We won't build on anything with this distance between us.*

You don't have that far to go. I'm just around the corner. Receiving this thought and rushing to stand, he practically stumbled through the entryway. She was sitting upright in her cloth cocoon. Her arms were wrapped around her like a butterfly awaiting transformation.

He moved closer to her, but didn't reach out to touch her, although it took all of his strength of will not to. "How are you feeling?" he asked.

"I'm all right." Her eyes rose up to his.

He risked reaching down to gently take her hand, unfolding it slowly. She responded to his touch with little resistance and he helped her to stand.

"Is this okay?" he asked, but he was already pulling her to him. He kissed her softly on the forehead and drew her in close. "Okay?"

She closed her eyes and didn't respond.

He moved to kiss her again on the lips and she startled. "I'm so sorry," he whispered.

She bit her lower lip and her eyes opened again to look up at him. Her lips were trembling but she stood up on her toes and leaned in, her lips ready to meet his. As soon as the contact was made he felt the sharp vibration and the brilliant surge like an echo ricocheting between them.

Then suddenly, as if in slow motion, she edged out of his grasp and backed away. She took his hand and guided it over her navel. Nothing changed but the instant warming under the cloth of her tunic and the skin underneath. He imagined the swirl of change occurring right beneath where his hand rested, and for a brief instant he thought he registered a glint of something.

"I know this all feels romantic and exciting, but all these changes," she paused and swallowed, pressing his hand against her, "it scares me. I mean we're not exactly living the ideal example of stability." She twisted her neck away from him.

The words that finally came were from the truest place inside of him. "Cue tried to warn me about this. I wasn't prepared to listen at the time, but you know what I think?" Heli paused and gripped her hand. Her eyes slowly floated back to meet his. "I think you and I have to create our own path. There's no recipe, we just have to play it out, make it our own."

A slight smile replaced the sad, empty gaze in her eyes. "She's hungry," Terra said, changing the heavy subject.

"She?" Heli asked.

"Just a hunch my mother had," Terra said, waiting for him to respond.

All he could expend was a lifting of his eyebrows. He took a moment to feel like he could breathe again.

"She's always had great intuition." Terra smiled.

"I question how well you fared with inheriting that intuition when it came to falling for me." Heli turned around when he heard someone approaching.

Justin stopped at the entry. "She's awake."

The news made Heli jump and then his attention was back on Terra.

"Did you hear that?" Heli leaned down so they were eye to eye. Her posture shifted as she straightened up to stand a little taller.

"Can we see her?" She was smiling.

"Hold on a minute, you're on bed rest. You're gonna have to let me…carry you or something." Heli leaned forward, ready to sweep her up.

"Your chariot awaits!" Dous careened around the corner wheeling Zuke toward them.

"How did you get that thing back here?" Heli asked, shocked.

"That thing has a name." He stared hard at Heli and leaned in to address Terra. "And Zuke would be honored to offer you a proper escort. Lord knows we could use some chivalry around here." Dous's eyes shot quickly to Heli then away again. "And I happen to be fortunate enough to have a girlfriend who is an Aquarius," he paused as if the words had slipped him up, "born practical, and she suggested that I bring him along just in case. He was loaded up in the back compartment of the Hov we abandoned when we arrived here." He shoved Zuke closer to where Terra stood leaning on Heli.

Terra was smiling back at Dous in the way she reserved solely for him.

"So she's your girlfriend now?" Terra eyed him teasingly as she reached to move onto the seat. She suddenly gripped her side. "Oh!" Heli jumped up close and quickly put his hands on her waist in case she might fall.

"You okay?" he asked as he helped her onto the seat.

"Yeah." Her eyebrows rose. "That was...different." Heli bent down in front of her on his knees to look at her directly. She finally released her stare from whatever had been holding her focus to look back at him.

"We can wait, if you need to lie down?" he asked.

"No, I'm good, it was just something...a flutter." She stopped and the slight swell of a smile came through on her face.

"You felt something? This early?" Heli asked.

Storgē

Terra leaned her head against the cot where Corinne lay sleeping, with both hands in a tight grip around her mother's.

Corinne's fingers twitched and she began to stir. Her eyes fluttered open.

"We were so worried," Terra said. Tears spilled down both cheeks as she lifted her head to look at her mother.

"I am so sorry, sweetheart." Corinne's voice came out as a ragged whisper.

Heli felt the uncomfortable moment picking at him and he edged in to stand next to Terra. "You have nothing to be sorry for. This was all my doing." He let out a long exhale. The shame actually burned in his chest.

Corinne looked up at him. "You had no idea I was there." She drew a long, strained breath. "I saw your face. I've never seen so much anger evolve into so much pain so quickly." She squeezed her eyes closed again and Heli could see the effort she was expending to get the words out. "You've suffered more than me I think." Her face paled in the laboring lack of oxygen and she closed her eyes once more. Heli could see the muscles in her forearms squeezing Terra's hands.

"You need to rest, Mother. I'm here. I won't leave you," Terra said.

Her mother's chest continued to rise and fall with turbulent fluctuations in her breath. "I'll rest, but you need to do the same. Promise me, sweetheart." She turned her head to look at Terra directly. "This isn't just about you or me anymore."

Terra looked up at Heli.

"Maybe we could move her in to be closer to you?" he offered.

"Could we?" Terra looked over her shoulder toward Justin and Mr. Cruise, who stood by, eyeing the monitors.

"We need to give her some time without disruption." Cruise squinted toward them.

"Dous and I can bring you here every day if you want. As long as you get enough rest in between," Heli said and looked at Dous.

"Zuke is at your service, m'lady. I believe he's had enough of my derriere," Dous said and gave a chivalrous bow.

"Then when she's ready you can move her?" Terra only half squatted with her arms against the arm-rests.

Heli touched her arm, caressing it lightly, and she sat down. *We'll bring her to you as soon as she's ready.*

Terra shook her head slightly and looked over at her mother again. "Are you in a lot of pain?"

Her mother smiled but kept her eyes shut. "It comes and goes. Sometimes it's difficult…to breathe."

Terra began to cry. "I don't want to leave you."

"It'll get better with time but right now you both need your rest," Heli said in the mildest tone he could muster. Corinne sucked in another ragged breath and Heli cringed watching her put forth the effort to hide the pain she was in.

They all watched as it only took a few seconds for Corinne to slip back into a coma-like slumber. "We can go now," Terra said quietly.

Heli felt the cold steely prick of Terra's listlessness in the time that it took for him to turn her around on Zuke and wheel her away from her mother. An itchy guilt worked over any happiness that had placated him earlier.

"I'll bring you back after dinner," Heli told her, but she didn't reply.

Numinous

"Well, here we are again, waiting," Dous said. He moved around Justin who stood pressed back against one of the pillars surrounding them. Mianna sat down next to him and reached a hand out toward him. He took it in his.

"Just another angle of control." Terra's voice streamed out with a frothy edge with her trailing thoughts. *He's pure evil.*

Heli still couldn't believe that they had Jacque locked up and now he was back in charge and roaming free again.

"All that matters now is that your mother is awake and getting better," Heli tried to reason with her.

Dous cut in, *I didn't want to say anything with all that's been going on, but Maisy's coming. Here. To see me. To meet you all.*

Well that's...wonderful news, Dous. Terra nodded.

It was Mianna who really pulled the strings. Dous smiled at Mianna and squeezed her hand. *She encouraged me to send a com-trip out to my parents.*

Heli stared back unsure of what to say. *And Jacque's okay with this arrangement?*

I don't really care if he's okay with it. I have every right to see my sister, Dous pressed back.

Mianna interrupted. "I just love the peace and quiet here." She rolled her eyes.

Oh yeah, and I hear you told Mianna about our little thing. Dous tapped his head.

"Yeah, it's always nice to clear the mind," Heli added, looking at Mianna. *She needed a little cajoling after that kiss. You totally left her hanging.*

You would've killed me if I had been the one to blow our cover, Dous projected.

Just be happy she knows or she'd think we we're all total weirdoes who like sit around and have polite conversation about the weather or something lame like that.

"How about this 'weather' we're having?" Dous looked bored. *There's more. We also put word out for Maisy and my parents to see if they could reach Emeal.*

Nice ruse the two of you have concocted, Heli thought.

Do you think she's still alive? Terra introjected with her thoughts.

We don't know, but Mianna told me that there was a secret hidden shelter located underground beneath the Frey. There's a chance that if she had any prior warning, she and possibly others may have escaped the Regulation's attack, Dous shared.

Heli looked at Mianna and acknowledged her with a courteous tip of his head. She nodded back while both wandering blue eyes landed on the tiny lens of the visuo-cam hovering in the corner.

With futile minutes creeping into what felt like hours, Heli knew why they had been summoned to the Query Room. Jacque would lay out the plans today and they would have to make a choice. His heart had already made his decision for him. Fortunately, there had been some time for Terra to rest after seeing her mother. Mutely Heli had already tackled the options in his mind, but he knew that the final call would be hers to make. He had been preparing himself for her likeliest reaction, bracing for the worst—knowing full well that she might somehow seek solace in blaming him again.

Dous turned to look at Justin. "Any idea when Jacque plans to make his appearance? I thought he was in some kind of a hurry."

"He'll be here momentarily." Justin was curt.

"I'm sure he's as eager to get on with this as we are," Heli shared openly.

I know, but I wish we could get on with it. Dous cursed in a mindful utterance.

"At least we have something to buy us some time." Terra lightly patted her belly and the usual flat depression of it seemed to be protruding a bit more lately.

Heli could feel the glacier of secrets grinding against his heart and he squeezed his eyes shut tight before settling in to tell her.

"What's wrong? There's something you're not telling me," she said, but before he could respond Jacque entered.

"Cozy little corner." Jacque walked around them offering little more than a distilled glance. Justin scowled, moving back into position up against the wall and aiming his stare straight ahead.

"My apologies, I didn't mean to interrupt the proceedings. Go on, Heli, you were about to share something?" Jacque said.

"He isn't going to let us wait this out. He intends on going forward with re-entry into the Strata on *his* time," Heli spilled and Terra shot him a shocked glance. She sat speechless with her mouth hanging open.

"You cretin," Mianna piped in and her face turned a ruddy shade of pink. "You're worse than my father ever warned."

"You should mind your own business, young lady, if you want me to have any reason to keep you around." Jacque spoke and Dous stood up.

"Don't provoke him." Heli drew a hand to signal for Dous to stand down and he turned to look at Terra. "This is no bluff. He has every intention to have us follow through with his plan. Your mother's recovery and our baby's life will depend on how we proceed. We have a choice to make." Heli lifted his head. "There's another option that'll pose less risk for you and the baby." He looked back down at Terra.

"You knew about this and you didn't tell me?" Terra's breathing became erratic and she slid away from him on the bench.

"Ah, young love. A shame it isn't non-penetrable." Jacque looked on with stoic resolution.

Dous interjected, "Heli didn't have a choice. He had to go along with this to get your mother the help she needed. And he threatened the baby if we don't go through with his plan."

Terra sat up straighter, her head swiveling from side to side. Finally, Heli watched as her features shifted from a frightened animal to that of a determined beast.

"You will never have control over this child," Terra said and her hand slid over her distended belly and she took a deep breath. "If it means the baby won't have to go in and can survive, then I'll go through with whatever you want." She swallowed.

Justin had been standing back. He nearly sprang off the wall to walk a few paces toward them before he spoke. "It's a method that will accelerate the development of the child. Physically, for you, it will be extremely taxing. It's been done before. We have the records of successful cases on file, but the body," he looked at Terra, "your body will be challenged to unnatural extremes. Either you go along with the uncertainty of the Strata, and one or both of you don't survive re-entry," Heli's chest stung with the mutiny in Justin's words, "or consider the greater chance that with a hastened birth you'll both come out of this okay. The decision is ultimately yours."

"You give us little choice." Terra looked up to stare directly at Jacque. He tipped his head back as if surprised by her acuity.

"I know what I want. For me, for this child, and for everyone here in this room. If our greatest chances are to move forward with this then I'll do whatever it takes. We opt to proceed with the treatment," Terra answered. Heli moved closer and she fell against him. He folded his arms around her.

"Well good. That worked out for the best then," Jacque said. Heli noted the flippant way he acknowledged their decision as if it were never theirs in the first place. He thought of all the signs, the hints of progression beyond the norm.

Heli dropped his head, shaking it then lifting it back up. "You've already started the treatment, haven't you?"

"Is that a question or did you need confirmation?" Jacque replied.

"You son of a—" Heli pressed his lips together on the final word and let go of Terra, who sat horrified. A vestige of fear returned to her pale, drawn face. He took one step toward Jacque.

"Careful. That would be your offspring's great-grandmother you nearly defiled." Jacque smiled, his crooked teeth flashed back at them, white soldiers on parade.

Terra gasped. "That's why I felt it. I didn't believe it could be anything this early but nerves." Terra's mouth gaped open and she stared at the floor.

Jacque angled in toward her. "All the confirmation I needed. Mickey assured me it would take."

"The tea." Heli realized and he looked at Justin.

Justin shook his head apologetically.

"Why would you do this? You and Mickey?"

"They don't have a voice for anything other than the mission. And with regards to that, they'll likely go to their graves before they'd tell you any of their deep, dark secrets."

Heli closed his eyes against the vision of so much betrayal.

"The perfect recipe," Jacque said.

"We never had a choice. You...already made it for us," Heli spit out.

"I would think you would've grown accustomed to this by now. I will always have the upper hand. But, you could show a little more gratitude. At least I gave you this much after what you did to me. I would say I've been fairly lenient having to wait even the few months this will require," Jacque said.

"How can you say that?" Heli flared. "Your reasons for wanting us to go back in there aren't without some merit. I know this because you're willing to risk everything to retrieve someone you actually care about. We're not that different, you and me. You'll even put her above your relationship with your own benefactors. Your bones can't be that brittle!"

"Do not presume to understand my motives or attempt to validate anything I do." Jacque's stare burned into Heli. "The survival of this child means very little to me, but I do need for Terra to be in good form for a successful retrieval," Jacque said.

Terra interrupted with a whisper. "I don't believe you. Heli's right. There has to be some part of you, somewhere deep, that sees what you're doing and knows it isn't right. That same part of you that sees Thryn. What you're after, by bringing her back, it's not going to fix anything. She'll never look upon you and accept you the way you are today. You'll continue to be as lonely and miserable of a human being as you are now."

Jacque looked down at her. He didn't utter a word in reply, but something in the twitch of his eye gave Heli reason to wonder.

Encasement

The turbulence of time beat down on all of them over the course of the next eight weeks. Heli hardly had a free moment to complain while he obsessively attended to Terra's every need. He had little or no tolerance for his own menial status, watching how difficult this was for her. Justin had helped move Corinne into a partition space right next to Terra's quarters so that they could be closer. Terra's mother was no longer bed-bound and despite the rest she still needed on her path toward healing, she was insistent about putting Terra's needs above her own.

The new arrangement placed a bit of a crimp on private interludes between Heli and Terra, but as the days wore on and the baby began to show more aggressive growth, he came to appreciate the fact that Terra had others to turn to. What he made sure of was that she got as much rest as possible and kept up with the nutritional regimen, or what Dous had endearingly called "the machine." Both Heli and Dous had watched her with amazement and a tinge of horror as she grazed on bits of this and that for a stretch of over three hours one morning. Dous shared openly that he was certain there was no one else on the entire planet that could scarf it in like he could. At least not until now. The nickname befitting her, she became a living, breathing facilitation of mass operation in a factory of blood, sweat, and tears. Heli would often sit back and watch her in amazement, imagining the network of organized systems and parts that would soon make up the whole of another living person. It was astonishing to stand outside this hidden world of change and recognize the incredible miracle really happening before his eyes.

She rarely slept through the night any longer. And Heli had been demoted honorably as her qualified runner. Waking him with an elbow in his chest, while her open thoughts spilled into his dreams, *I need something to eat, sorry.* It wasn't until Justin revealed his brilliance with the idea that synthanutrients were a viable option at night to keep up with her requirements that Heli began getting any sleep at all. By that time, she had popped out so much that he felt like a third-party lobbyist vying for room in the hammock. The moving, the adjusting…and the pillows? Heli could not for the life of him understand her new fancy for pillows propping her up, under her arms, and between her legs.

Days dragged on while Heli recalled their earlier times at IDEA with the Probatory Scenario Training, and what Tracy had termed PST. It had zapped them of all energy in the same way this experience had.

There was nothing to say about it when a cot suddenly appeared one day out of the blue next to Terra's hammock. Heli stood staring at it numbly, understanding that someone had obviously taken pity on him.

Corinne tiptoed in around the corner that morning. "Terra's not the only one who could use some shut-eye. We wouldn't want you rough around the edges when the time comes." She smiled at him and his attempt to smile back came out more as a pathetic grunt than anything intelligible. He set up camp on the cot that evening and had the best night's sleep he'd had in weeks.

More tempered activities became a part of their everyday routine. The quiet sparked creativity for Heli as he unearthed sheet after sheet of new music to play for her on his whistle. He would join her in her hammock, demanding that the pillows make room for him, and she'd reluctantly toss them out. In exchange he'd roll in and she'd curl up in the crook of his arm while he played. These times between them, Heli was coming to realize, were precious and fleeting.

Dous and Mianna had their routines and always shared meals with them. They would often join them in the early evenings for short walks or games on the patio.

Mickey was on food patrol while Justin seemed to somehow miraculously keep Jacque busy enough that he didn't bother them. All Jacque needed were reports that everything was progressing and assurance that the time would be soon.

Terra began to experience considerably strong pre-term contractions and Corinne would explain that they were a normal stage in a traditional-term pregnancy but that hers were likely more intense because her body was having to adjust more rapidly.

Her mother explained, "Braxton's, they're called. Every woman's tolerance is somewhat different. It's been some time, but in my case, carrying you, I never really noticed them. I was reading some of the reports from the trials they conducted during the time of the Blend and many of the women in the sample group reported these sensations as their bodies were preparing for childbirth. They had also reported to have developed a higher threshold for the discomfort," she explained.

"Like a practice round?" Terra's voice squeaked a bit.

"I wish it were that simple. The pain you're experiencing now with these contractions, although in your case above the standard for most natural-term women, would be extremely mild compared to what you'll feel when it's for real." Her face twisted with a reliably honest grin.

"But I had one the other day that took me to the ground." Terra seemed as if she might burst into tears and Heli flinched with the image of her crouched down in a squat on the path as they were walking to dinner.

A master in the art of soothing, Corinne replied, "I've prepared an herbal salve that can help with the discomfort of the stretching and muscle aches as you get closer to delivery." Heli listened, taking mental notes. She slid her hand over Terra's distended belly and withdrew a device that worked like a pen to draw a line that hovered and stretched in a vertical cross-section along Terra's torso. "43.7 centimeters!" Corinne exclaimed, smiling.

Heli had no idea what the numbers meant, but the news must have been good.

"Here, Heli." She handed him a pestle containing what he could only describe as some kind of rusted jelly with bursts of tiny green flecks mixed in. At least it smelled good.

She was obviously able to read the look he returned. "You rub it on there." She pointed to the bulbous display of Terra's extended frame. She looked down at her smiling daughter and moved out to leave them alone.

He dipped his fingers into the salve and dripped it over her belly button. Her eyebrows rose as his hand made contact.

"How is it?" he asked.

"Cold." She sucked in a breath.

He knew she was watching him but he didn't look at her as he rubbed the mixture over the expanded skin of her curving center. Soon he could feel warmth spreading. He lifted his hand and frowned.

"It's not you, don't worry, it's the lavender and eucalyptus. I think she may have added a drop of peppermint as well. It's supposed to feel warm as you apply it." Her hand reached for his and he let her take it. She placed it back on her bulging center.

"We're almost there. You're doing great." He watched her smile while his hand drew hypnotic swirls on her tight skin.

"I know. I can't believe how fast it's going." She swallowed and Heli bent down to kiss her.

"I think the prospects of this might be scarier than re-entering the Strata," she admitted.

"I know. I wish there was more time."

"Don't blink, right?" She stared into his eyes.

He winked at her, closing both eyes. *Too late. We're still here, now, in this moment. Let's hold onto that, okay? We meet tomorrow when tomorrow comes.*

Her arms wrapped around his neck and she pulled him close. Nose to nose he could hear her thoughts muttering while her lips met his. *We live in this moment.*

Covenant

They're on their way here. Dous looked at Heli.

They? Then Emeal made it out? Heli asked.

Wait till you hear what happened down there. I don't want to talk about it in front of Mianna. Dous's eyes drifted over to look at her. He nodded and Mianna smirked, obviously fully aware of their private conversation. She rolled her eyes slightly and positioned herself a few inches away from them, keeping herself entertained by the flashing images on her CS card.

Justin's helping arrange the rendezvous point toward the rear of the grounds. The same entry point I came in by the waterway ditch when we arrived. He's made plans to shut off the valve so they can enter easily. My parents are staying back. They've been helping Emeal get the word out to other factions and Maisy insisted on coming to see me, Dous projected.

Jacque doesn't know? Heli sent and pressed back from his seat at the table.

Emeal's been in contact with others who see this as the time to act. We won't be able to hide them once they're here, but he has no idea that they're coming. Dous looked up at him.

Others? Are you talking about a revolt? Heli projected. *The baby could come any day. Jacque's already on pins and needles, obsessed with us going back in. What if he finds out? This could be bad for us.*

Emeal has a plan, to get us out. The reinforcements are intended to aid in our exit. Dous looked at Heli from under his long lashes.

You're talking escape? From here? Heli's thoughts projected while he lifted his eye brows and Mianna looked at him uncomfortably.

Emeal knows of other places like the Frey where we'd be safe and Terra and the baby wouldn't have to be separated. We could leave and never have to go into that thing again. Dous lifted his head.

Mianna sat up taller, giving in to the silence to speak. "How's Terra doing?"

Dous looked back at her with an apology written on his face.

"She's doing okay," Heli said. "It's getting harder every day but everything's moving along as far as I can tell. She's pretty uncomfortable at this point. Could be any day now."

"Is her mother prepared to handle the delivery?" Mianna asked. She looked up at Heli.

"I hope so, she's all we've got," Heli answered and realized how he hadn't really contemplated preparations for the actual event of the baby's arrival.

"I shadowed Emeal from time to time with some of the midwifery duties in the Frey. Maybe I could help?" Mianna offered.

You actually think we're gonna smuggle anyone else in without initiating our own war? Heli sent a passing thought to Dous.

Dous squeezed Mianna's hand. "I'm sure Corinne would welcome any amount of helping hands she can get. It's getting late. We should get going." Then his thoughts projected through his shrouded gaze. *Meet us in the Query Room in one hour.*

***

Heli had never told anyone, but he was absolutely terrified of a moonless night. Something about the absence of light, staring into an abyss of stars—nothing to stave off the macabre glare of desolation that seeped in all around him. Heli sat outside Terra's quarters on a patch of grass. He could see the glow from her CS card filtering out, and despite the inky night encasing him, the air held a mixture of humidity and warmth that kept him comfortable.

Three full cycles of the moon, nearly thirteen weeks, had passed. He stared up at the sable sky just visible above the low light of the building, an opening to the heavens, and he dared himself to hold his focus. If Dous was right and Emeal could get them all out, they could raise their child free from IDEA's gates and avoid the possibility of ever having to enter the Strata again.

Her voice diffused into Heli's thoughts. *I was looking for you.* It floated along with the temperate air. Heli shivered when it reached him. He looked back over his shoulder to see Terra approaching.

"What are you doing out of bed?" he asked. He could tell she must have sensed the gentle chiding in his voice, but she couldn't hide the news in her eyes. She slowed her pace and he noticed how she was holding herself under the curve of her belly. He quickly pressed up from his seated position on the ground to move closer to her.

She was standing unnaturally still. He lunged and nearly fell into her, searching her eyes and gripping her around her waist. "What's happening? Are you okay?"

"I'm a bit of a mess. It woke me." She looked down and he could feel her tensing in the shoulders where he had a solid hold on her. He followed her gaze down to see the watery stain against the bottom edge of her tunic.

"Your water broke?" he asked and heard his own voice croak.

"I think so." Her voice was a soft drum and like a dream she looked up at him with her mouth parted slightly. "How do you even know about all this?"

"Your mother's a nimble tutor." He edged his way around her with his arm still secure against her lower back. "We need to get you inside and lay you down." He struggled to start her moving as she stood firm.

"No, I'm not going anywhere," she said, and she started to bend over to angle down toward the ground.

"What? Here? Right here?" He pointed a fierce finger at the earth, still holding her under one arm as she had made it midway to a seated position.

"I need to get you to your mother!" Heli pulled her up a bit. She fought against him, shaking her arm free.

"No! I stay here! You go get her. This is happening right here!" Her breathing changed and she was suddenly panting like a wild animal as one hand and her rear met the earth in a clumsy side roll.

Heli shook his head, kneeling in front of her. "I'm not going to leave you out here!"

"I'll be fine. We have time. Trust me," she said. Heli watched her as she moved forward and back again on her hands and knees on the blanket of grass.

"Oh my god. You're not kidding. You want to do this here?" He didn't have time to argue. He aimed to reach Dous, *Dous! Where are you? The baby is coming!*

We're on our... and the thought was cut off as Terra let out a grinding screech.

Heli panicked, "I'll go get your mother and the others. I'll be back as soon as I can." He stood up and stalled for a second watching her writhe in pain with her hands in fists around the grass.

"Go!" she screamed. Her voice was so visceral that he half wondered what had possessed her.

He ran as fast as his legs could carry him into Terra's quarters, yelling for Corinne. Just as he passed through their chamber into the next, he collided with an armload of linens and instruments that barreled into him and then exploded out and up. He and Corinne met on the floor.

"Here, grab the towels! I've got the rest!" Corinne stood up and reached down, busily picking at the assortment of tools and monitoring devices, their screens on and pulsing with life already. Heli scanned the floor tiles until he saw the semi-folded towels and blankets that had flown over his shoulder and were now strewn in piles along the edge of the wall. He scooped them up under his arm and tucked them into a proper football hold.

We're on our way! Heli sent, hoping Terra was open to his thoughts.

Don't worry, I'm okay. Everyone's here, she sent back.

Heli stopped in his tracks for a moment. Terra's mother was already out of sight when he realized the "everyone" she must have been referring to.

He took off after Corinne and as soon as he had made his way to the garden he could see the shadows surrounding Terra. She was still on the ground. Heli recognized the all too familiar position she was in with her legs folded under her and her arms stretched out in front of her as if in prayer, her forehead pressed against the ground. He slowed his expeditious pace.

When he met up with her audience it was the striking silver hair almost casting its own light in the dark that caught his attention first. Emeal knelt next to Terra, rubbing her spine and humming softly. She raised her head as Heli approached and smiled up at him, never faltering with the tune.

He knelt where Terra's head met the earth and placed a hand on top of one of hers. She turned her palm up to grip his hand and squeezed.

Everyone came. They're all here. Emeal's alive! Her head swiveled slightly against the ground and he could see by looking at her rounder cheeks that she was smiling. She adjusted some to bring her head up, still sitting on her legs with bent knees, and released his hand.

"Have you met Maisy?" Terra's face appeared flushed, but she looked happy. As happy as he had ever seen her. A contagious giddiness spilled out of her and onto him. He couldn't help but smile back. When he looked up at the others surrounding them, he saw Dous and Mianna and Dous's sister Maisy encircling them. Dous was holding tight to one of each of their hands. All eyes were alight with anticipation.

"I had a feeling we'd get lucky tonight." Dous stared at Heli and smiled. He shook the hands he held with both hands and the girls' laughter slipped into the night air.

Terra was smiling and then suddenly a switch flipped, her smile disappeared, and her eyes grew wide. Heli watched as the glow was replaced by a tornado. She screeched as if her side were splitting. The howling rip of her scream sent the hairs straight up on Heli's neck, cutting in at him from the root down.

"Another contraction?" Heli asked.

Corinne pulled him back to move in and she and Emeal went straight to work. He felt Dous's hand reach to grip his shoulder. The two women had swiftly moved Terra onto her back and the others had moved away beyond the periphery of chaos.

Stay with me! He heard careening through his mind only to realize that he was the one sending the message.

The same message Heli had succumbed to chanting profusely when they had all entered the Strata together. He felt the swell of heat pouring through him and the quick release of his friend's hand from his shoulder as he felt them all press back in a wall surrounding them.

Yelling and confusion rained down and there was a taste of something bitter burning in the air, like he was in a trance and time had somehow slowed. He could see the figures of two others making their way toward the protective herd.

Heli couldn't bear any more of it and he stood, marked for vengeance. His hands were a blood red riptide of explosive heat as he looked out and saw Jacque making his way toward them with Justin at his heels.

"Stay the hell away!" Heli growled.

Justin stopped mid-step.

Jacque slowed his quick pace but continued to move forward. He held up a hand. "I won't intervene, but I'll be talking to that one when this is over." Jacque pointed to Emeal.

"Really bad timing." Heli clenched teeth while he listened and nearly shriveled to the ground with Terra's next yowl.

"I have every right to be here." Jacque nodded.

"The least you can do is give us this! Leave us be!" Heli screamed.

"I'll go. But he stays," Jacque pointed to Justin, "to report to me when this is all over and to apprehend our uninvited guests." He stared at Emeal and she rose up from her position by Terra to address him eye to eye.

"You saw fit to take away the only place I call home. As I see it my arrival here is warranted being that it's the only other home I know."

"So be it. But when this is over with, you and I will be catching up." Jacque turned from them and Heli suddenly woke to the silence around him.

The penetrating screams that had saturated the air had gone mute. Terra was quiet. Too quiet. Heli turned around and could see from where he stood how she lay sprawled out in the massacre of the stolen moment. And from what he was witnessing now, these had been critical moments. Dous and Mianna both kneeled on the ground by her side. Terra moaned and Corinne looked down at the bundle she held in her hands, and with ripe tears streaming down her face she spoke softly. "Hold her."

His hands were shaking as he reached over Terra to join her in receiving their daughter. In the instant they touched their child he could feel the transfer of her weight, light as a feather, yet she somehow carried the weight of the world. Wrapped up under a blood-stained cloth, small words escaped his mouth. "She's beautiful." Terra closed her eyes as tears streamed down her cheeks and his attention returned to the baby. Mesmerized by the rosy, purple blotches of her newborn skin, his finger trailed down her tiny arm. Her hand hung there limply. His finger found its way into her curled-up fist. This life, their future, every possible moment until now—gone. And he could feel that she *was gone.* Cradled in his hands she lay in the purest of silence. Silence of a different quality, syrupy and invasive with its presence.

He could only recall one other moment like this in his life—the moment he had entered the Strata. A place where nothing remained but the shell of a soul-draining loss and the gut-wrenching screams that thrust a dagger of realization and release of his own heartbeat. He closed his eyes, unable to bear witness to the unkind reality and at the same moment a spark dripped from his fingertip into his daughter's palm.

Beholden

I open my eyes.

Hope, like a blunt force, strikes me from all angles. Who I was, who I might have been is now in someone else's hands. Everything I know about this moment is suddenly transformed, cascading out of the sound of Terra's shrill screams. She is so light on my hands, yet I can feel the weight of her spirit. I reach, and I am built back up in the instant that I touch her tiny palm. Slight as the movement of the air, her fingers curl. A single tear stings my cheek—a cooling resolution to the agony. She's alive! Warmth returns as Terra's thoughts whisper her name...Zenith. Others who matter are surrounding us, but never in all of my life has anyone captured more of my attention than She at this moment.

She, who will light the dawn and transcend the darkness. I watch, a flush of pink to her fair skin as she fights to take her first breath in this world.

"The future depends on what we do in the present."

~Mahatma Gandhi

About the Author
Sheala Dawn Henke

Sheala Dawn Henke has worked as teacher in Fort Collins, CO for over fifteen years and stays busy raising her two boys Canyon and Cache with the help of her husband Jay. She believes in the alchemy of thought and the power of words to manifest conscientious change. In her stories she creates worlds imagined that can empower young individuals to become the catalyst to positive action and the markers of hope for a brighter future. She whole-heartedly believes that between the realms of fantasy and fiction we create our own reality.

www.ingramcontent.com/pod-product-compliance
Lightning Source LLC
Chambersburg PA
CBHW051440260626
47162CB00001B/174